Crescent City Ghost Tours

Carrie Pulkinen

This is a work of fiction. Names, characters, places, and incidents are either the product of the author's imagination or are used fictitiously, and any resemblance to actual persons living or dead, business establishments, events, or locales, is entirely coincidental.

Love & Omens

COPYRIGHT © 2019 by Carrie Pulkinen

All rights reserved. No part of this book may be used or reproduced in any manner whatsoever without written permission of the author except in the case of brief quotations embodied in critical articles or reviews.

Contact Information: www.CarriePulkinen.com

Edited by Krista Venero
Cover Design by Carrie Pulkinen

First Edition, 2019

CHAPTER ONE

A crisp February breeze rolled down Frenchman Street, biting at Sydney Park's cheeks. She flipped up the collar of her leather jacket and angled her face toward the sky, letting the midday sun warm the chill from her skin.

Her phone buzzed on the table, and a text from Eric lit up the screen: *Where are you?*

She replied *Upstairs,* and her coworker's response came through as she set the device down: *Coming up.*

Leaning her arm on the pink wrought-iron railing, she peered over the gallery at the activity on the street below. New Orleans tourists and locals alike bustled about, grabbing lunch or drinks and chatting before moving on to their destinations.

Crescent City Ghost Tours held their weekly planning meeting over lunch at Dat Dog every Tuesday, and while the chill in the air sent most patrons indoors, Sydney snagged a table on the gallery upstairs, away from the interior noise.

Her boss, Sean, had something important to announce

to the group, and for once, she hadn't seen it coming in a vision. Her family curse made surprises few and far between, and a little flush of adrenaline caused a bubbly sensation in her chest, a tingle shooting up her spine as she awaited the news.

She inhaled a deep breath and let out a contented sigh, basking in the mix of cool air and warm sun as the jazzy music from a street band a few blocks away drifted on the breeze. A snare drum tapped out a quick rhythm, and a marching tuba, catching the sunlight in glints as its player danced, blew a deep bass while a trumpet blasted out the melody.

She'd barely had a chance to take in another breath when her skin turned to gooseflesh. The tiny hairs on the back of her neck stood on end, and her peripheral vision took on a blue and gold kaleidoscope effect.

Dammit, that feeling was short-lived. The mosaic pattern grew, tunneling her vision into a swirling phantasmagoria of cut glass, light, and shadow. Her perception of the real world disintegrated as a sinking sensation pulled her down the rabbit hole into a premonition.

As the kaleidoscope in her mind's eye cleared, she focused on her surroundings, taking in as much information as she could. When her brain tumbled into a vision of its own accord, she never knew how long she'd be under, how much time she'd have to figure out what the universe wanted her to know.

And why it wanted her to know it? That was a mystery she'd never solve.

Normally, when the scenery came into focus, the blue and gold stained-glass ring sparkling in her peripheral was the only thing distinguishing the life-like "Wonderland" from reality. This time, something about the vision felt… off…like it wasn't fully formed.

In her mind, she saw herself standing in a cemetery, her head bowed, a deep sob racking her body as Sean held her close to his side. Rows of above-ground tombs dotted the landscape, some standing five feet tall, others soaring to twice that height. A murkiness in her vision obscured the markers, and their forms wavered, making it impossible to decipher their exact shapes.

A crowd gathered around a coffin, and warm, humid air pressed down on her, squeezing the breath from her lungs. Forcing herself to move closer in her vision, she rotated the scene in her mind so she could see her own face.

Fresh tears streamed down her cheeks, following the paths of the others that had long since dried. Sean's red-rimmed eyes flicked toward the casket, and he swallowed hard, shaking his head as he sucked in a trembling breath.

She scanned the scene, searching for familiar faces, trying desperately to figure out who occupied the coffin in the distance, but the vision grew stagnant, the people blurred. She pushed forward, trying to move deeper into the cemetery toward the tomb, but an invisible wall blocked her path. The blue and gold kaleidoscope pattern dancing on the edges of her vision grew, encroaching on her view of the scene.

"You okay, Syd?" Sean's voice echoed in her mind as Wonderland shut down, jolting her into the present.

Time behaved differently in her visions, and while her visit to the cemetery felt like it lasted a good ten minutes, her check-out from reality had likely stolen no more than a few seconds from her day. She blinked, shaking her head and brushing her dark hair from her eyes. Sean slid into the seat next to her, and Eric and Jason sat on the opposite side of the table.

"Hey." Sean rested a hand on her left arm and tapped two fingers against it. "Anything I need to know?"

Though her jacket covered her *Alice's Adventures in Wonderland*-themed tattoo sleeve, her friend's gesture held the same meaning: a silent question whether her spaced-out expression was from a premonition or if she'd simply been lost in thought.

"No." She slipped her phone into her pocket as the server delivered their lunch order. "I'm fine…still processing it."

"Are you sure?" Eric pulled a knit beanie over his dark brown hair. "You picked a table on a windy balcony in the dead of winter. Seems more crazy than fine."

"Please. It's sunny and sixty-three degrees. Don't be a baby." She snatched a fry from his plate and shoved it into her mouth.

"Hey! You've got your own."

"I know." She shrugged. "I'm getting even for last time."

"All right, kids, eat up," Sean said. "We've got a lot to talk about, and my wife is so pregnant she's about to burst. I could get called away at any second, and this is important business." He smiled, but it didn't mask the worry in his eyes.

Even though Sydney had seen his kids—this one and the one who would be coming in a few years—in her visions, he'd been on edge since the third trimester began.

That premonition had been a happy one. If all her visions went the way of the ones she'd had about Sean lately, her life would be a hell of a lot easier. Unfortunately, ones like the nightmare she'd just had always slipped in the moment things started running smoothly.

"Still no visions about the actual birth?" Sean's brow knit over his dark brown eyes, and she couldn't help but grin at his new-father anxiety.

Even if she hadn't known him her entire life, his concern alone was enough to prove he'd be a great dad. His wife and soon-to-be daughter were two lucky ladies. "No, but everything is going to be fine. I wouldn't have seen you guys a few years down the road if there were going to be issues. Don't worry."

His shoulders relaxed as he nodded. "The vision you just had…?"

"It wasn't about that." She picked up her hot dog and took a massive bite. The savory flavors of Polish sausage and dill relish danced on her tongue as she stared out across the street and ran the premonition through her mind again.

The coffin had been full size, so nothing had changed about the baby's birth. But Sean had been there, red-eyed and sobbing right along with her. Whoever was going to die, they both cared deeply for the person.

"So, what's the news?" Jason bit into his burger and stared at Sean with wide, blue eyes.

"Yeah, man. Don't leave us hanging," Eric said.

Sean grinned. "We've been talking about expanding the business for a while now, and…it's happening. I'm taking on a partner."

Sydney nearly choked on her Dr. Pepper, her quick inhale sucking the bubbles up the back of her throat to sting her nose. "Now? I thought you were going to wait until things settled down with your home life. You're about to have a baby."

"I know." He held up his hands. "But the opportunity presented itself, and I couldn't pass it up. I wouldn't have done it if I didn't think my awesome employees could handle it."

He had a point. They were more than capable of taking on a new tour or two, and Sean had been discussing it with her for months. But their conversations never alluded to him bringing in a new partner.

She crossed her arms. "What's this person bringing to the table that we can't do on our own with a few extra guides?"

"That's the exciting part." Sean's eyes gleamed. "We're going to start a line of tours that focuses on true crimes, whether they've left behind a haunting or not. People are mesmerized by the seedy underbelly of the city and all the gruesome things that have happened in our history: The Axeman, the Trunk Murders, the Vampire Brothers… We'll guide them around the city to show them the locations of the crimes, and the tour will end at our new Museum of the Macabre."

"I like the way this sounds." Eric leaned forward, resting his elbows on the table. "What's going to be at the museum?"

"Let me guess." Sydney turned to Sean. "Murder weapons? You found someone who could get ahold of an actual trunk from the murder scene? An axe used by The Axeman himself?" Which, in all honesty, sounded pretty cool. She could get on board with this, as long as the new partner wasn't an ass.

"Exactly. He's even procured a coffin dating back to the 1700s. We're thinking the tour will start…"

The guys continued the discussion, but Sean's mention of a coffin had Sydney's mind drifting back to her vision.

She needed to go home and meditate on this, see if she could open the door and slip back into the scene. The only people who weren't blurry in the premonition were herself and Sean, so that left the possibility of death open to at least five or six others.

Then again, if the cemetery were going to be a stop on the new tour, they could have simply arrived during a stranger's funeral in her vision. But that didn't explain the obvious tears on her face.

There was no need to panic yet. The grave could have been metaphorical. Sometimes her visions weren't literal. They were occasionally downright strange, hence the nickname of "Wonderland" she'd given to them. Between the sinking sensation and the kaleidoscope patterns tunneling her vision, she'd always felt a bit like Alice falling down the rabbit hole when they started.

She had time to figure this out. The weather had been warm in the cemetery, and according to the local weatherman, the current cold snap would last at least two more weeks. She'd put the pieces together by then.

And who knew? Maybe this coffin was symbolic like the tiny one she'd flushed down the toilet in a vision she had as a teen. She'd been certain her purple betta fish, Hatter, was about to kick the bucket, when in reality, the coffin had been an omen, a sign of what would happen to her chemistry grade when she chose a Foo Fighters concert over studying for an exam. That trip to Wonderland had been blurry around the edges like this one.

"Syd?" Sean nudged her with an elbow, and she tucked her hair behind her ear, nodding to feign listening. "You're good with the extra responsibility?"

"Of course." She had no idea what he'd said, but she'd

handle whatever it was. "Just tell me what to do, and it's done."

Sean gave her a quizzical look before shaking his head. "Who's on tonight?"

"It's you and me, right, Eric?" She glanced across the table, and Eric nodded.

"Okay. He'll be following the eight o'clock tour, and I'll tag along too. Hopefully the merger will become official shortly after." Sean looked each of them in the eyes. "Is everyone on board with this?"

"Hell, yeah." Eric reached across the table to fist-bump Sean.

"Absolutely," Jason said.

They all looked at Sydney, and she swallowed. She'd heard less than half of what they said, but she trusted Sean to make the right decision for the company.

"Yeah. True crime. Museum of the Macabre. Sounds great." She flashed a small smile and stood to throw her trash away.

"All right. Class dismissed." Sean stayed in his seat as Eric and Jason said goodbye and shuffled inside the building.

"I'll see you tonight." Sydney took one step toward the door before Sean stood and put a hand on her shoulder.

"That vision you had…"

She pressed her lips together and forced her gaze to his. "I'm not sure what it means. I'll let you know if it's anything important."

He dropped his arm to his side. "It wasn't Emily…?"

"No." She shook her head adamantly. He'd already been through one death after a vision of hers, and she wasn't about to let him worry again. "Emily wasn't in it. She's…"

He held her gaze, his dark eyes searching hers.

She couldn't lie to him. Honestly, she had no idea what the coffin contained. Maybe it wasn't even a body. Maybe it signified the death of the company if he went through with the merger. She'd have to do a lot more digging to find out, and there was no point in worrying anyone until she knew the whole story.

"It's not like last time, okay? I'd tell you if it was." She'd seen his first wife's death in all its horrific detail, and neither one of them had been able to stop it from happening.

He nodded. "Thanks, Syd. And thanks for taking this on. I don't know how much I'll be around when Sable makes her appearance, but I know the company will be in good hands with you in charge."

"No problem. I'm looking forward to the challenge." What on Earth had she agreed to?

It didn't matter. She could handle anything the job threw at her. Right now, she needed to figure out what kind of death that funeral represented and how she could stop it from happening.

CHAPTER TWO

A smile tugged on Blake Beaumont's lips as he stood on the bank of the Mississippi River, overlooking the muddy water. A white steamboat docked a few yards away added to the picturesque view of the Crescent City Connection Bridge illuminated against the dark night sky.

The evenly spaced lights spanning the length of the bridge cast a reddish-gold glow on the water's surface, and the smooth sounds of a street performer playing the saxophone echoed in the distance. A couple sitting on a park bench laughed behind him, the happy sound mixing with the faint music to create a soothing, welcoming melody all its own.

Man, it felt good to be home.

The February wind stung his cheeks, but he'd take New Orleans' two weeks of fifty-degree winter over the months of frigid ice and snow he'd endured in New York. His time away had been a necessity, but he was home now and here to stay.

He jogged across the railroad tracks and slipped his hands into his pockets as he crossed Decatur Street and entered Jackson Square. The plaza buzzed with activity as crowds gathered for the nightly ghost and vampire tours, and psychics set up tables along the walkway, offering passersby spiritual advice and glimpses into their futures.

Some of the fortunetellers in the Square had actual psychic abilities, while others relied on mentalism and a keen eye for reading body language to tell people what they wanted to hear. Who was who, he couldn't tell anymore. He'd been away for far too long.

He smiled and nodded at a woman with a floral head wrap and matching dress. Four-inch tarnished gold hoop earrings and a set of bangle bracelets clinking on her arm as she waved her hand over her crystal ball added to her gypsy-like appearance.

If this venture didn't work out, he might be forced to set up his own table and offer readings. He could don a wizard's cape or some other ridiculous costume and amaze people with his ability to read the energy in objects, but therein lay the problem. His psychic power was dependent on customers actually having an object with them that he could read.

Not to mention, the thought of putting his ability on display made his skin crawl. Once people found out what he could do, they wanted him to become some kind of freak show act, performing for all their friends. That, or they called him a scammer and a fraud. *No thank you.*

His talent would better serve him on his current path, and joining forces with the most popular tour company in the French Quarter would ensure that path led to success.

He spotted his old high school buddy leaning against the fence, and he lifted a hand to catch his attention. "Hey, Sean."

"Blake." Sean pushed from the fence and sauntered toward him. "Glad you could make it."

"I'm looking forward to it. You know, I've lived in New Orleans all my life…aside from the recent years… and I've never been on a walking tour." He stepped around a performer who'd painted his entire body gold and followed Sean toward the St. Louis Cathedral.

Built in 1794, the massive church boasted three steeples, with an enormous clock adorning the center one. A crowd huddled near the steps, forming a semicircle around a man in his early twenties with brown hair and a trench coat.

Sean stopped behind the crowd and nodded at the man. "It can be hard to think like a tourist in your home city. We tend to take what we see every day for granted."

"No kidding." Blake had moved away with *good riddance* on his mind, but he never fathomed how much he'd miss this place until he left. "I've been thinking like a tourist for the past six months, since I moved back."

Sean waved, and the man on the steps strode toward them. "Your ideas are genius. I really think this is going to work out."

He couldn't fight his smile. That was exactly what he wanted to hear. "Is the rest of your team on board?"

"I had a meeting with them this afternoon. They're in."

"Sweet." When he'd first had the idea of setting up the museum and adding a tour to go with the artifacts, he'd asked around in the community. He hit the jackpot when he discovered the most reputable company belonged to his childhood friend.

He'd pitched the idea to Sean, and they'd been discussing the details for the past month. If the tour tonight proved as good as the rumors, Blake would be ready to sign on the dotted line. The Big Apple may have sent him running with his tail between his legs, but the Big Easy was his home turf, and if he could make this venture work, he'd be set.

If it didn't work, his savings would run out eventually, and he'd have to get a "real job." Sitting in an office all day long would kill him, and after his career-ending mistake at the NYC Museum of History, starting his own exhibit was the only way he could continue using his college degree… and his ability…to earn a living.

"This is Eric." Sean clapped the man on the shoulder, and Blake shook his hand.

"I can't wait to investigate the museum. With all those artifacts, the activity must be off the chain." Eric's eyes gleamed with excitement.

"It hasn't been too bad yet." Nothing out of the ordinary for the most haunted city in America, anyway. Occasional knocks and sounds of footsteps were part of the charm of the nineteenth-century buildings in the French Quarter. As long as he didn't bring anything sinister into his home, he could handle sharing his space with a ghost or two.

Eric pulled his phone from his pocket and glanced at the screen. "Syd's ready. Enjoy the tour. I'm looking forward to working with you." He nodded at Blake and jogged into the crowd.

"We've got two tours running tonight." Sean guided him into the group. "Identical routes, but Syd will run in reverse, so they never hit a stop at the same time."

Blake nodded. "Sounds logical. Keep the groups smaller. More intimate."

"Sydney's a rock star. You're going to love her." Sean

gestured toward the woman leading the second tour, and Blake's heart tumbled into his stomach.

"Is that Sydney Park?"

"Yeah. You know her?"

Talk about a blast from the past. Blake drifted forward to get a better look, his throat thickening as the memories came flooding back. "*Knew* her. I haven't seen her since college."

With her torn jeans, black leather jacket, and Converse shoes, her style hadn't changed a bit. Her hair was shorter, cropped above her ear on the left side and hanging down to her chin on the right, but the shiny black color still reminded him of a raven's feathers glinting in the moonlight. She had flawless light brown skin, a delicate nose, and a light coat of makeup accenting her dark brown eyes. A tourist said something humorous, and as Sydney's mulberry lips curved into a smile, Blake's heart sprinted like a racehorse out of the gates.

As she climbed to the top of the steps, she raised a hand and addressed the crowd with the same strong, confident voice that had drawn him to her all those years ago. "We're going to divide you into two groups. Eric will take half of you…" She gestured to Eric like a gameshow model. "And I'll take the rest. Any questions before we get started?"

A man in his sixties wearing an *I got Bourbon faced on Shit Street* t-shirt raked his gaze down her body and narrowed his eyes. "Yeah. What are you?"

She gave him a tight-lipped smile. "I'm a tour guide." Holding her arm straight in front of her, she descended the steps, making a path through the crowd.

The man stumbled as he turned, his speech slurred. "No, I mean where are you from?" He pointed, wiggling his finger at her face, and Blake instinctively stepped toward them.

Sydney dropped her arms to her sides and faced the man. "I'm from New Orleans. Born and raised." She cocked her head, her annoyance clear in her expression, but her confident posture said she had plenty of experience dealing with people like this.

The man took a gulp of his yard-sized beer. "Naw. What nationality are you? Where are your parents from?"

Eric moved in closer, as if ready to defuse the situation. Blake started forward again, but Sean stopped him with a hand on his shoulder. "She's got this."

Sydney crossed her arms and looked the man hard in the eyes. "I'm American, and both my parents were born here in Louisiana. Any *other* questions?"

The man's mouth opened and closed a few times, his shocked expression making it clear he was used to having the upper hand. Blake chuckled. No man ever had the upper hand with Sydney Park.

"You're in that group." She pointed, and the man sank back into the crowd.

Eric laughed and lowered his voice as he followed Sydney to the back of the swarm…toward Blake. "Wouldn't it have been easier to tell him your dad is Korean?"

Blake tensed as she approached; with her attention focused on her coworker, she hadn't noticed him yet.

"My mom is Irish and Haitian. Should I have to explain that too? Why would I make his ignorance any easier for him?"

"Good point." Eric raised his hand. "Y'all on this side, follow me." He led his group to the opposite end of the church.

"I told you she's a rock star," Sean said.

"Feisty as ever." Blake fought his smile. Even after all these years, the woman still made his blood hum.

She shouldn't have. Not after the way she left him. But he couldn't deny the glowing embers reigniting in his core. He could either fan the flames or stomp them out before she burned him to ash again. Which would it be this time?

Standing on her toes, she mouthed the numbers as she did a quick headcount. When she reached Sean, she grinned, but as her gaze locked with Blake's, she faltered. Her eyes widened, her mouth falling slack for a moment before she snapped it shut, swallowed hard, and continued her count.

Her reaction lit another spark inside his chest, stoking the coals that should have burned out long ago.

"Okay." She tapped the screen of her iPad and turned it around to show the audience a square QR code. Her gaze flicked between Blake and Sean a few times before she continued, "I'm going to walk around and let y'all scan this with your phones. It will sync with the presentation so you can see the photo and video evidence of the hauntings up close as we tour."

She shuffled through the crowd, stopping in front of each person with a phone before turning around and ignoring Blake as she moved toward the steps.

"Hey, Syd," Sean said. "Blake's never done the tour. Bring the code over here for him to scan."

"Right." Her eyes tightened, and her smile seemed forced as she glided toward him.

"Hi, Sydney. It's good to see you." He scanned the code, and the Crescent City Ghost Tours logo illuminated his screen.

"Hi, Blake. It's been a while." She looked at him, and her eyes softened, her lips parting slightly.

He could almost taste the strawberry lip balm she used to wear, and he was filled with the sudden urge to find out if she still used it. He swallowed the phantom flavor from his mouth. His emotional coals didn't need stoking. They were already ablaze.

She looked at Sean. "You didn't mention Blake was the friend you were teaming up with."

He tilted his head. "I told you at lunch today."

"Oh, right." She blinked. "It must have slipped my mind. Well…" Her gaze landed on Blake, and he tensed. "Enjoy the tour."

She trotted to the front of the group and began her speech as if he were just another visitor joining the outing…like what they'd shared had never happened.

"Slipped her mind, my ass," Blake muttered as he followed the group into Pirate's Alley.

Of all the times for Sydney to tune Sean out, it had to happen at lunch today. If she'd even been halfway listening to the conversation, she would have heard Blake's name mentioned and been prepared…or at least aware she would have to face him tonight.

Nothing could have prepared her for those piercing blue eyes or the way his gaze bore into her, slicing her open and latching onto her heart. And now she had to work with the man…

She turned the corner onto Dauphine Street and led her group to the Sultan's Palace. On autopilot, she told the story of the alleged massacre, the blood running out the door and onto the street, and the Sultan being buried alive. The presentation revealed the spirit evidence they'd captured on an investigation, and while she told the tour group the story of the Sultan was merely a legend and the ghosts occupying the building had nothing to do with the horrifying tale, they always preferred the gruesome lore to the reality of the haunting.

And now the reality of her past was back to haunt her...

Two tours a night, five nights a week, fifty-one weeks a year for the past six years. To say she was used to people watching her was an understatement. But something about the look in Blake's eyes every time she accidentally caught his gaze made her throat close up and her palms sweat.

He kept his light brown hair sheared short on the sides and long on top in a messy wave. He had a strong jaw and sharp cheekbones, but those full, kissable lips softened his features, making him look like he stepped right off the page of a men's cologne ad.

She delivered her speech at three more stops on the tour, and the patrons *oohed* and *ahhed* at the video evidence as usual. But Blake kept his eyes trained on her, barely glancing at his screen.

The heaviness of his gaze weighed on her conscience. How could he stand to look at her after she'd treated him so badly?

In her defense, he was going to treat her just as badly —she'd seen it in a vision. She'd simply ended the relationship before he got the chance to hurt her.

The real question was: how could he still stir butterflies in her stomach after all this time?

It didn't matter. He'd planned to stand her up on what

was—at the time—one of the most important nights of her life: her induction into the Krewe of Horae, for goodness' sake. Only a select few were allowed to join the all-female Mardi Gras group each year. It was a huge deal, and any man who would treat a woman with that kind of disregard wasn't worth wasting her time on.

Besides, eight years had passed since they broke up. He'd moved to New York and started a new life, and she'd moved on. They were adults now, not college kids. They could be professional.

As the tour concluded, she thanked the guests and accepted the tips they offered. Blake stood with Sean on the sidewalk a few feet away, and they shook hands, the excitement in their eyes indicating the deal had been sealed.

The flutter in her stomach rose up to meet her sinking heart as she swallowed the dryness from her mouth. Hopefully she wouldn't have to work too closely with Blake. Sydney was in charge of tech, so as long as ghosts weren't involved on Blake's side of the company, he wouldn't need her for much. No paranormal evidence to present meant no tech on the new tour. *Hopefully.*

She said goodbye to the last tourist and turned toward the men, squaring her shoulders and lifting her chin. If Blake didn't mention their breakup, she wouldn't either. There was no need to delve into the past when the present was the only time they could control. *Keep it professional, Syd.*

"That was an impressive tour." His smile weakened her knees, so she locked them. "Sean says you designed the accompanying presentation from scratch."

She sucked in the breath he stole from her lungs. "It makes the tour more interactive. The customers love it."

Her voice was steady, strong, masking the way her insides trembled.

"I bet." He caught her gaze and held it, but he wasn't looking *at* her. Something about his expression, his body language…his aura in general…made it seem like he was looking *inside* her.

It was part of his charisma, the way he always made her feel like she was the most important person in the room. Blake had a magnetic personality, but his charm wouldn't work on her this time. They were coworkers now. Technically, if he and Sean were partners, that made Blake her boss. She knew better than to date the boss.

If she could convince her body to stop reacting like it was a sweet tooth and he was the last piece of candy on earth, she'd be okay.

Sean cleared his throat. "I want to schedule a lunch meeting with the whole team tomorrow to iron out the details. Then we need to plan a time to investigate the museum. The building itself has a residual haunting, but it will take some time to figure out if any new spirits have come in with the artifacts being collected."

Blake glanced at Sean before looking at Sydney again. "Sounds good."

"And you two will need to spend some time together working out the new tour and the interactive displays for the museum," Sean said. "Is that going to be an issue?" He arched a brow, his gaze flicking between them.

Sydney fought to keep her expression neutral. That was way more time than she cared to spend with Blake, but if she brought Eric or Jason along as a buffer, she could handle it. She forced a smile and tore her gaze away from Blake's deep blue eyes. "Why would it be an issue?"

"I'm looking forward to it," Blake said, his eyes still on her.

Is he, now? I'm sure as hell not. "Oh, but lunch tomorrow doesn't work for me. My krewe is meeting to discuss our masquerade, so you'll have to do it without me. Mardi Gras is a busy time of year." She pressed her lips together, mentally smacking herself upside the head. Why did she have to bring *that* up?

Blake's brow lifted. "The Krewe of Horae?"

She nodded, holding her breath. *Please let it go.* She did not want to revisit that near-disaster right now.

His lips twitched. "I remember when you first joined. You were so excited for your induction. It's been what? Eight years now?"

Oh, lord. He went there. She clenched her teeth. "Something like that."

"We'll do it in the afternoon then." Sean fished his buzzing phone from his pocket. "Three o'clock? I need you there, Syd. You'll be taking over my duties for a while when the baby comes."

She let out her breath in a slow hiss. There was no way out of this. "I'll be there."

"Good." Sean froze, staring at his screen. "Oh, God."

"What is it?" she asked.

He blinked. "Emily's water broke." His jaw went slack, his gaze darting from the phone to Sydney to Blake.

Sydney grinned. "You're having a baby."

"We're having a baby." He stood there, unmoving.

She laughed and gave him a shove. "Go get your wife and take her to the hospital."

"Right. Umm…"

"I'll handle the meeting tomorrow. Go meet your baby."

He nodded. "Thanks, Syd. Blake, I'll be in touch." He turned and jogged up the sidewalk.

"That's exciting." Blake caught her gaze again and shoved his hands in his pockets. "Sometimes I wonder what my life would be like now if I'd never gone to New York."

That was her cue to leave. "It is what it is. You can't change the past, so there's no use dwelling on it." And he *did* go to New York. Even if he hadn't planned on standing her up, he had planned to move across the country. Her heart would have been broken either way.

His gaze danced around her face, pausing on her lips a moment too long. "If I could see the future…if I'd known how it would turn out…"

"If ifs and buts were candy and nuts…"

"I wouldn't have gone."

"But you did." She shrugged. Blake didn't know about her ability. Everyone *thought* they wanted to see the future, but would he really have done things differently? Doubtful. Whatever reason he'd had for standing her up must have been more important than their relationship. Anyway, he wouldn't have missed grad school for her. She wouldn't have let him.

Pain happened, whether she could see it coming or not, and if she could give up her ability and never see the future again, she'd do it in a heartbeat. But *ifs* weren't worth the breath they were uttered on.

She crossed her arms, doing her best to ignore the regret softening his eyes. "Where are we meeting tomorrow?"

"At the museum." He hesitated. "What's your number? I'll text you the address."

She recited the digits as he punched them into his

phone. Hers buzzed in her pocket, and she pulled it out to glance at the screen. "Got it. I'll let the guys know." She took two steps backward, hoping to break the magnetic hold he had on her.

He didn't move. "I'm looking forward to working with you."

She forced a smile, nodded, and turned away.

CHAPTER THREE

It looked like Blake was getting a second chance with Sydney, but did he want to risk it again? Judging from the spring in his step as he strode down Dumaine Street toward his home, at least part of him did.

Then again, his blood always carried a little flush of excitement during Mardi Gras season. The entire city buzzed with energy this time of year, and he slowed his pace to admire the decorations the residents had put up in honor of New Orleans' most celebrated holiday.

A wrought-iron fence with fleur-de-lis posts hung heavy with thousands of strands of plastic beads in shades of green, gold, and purple, and a yellow cottage with blue shutters boasted yards of garland in the same colors with matching wreaths and giant fleurs-de-lis hanging in the windows. Across the street, shiny, scalloped fabric in the signature festive hues draped from a second-story balcony, and oversized beads and carnival masks hung from the shutters.

He made a left on Bourbon Street and side-stepped around a group of women celebrating a bachelorette party.

The bride-to-be wore a white veil attached to a headband, and the silver glitter on her dark skin glinted in the streetlights. Her entourage wore pink sashes with "Bride Tribe" emblazoned across them, and they all carried yard glasses filled with syrupy daiquiris.

"Hey, cutie." A blonde shuffled toward him, her ankles wobbling in her five-inch heels. "Do you live here?"

"Yes, ma'am, I do. Are you lost?"

"No." Her laugh came out as a snort, and she covered her mouth. "We're doing a scavenger hunt, and we need a picture with a local." She pulled out her phone and squinted at the screen. "A local who doesn't work in a bar. Do you work in a bar?"

"No, but I—"

"Hey, Denise, I found one." She stumbled into him, catching herself on his shoulder.

Blake clutched her arm until she steadied and then stepped away. The bride sashayed toward him, her stilettos in her hand, and he cringed at the sight of her bare feet on the pavement. "You really should wear shoes out here. No telling what you might step on."

She ignored his comment and posed next to him, holding two fingers up near her face. "I'm ready."

"Hold on." Blake backed away. He'd faced the wrath of a jealous lover before, and he wasn't about to let it happen again. "I'd really rather not."

"Please?" The blonde batted her false lashes, revealing the sparkling pink shadow on her lids. "It's just one little picture."

"And then her fiancé sees it and comes after me? No, thanks." While their behavior was typical for a bachelorette party, there was no way he was setting himself up to be the target of a jealous rage. Not again.

"What if we're all in the picture?" the blonde asked. "We can't go back to the bar until we get this. Pretty please?"

The rest of the tribe gathered around the bride and said, "Please," in unison. A woman with long braids lost her balance, falling face-first into her friend. The other woman caught her, and the whole bunch burst into a cacophony of laughter.

He turned to make his escape, but the blonde clutched his arm. "Hold up, cutie pie. We haven't got the picture yet."

Blake sighed. "All right." He joined the group, standing rigid and shoving his hands in his pockets to look as innocent as possible.

The blonde leaned in and snapped a selfie with them. "Thank you. You're awesome." She slipped a strand of pink beads over his head before the group headed toward the next bar.

Blake picked up his pace, making a right on St. Ann and heading home. Two blocks away from New Orleans' most famous street, Blake's apartment and museum sat in a prime location for both living and running his business. The brick façade with maroon shutters gave the downstairs portion of the building just enough creepy curb appeal to draw in potential customers, and the eerie window displays featuring items used in magical rituals as well as embalming supplies were sure to catch people's attention.

He'd covered the windows in brown paper, for now, piquing visitors' curiosity as he waited to settle on a grand opening date. Now that his merger with the tour company was finalized, things were starting to look up.

It had to be fate. Everything that went down in New York

must have happened for the sole purpose of sending him home. Sure, it could have been coincidence, but what a crazy bit of serendipity for him to see Sydney again when he had.

He'd been back in New Orleans for six months and hadn't run into her until tonight. If they'd met earlier, she'd have turned up her nose and walked away like she had all those years ago when he'd told her his plans to move to New York.

Now she'd have to talk to him, and maybe…maybe he could convince her to give him another chance. He had no plans of leaving this time, and his feelings for her were already clawing out of the grave he'd buried them in eight years ago. Then again…

He may have deserved to be dumped, but not the way she did it. Nobody deserved to be ghosted.

Besides, they would be working together. He'd learned the hard way that office romances never worked, and he refused to make that mistake again.

He shuffled toward the side entrance leading upstairs to his apartment and found Claire, his cousin's daughter, sitting sideways on the porch steps, her shoulder against the wall, her finger tracing the bottom panel of the wooden door.

Stopping in front of her, he fished his key from his pocket and waited for her to notice him. She appeared lost in thought, her brow furrowing, the sadness in her eyes tugging at his heart. At nineteen years old, Claire had endured more tragedy than anyone should ever have to. He cleared his throat.

"Hey, Blake." She dropped her hand into her lap and smiled, but it didn't reach her eyes. "I was wondering how long you were going to stand there."

"What are you doing?" He sank onto a step next to her.

"Waiting for you." She tucked her brown hair behind her ear. "How'd the tour go?"

"Good. It's a done deal. We're a museum and tour company now."

"That's great." Her eyes brightened. "I did some more research on The Axeman murders. It looks like he had more victims than they originally thought. There might be more weapons out there. Do you want me to do some digging? See if they're in anyone's private collections?"

"We've got an axe and a cleaver. That's enough for that particular crime, and anyway, you need to focus on your studies."

She scoffed. "Please. My classes are so easy I can make A's with my eyes closed. I sleep through half of them."

"They'll get harder."

"Doubt it. Did you know The Axeman snuck in by removing a panel in the door? What kind of a person sneaks into someone's house, unarmed, and uses the victim's own tools as a weapon? That was one twisted individual. I bet he got off on it."

Blake cringed. "A lot of people think it was mafia-related. A hitman, not a serial killer."

She shrugged and picked at her fingernails.

"Maybe you should lay off the crime research for a while. I don't think it's good for you right now."

"No, I need this." Her eyes widened, and she sat up straight. "It helps me feel…less alone. Knowing that Brooklyn wasn't the only victim of a senseless killing helps me cope. Moving here may have taken me away from everything that reminds me of her, but it will never take her out of my mind. She'll always be with me."

The passion in her words tightened his chest. He couldn't imagine what she'd been through. "Your dad is worried about you."

"Step-dad. Anyway, do you want to watch a movie or something? Hang out?" Her tone flipped from intense to casual in a beat, something her parents warned him to look out for when she moved here.

"Claire, you're nineteen."

She crossed her arms. "And you're thirty. What's your point?"

"You've made friends in the dorm, right? What about your roommate? Don't you want to hang out with her? At least *try* to have a good time so I can tell your parents you're making an attempt?"

"Working for you *is* my attempt. I have a job. I'm acing all my classes. That's enough."

"School has always been easy for you, but you need to learn to enjoy life again."

"The way you enjoyed your boss at the museum until her husband got fed up?" She arched a brow, challenging him.

"They were separated when I dated her." He gritted his teeth, attempting to quell his frustration. Claire tried his patience to no end, but after everything she'd been through, he let it slide.

"You lost your job, but I guess that's okay, since you enjoyed doing it." She inclined her chin.

Blake blew out a slow breath through his nose, his nostrils flaring as he counted to ten in his mind. "This conversation isn't about me. Honestly, Claire, I'm worried about you too. It's ten-thirty at night, and you've been sitting on my doorstep all evening. Are you sure you're okay?"

She visibly shivered and rubbed the back of her neck before squinting at his chest. "Nice necklace."

He glanced down at the beads. "I was ambushed by a bachelorette party on my way home."

"That explains the dicks."

"Dicks?"

"The beads are dicks." She laughed. "You've been walking around the French Quarter with a bunch of dicks around your neck."

"Seriously?" He took off the necklace and examined it. Sure enough, what he'd thought were simply cylindrical-shaped beads were actually tiny pink dicks with well-formed ball sacks threaded end-to-end. "They're awfully detailed for being so small."

Claire picked up the other end of the strand. "Look at that. They even have a little ridge around the head. How cute. Tiny, but cute."

Blake chuckled. "Well, size doesn't matter anyway, right?"

She snorted. "The only people who say that are men with small dicks and the women who love them… They love the men, I mean. Nobody loves a little dick. Can I have it?"

"Be my guest."

She slipped it over her head and slid a thumb across her phone screen as she stood.

Blake rose to his feet. "Where are you off to?"

"My roommate just texted. Looks like I'm going to a party. What time should I come in tomorrow?"

"Regular time. Sean's team is coming in at three."

"Great. I'll see you then. Ah!" She squealed and jumped as a black crow swooped down from the street, landing on the steps in front of Blake's apartment. "What is that?"

He waved an arm at the animal to shoo it away, but it barely flinched before ruffling its feathers and screeching at him. "Damn crow's been hanging around for the past week."

Claire inched toward it. "They say crows are bad omens, you know."

"They're pests is what they are." He stomped on the wooden step, and the bird flew away. "It keeps dragging trash out of the can and dropping it on the sidewalk. I might have to invest in one of those plastic barn owl decoys to keep it away once the museum opens." Then again, a crow would add to the creepy vibe he was going for.

"Good luck with that. See you tomorrow." Claire turned and strode away.

"Be careful out there," he called before she rounded the corner.

"Yes, sir." She grinned and gave him a mock salute before disappearing behind a building.

Blake shook his head and unlocked the door, trudging up the steps to his second-floor apartment. He'd promised his cousin he'd look out for Claire when she started college. Giving her a job at his museum had seemed like a good way to keep tabs on her, but he'd been second-guessing his decision lately. A less hands-on approach might have been better, but it was too late for that now. At least she was finally making friends. Her parents would be thrilled to hear about her progress.

He slipped out of his jacket and tossed it on the couch before kicking off his shoes and padding into the bedroom. Pulling the string to turn on the light, he peered at the top shelf in the back of his closet. A small cedar box sat wedged in the corner behind a stack of old CDs he couldn't bring himself to part with.

The box scraped across the shelf as he tugged it down, but a loud *bang* reverberating through the bottom floor overpowered the sound. He jumped, nearly dropping the container, but he tightened his grip on the smooth wood and carried it to the dresser.

Setting it down, he stood still, breathing deeply to calm his sprinting heart and listening for any more phantom sounds. Sean had warned him that bringing in all these artifacts related to tragedy might attract ghosts—ones attached to the objects as well as wandering spirits.

The heater hummed as it kicked on, and someone outside shouted. Otherwise, the room was devoid of sound. He shook his head, chuckling at himself. *Get a grip.* Ghosts were simply people without bodies. Sean had assured him of that. But…what if the disembodied person were a murderer in life?

The sound of light footsteps emanated from the living room, a sound he'd heard every night since he moved in. This was part of the residual haunting he'd been told about. Spirit energy from a ghost that had already moved on to…wherever…lingered in the building, repeating the same motions at the same time. It wasn't intelligent, and he couldn't do anything about it.

That didn't stop him from tiptoeing into the hallway. He held his breath as he peered around the corner, half-expecting to see the ghost of The Axeman standing in his living room. As usual, the space sat empty.

He exhaled a curse and shuffled to his bedroom. He'd lived in this city twenty-two years of his life, and the idea of ghosts had never scared him before. But Claire's research on all these crimes, particularly the gruesome murders, had him jumping at every damn sound he heard.

Once the team did their investigation and reassured him nothing was dangerous, he'd sleep better. Until then, he'd have to get used to sharing his space with unknown ghosts.

His gaze locked on the cedar box he'd retrieved from the closet, and his pulse quickened. He carried it to the bed, sinking onto the edge of the mattress as he lifted the lid. His expired passport sat on top, and he moved it aside, shuffling through various mementos until he found what he was looking for: a pewter sundial pendant hanging from a strip of black leather.

He set the box aside and held the necklace up to the light. He hadn't thought about this pendant in ages. When he first returned to New Orleans, Sydney had crossed his mind a few times. He'd considered looking her up to see how she was doing, but she'd it made it crystal clear she was done with him when they broke up, so he'd dismissed the idea as quickly as it had formed. It was a good thing too.

Seeing her tonight had stirred up emotions he'd thought were dead and buried. Hell, he'd only been fooling himself. He used to think Sydney was *the one*. He may have succeeded in concealing the emotions, but they were still alive and kicking.

He should've tried harder. Sure, she'd blocked his number and changed her routine so they didn't cross paths, but he'd only made a few attempts to contact her. He'd talked to a couple of her friends, but all they'd tell him was that Sydney didn't want to see him.

He should have gone to her house and waited outside her door, but his pride kept him from sinking to that level.

He was graduating, moving to New York to get his Master's degree, and Sydney was a freshman.

She'd broken his heart. He'd have done whatever it took to make their relationship work. He'd have flown home every weekend to see her if that's what she wanted. If she'd have just talked to him…

But she didn't. She dumped him via text and never spoke to him again. *Who does that?* He'd turned his devastation into anger and headed for New York without looking back. Without realizing what he'd left behind.

He clutched the pendant in his palm, closing his eyes and focusing on the energy. His skin tingled as he opened himself to the stories it had to tell. In his mind, he saw the day Sydney gave the necklace to him. They'd been dating for a little over a month, and he'd always admired it. She said the sundial had significance, though she wouldn't elaborate on why, so when she'd taken it off and clasped it around his neck, the gesture seared into his heart.

She had cared for him at one time. Her emotions, though faint, still seeped into his skin as he focused on the necklace.

His own energy attached to the object was much stronger. He'd worn the damn thing for two and a half months after she dumped him, hoping she'd change her mind and at least tell him goodbye before he left.

He never heard from her again, and the hurt and anger he'd used as fuel to propel himself out of the state felt as vibrant as if it had happened yesterday. These were the emotions he needed to focus on. He had to remember the pain, or he'd fall for her all over again.

It was time to snuff out the burning embers of their past. They were coworkers now, and that was all they'd ever be.

CHAPTER FOUR

Sydney left Antoine's with a full stomach and another big item marked off her to-do list. With the plans for her krewe's annual masquerade finalized, all she had left to worry about for Mardi Gras were her costumes for the parade and the ball. That and the stress of navigating the busy streets and keeping her tour groups together when the mass of tourists descended upon the city, but she'd been handling that for years.

Her phone buzzed as she made a left on St. Ann, and a text from Blake illuminated the screen: *Are we still on for 3:00?*

A weird flitting sensation formed in her chest as she typed her reply: *On my way.* She waited a few seconds for a response, but nothing came through, so she shoved her phone into her pocket. Had he texted Eric and Jason too, or was he afraid she'd skip the meeting because of their history? Probably the latter.

To be fair, faking food poisoning had crossed her mind. Migraines were always convincing excuses, but she was a professional. So what if her heart flip-flopped in her chest every time he looked at her? She'd get over it eventually.

She refused to be the reason the company died, so she had to.

The moment the thought crossed her mind, her vision tunneled, the blue and gold kaleidoscope eclipsing her perception of the real world, the sinking sensation dragging her down to Wonderland at record speed.

As the cut-glass mosaic cleared in the center of her vision, she stood in the cemetery again. She spun in a circle, trying to assess her surroundings, to at least figure out *which* cemetery she was in, but the sparkling, dancing colors in her peripheral blocked her view of anything but the funeral. She pushed forward, the sensation of trudging through molasses making it impossible to reach the coffin. Standing on her toes, she glanced over a blurry shoulder and found the casket closed.

Nothing discerning about the location stood out, but as she turned, a blurry figure standing next to Sean became crisp: Eric.

The menacing sound of beating wings drew her attention to the sky, and a swarm of black figures obscured the sun. A flock of screeching crows roosted on the top of a massive tomb, their beady eyes boring into her, driving their portentous message home.

A car horn sounded, and Sydney's vision eclipsed again. She blinked, and Bourbon Street came into focus. A man in an expensive suit rammed into her shoulder as he passed, but he kept his phone pressed to his ear, not even muttering an apology as he paced up the sidewalk. She shook her head and continued across the street.

That damn vision was driving her crazy. She'd meditated on it for an hour last night, but even with complete focus and an intentional trip down the rabbit hole, she hadn't been able to glean a single bit of new information. And now, randomly, as she walked down the street—which was not the safest place to black out—the universe decided to show her more?

At least Eric was in the clear, and she could rule out the death of one more friend. *Two down, only four or five to go.*

A sickening sensation formed in her stomach. The last time a vision had been this difficult to expand, Courtney, Sean's first wife, had died. Sydney had seen the car wreck over and over in her mind, but every time she tried to pull back from the vision and get a better view, she'd been thrown out of it as if she weren't meant to know.

She couldn't say when or how it would happen, only that it would. Sean convinced Courtney not to drive for a couple of months, but the vision didn't change. Courtney got fed up and crashed into an eighteen-wheeler shortly after.

Of course, Sydney's mom had used the ordeal as a hammer to pound the curse theory deeper into her mind, insisting that she couldn't stop the hands of fate when a soul was called home, so she should keep her premonitions to herself. People weren't meant to know, much less change, the future the universe had planned for them.

So why the hell did she have the visions if she wasn't meant to affect the future?

Sydney had learned to be more careful when sharing her premonitions after that. Most people didn't even know she had them, and she preferred to keep it that way.

But this new vision… Those crows… Her hope that the coffin was a metaphor began to dwindle, the nagging notion that someone she loved was going to die weighing heavy on her heart.

She pushed the idea out of her mind before it paralyzed her. Living in fear would do her no good, and until she figured out exactly what the universe was trying to tell her, there wasn't much she could do.

She slowed her pace as she reached Blake's address. This time, her sprinting pulse had nothing to do with the ominous vision and everything to do with the man she was about to face. With Sean temporarily out of the picture, it was up to her to make sure nothing bad happened in his absence. Getting involved with her ex would make for glitchy working conditions, and she wasn't about to throw a line of bad code into their perfectly calibrated program.

"No matter how hot he is or how nice he seems, he was going to stand you up. Remember that, Syd." Not to mention she couldn't shake the feeling that this merger could be the reason someone she loved was going to die.

As if in answer to that thought, a single crow flew down, landing on the sidewalk in front of the entrance. It puffed out its obsidian feathers and let out a grating caw.

"I've received the message loud and clear, so unless you have new information for me, you'd best be on your way." She stopped and fisted her hands on her hips. "Now I'm talking to birds. Fantastic."

The crow cawed again, and Sydney waved her arms, chasing it away from the entrance. Enough with the omens. If the universe wanted her to do something about that vision, it needed to step up its game. The bird perched on the windowsill and eyed her as she straightened her shoulders, took a deep breath, and stepped through the door.

The dark-stained concrete floor gleamed beneath the track lighting above, and marble-looking pillars lined the massive open space, the empty plexiglass boxes sitting atop them polished and ready to hold Blake's collection of macabre artifacts. A heap of cardboard boxes filled one corner of the room, and Eric and Jason peered into a container, flipping through a stack of what looked like vinyl albums.

"Hey, Syd." Jason waved, and Eric nodded hello before returning his focus to the box.

She shuffled deeper into the room, and Blake stepped through a doorway from the back. The slight fading on the front of his dark jeans drew her attention to his muscular thighs, and his deep blue t-shirt enhanced the color of his eyes, making them even more breathtaking.

Old, familiar feelings fluttered to the surface, but she put a lid on them before they could boil over. Even if he wasn't a self-centered jerk who planned to stand her up and then abandon her for New York, he was her boss now, and she would keep reminding herself of that until she believed it mattered.

He took two steps toward her and stopped, the hard set of his eyes softening into an expression that made her lightheaded. "Hey, Sydney. I'm glad you could make it."

Her weight shifted to her toes, her body involuntarily drifting toward him before she clenched her fists and regained her composure. She glanced at a clock. Ten 'til three. She was early as usual, though the guys must have been beyond excited about this venture to show up before her.

"I never miss a work meeting unless I'm on my deathbed. And even then, I'd call if I couldn't make it." She arched a brow, hoping her point hit home.

He blinked but didn't miss a beat in his reply. "I'm glad to hear that. Giving a reason for your disappearance is the decent thing to do."

Okay, she deserved that. Her statement had been unfair and unprofessional—not at all the way she should behave. She opened her mouth for a rebuttal, but a tall woman with long brown hair and brown eyes entered from the back room.

"Wait. This is who we were waiting for?" She marched toward Blake and backhanded him on the bicep. "When you guys said 'Syd,' I thought you were talking about a guy."

Blake cleared his throat. "Sydney, this is my cousin, Claire."

Her eyes rolled so hard her head moved with them. "Second cousin by marriage only. It's so nice to meet you."

"Nice to meet you too." Sydney held out her hand to shake, but Claire pulled her into a bear hug instead.

"I am *so* thrilled that you're a girl." Her chin moved against the top of Sydney's head. "I thought I was going to have to keep all the boys in line by myself."

Sydney patted her back and unwedged herself from Claire's embrace. "We'll work on them together."

"Claire has been helping me set up the museum and doing research on the artifacts for the displays." As Blake held Sydney's gaze, confliction danced in his eyes. He opened his mouth to say more, but he pressed his lips together and gave her a tight smile instead.

"I can only imagine what kinds of ghosts we've brought into the building with everything Blake's found. So much murder and mayhem in one place." Claire's eyes gleamed.

"That's what we're here for." Eric shuffled forward,

holding a pair of antique forceps, opening and closing them as he spoke. "We'll gather the evidence to convince the customers the place is haunted, but only Sean can tell us whose ghosts are really here."

Blake nodded and looked at Sydney. "Do you need to wait for him to do the investigation? I was hoping to get the place checked out sooner rather than later. The activity is starting to pick up."

"Are you afraid of a little spirit energy?" He should have stayed in New York if he was. Lord knew her life would be a lot easier if he had.

Blake straightened. "I'm not afraid, but I'd like to know what's been making all the noises I'm hearing at night."

She watched his lips as he spoke, remembering the way they'd felt gliding along her skin. They'd made plenty of their own noises at night back in the day... *Stop it, Syd.* She clenched her teeth.

"We can start without him." The sooner she could get this over with, the better. "Sean can do his thing any time of day. We need to be here at night, when there's less interference from outside sounds."

"Can I help?" Claire bounced on her toes.

"Since we've never investigated this building before, we need to do it alone," Jason said.

Claire's shoulders slumped, and Blake wrapped an arm around her. "But the second time, I'm sure you can." He looked at Sydney, his concern for his cousin evident in his expression. "It takes time to figure it all out, right? You'll be doing multiple investigations?"

"Most likely." *Unfortunately.* "Once we get our baseline readings and do the initial investigation, we'll ask both of you to come in so we can see if the activity changes with you here."

Claire smiled. "Awesome. I hope The Axeman is here."

Eric's brow furrowed, and he gave Sydney a strange look before focusing on Blake.

Blake motioned toward the boxes in the corner. "Let me show you some of the artifacts we have."

"What are these barbeque tongs for?" Eric clicked the forceps. "Did somebody get roasted?"

Claire snickered.

"Those are forceps." Sydney fought the urge to smack him upside the head.

"They're used to pull a baby out of a woman's vagina." Claire laughed.

Eric wrinkled his nose and set the instrument on top of a display case, jerking his hand away as if it shocked him.

"Those belonged to a doctor who did exploratory surgeries on pregnant women." Blake's face was grim. "He *accidentally* killed several of them and their unborn babies."

Sydney shivered. She'd heard the tale many times, but it didn't make it any less gruesome. This particular story was merely a legend, though. No physical proof had been found to corroborate it, so Blake couldn't possibly know for sure that was what the forceps were used for.

They moved to the back of the room, and Blake showed them several more artifacts from murder weapons to antique embalming tools to various suitcases and other personal belongings of victims or perpetrators of infamous crimes in the city's history.

"Where did you find all this stuff?" Eric asked.

"A lot of it came from people's private collections. Some are on loan, and others I bought outright. I've also acquired things from evidence storage when the crimes were past the statute of limitations."

"Fascinating." Jason ran his hand along the arm of a wooden chair. "How do you know this stuff is real? I mean, aside from your museum background and your experience with antiques. How do you know this chair was actually used by the Vampire Brothers in the thirties?"

Blake leaned an elbow on a stack of boxes. "I guess Sean didn't tell you about my ability?"

Sydney raised her eyebrows and looked at Blake. This was news to her. They'd dated for four months, and he'd never mentioned having any sort of psychic ability. What other secrets had he kept from her? She mentally added this to her list of reasons why dumping him had been the right thing to do. Relationships were nothing without honesty.

Her jaw clenched involuntarily. She'd never told him about her own curse either.

"I use psychometry," he said.

"He can read the energy in objects." Claire bubbled with excitement. "He just has to touch something, and he can tell you who owned it and what they did with it…and sometimes even how they felt while they did it. He's amazing."

Blake let out an embarrassed chuckle. "I don't know about amazing." He flicked his gaze between Sydney and his cousin. "Don't you have a class to get to, Claire?"

She groaned. "Yeah, I do. Don't plan too much without me, okay? I'm super excited to be a part of this."

"We're glad to have you on board." Sydney waved as Claire pranced out the door.

Blake eyed Sydney, trying to gauge her reaction to his psychic power. He'd wanted to mention it when they were dating. Hell, he'd wanted her to know everything about him, but he'd been afraid his weird talent would freak her out.

He was still testing the waters back then, and he learned the hard way what could happen when sharing his gift backfired. Few people knew about his ability, and he hadn't decided if he wanted it to be common knowledge among their potential customers. He'd already been called a fraud and a liar—among other things—but for this venture to be a success, his team needed to know what they were dealing with.

Sydney's only reaction to the news had been a slight eyebrow raise that looked more like a *Why didn't you tell me?* than disgust or weirdness. She hunted ghosts, and her boss was a psychic medium...she was probably used to weird.

"Where is she from?" Sydney ran her hand along the top of a box, avoiding his gaze and the subject of his ability. "She has a slight accent, but it's not very strong."

"New York."

She cocked her head. "Oh, you ran off to New York and came home with a girl?" Something Blake wanted to call jealousy briefly sparked in Sydney's eyes before she slipped on her mask of professionalism, straightening her spine and turning her attention to the box.

Something he *didn't* want to call anticipation fluttered in his chest at the idea she might still harbor feelings for him after all these years. "She's my cousin's kid."

"Is she...okay?" Eric asked. "I was picking up some strange vibes from her. Emotions all over the place."

"I was wondering why you weren't hitting on her."

Sydney nudged a table with her hip as if testing its stability before sitting on the surface. "She looks like your type."

Eric leaned on the table next to her, crossing his arms. "I don't have a type."

"She has boobs, and she's breathing. She's your type." She mussed his hair, and he swatted her hand away.

"Are you sure you want to be a part of this group?" Jason shook his head. "Those two bicker like siblings."

Blake smiled. He absolutely wanted to be a part of this group. It was no wonder their company was so successful. They had a Grade A tour with some astonishing evidence to back up their haunting claims, and the four of them fit together like olive salad on a muffuletta. They just…worked.

Sean obviously called the shots, but Sydney played the unspoken role of second. Jason and Eric knew their place in the hierarchy, and everyone seemed satisfied with their group dynamic. Blake would have to figure out a way to fit into their machine without slipping any gears.

"I think we're going to make a great team." He locked eyes with Sydney, and an invisible cord drew him toward her. He *hoped* they'd make a good team, but he'd have to keep his feelings for her in check. The spark was still burning, and from the way she looked at him, she had to feel it too. She was denying it, though, and so would he. This merger was too important to risk it.

He grabbed a folding chair and sank into it. "Tell me about these vibes you're picking up from Claire. What exactly do you mean?" He rubbed his palms on his jeans and rested his hands on his knees.

"I'm an empath," Eric said. "I can read people's

emotions, and hers were all over the place. No offense, but she seems pretty messed up."

Blake nodded, his heart sinking at Eric's observation. "At the end of her senior year of high school, her best friend was brutally murdered. They still haven't found the killer."

Sydney's mouth dropped open. "How awful. She must be devastated."

"She is, but she's getting better. I *thought* she was, anyway. Maybe she's just getting better at hiding it." He stared straight ahead, his gaze losing focus for a moment before he shook his head. "Her step-dad is my cousin. Her family thought it would be good for her to get away, so when I moved here, they asked if I'd look out for her. The change of scenery seems to have helped, and she's away from danger in case she was mixed up in whatever her friend had gotten into."

"Wow." Sydney looked into his eyes, and the invisible cord tugging him toward her pulled harder. She'd always had a way of drawing him in with her gaze, making the rest of the world disappear. It seemed she still did. "That's really sweet of you to look out for her. Does she live with you?"

"She lives in the dorms. Between her friends, her studies, and helping me with the museum, she stays busy. Out of her head, I guess." He shrugged.

The corners of her lips tugged into a tentative smile, and her mask of professionalism slipped, her eyes softening as she held his gaze. His fingers twitched with the urge to reach for her, to see if she fit in his arms the way he remembered, if her lips still tasted like strawberries.

He cleared his throat, breaking the trance she'd pulled

him into. "So, Eric, can you sense everyone's emotions all the time? Or do you have to focus? How does it work?"

Leaning on the table, Eric crossed his legs at the ankles. "I *could* feel it all the time, but I've figured out how to put up shields so I don't get overwhelmed. And some people I can't feel at all."

"Why do you think that is?" Blake had never picked up an object he couldn't get at least some kind of history on if he tried hard enough.

Eric lifted his hands. "Sometimes people are good at hiding their emotions. They're closed off for whatever reason, like they're inside a bubble."

"Have you ever tried to pop the bubble and get inside?"

He shook his head. "Knowing what everyone else is feeling isn't always a good thing. It's nice to be around people who don't affect me on a psychic level sometimes. Like Sydney here." He lightly punched her on the shoulder. "She's about as closed off as a floodgate during a hurricane."

"Lucky me." She hit him back.

Interesting. In the time they'd dated, he felt like he'd only scratched the surface of her complexity. Good to know he wasn't the only one. "So, you can tell how I'm feeling?"

Eric chuckled and glanced at Sydney. "Yep."

Fantastic. "And you get nothing from her?" He gestured toward Sydney.

"Not a thing."

Damn. There went his one chance at finding out if she still had feelings for him. Now he'd have to do it the old-fashioned way and ask her himself. Wait. What was he thinking? *Keep it professional. Don't go there again.* "Well, aren't we an interesting group?"

Eric raised his eyebrows at Sydney, and her knuckles whitened as she clutched the edge of the table.

"I'm the only normal one here," Jason said, and Sydney gave him a hard look.

"You have an ability too?" Blake asked, but she clamped her mouth shut and inclined her chin.

"She can see the future," Eric said.

"Can she?" He glanced from Eric to Sydney.

Her annoyed expression made it clear she didn't want Blake to know about her ability. "She can…sometimes." Her tone was indignant. "Can we finish up this meeting? I've got two tours to run tonight."

His curiosity piqued, he opened his mouth to press her for more explanation, but the door to the back room slammed shut, making him jump. His pulse sprinted, but the heat creeping up his neck came from the embarrassment of letting it get to him in front of a group of seasoned ghost hunters. Thankfully, the sound startled the others too.

Sydney shot to her feet and strode toward the door, running her hand along the jamb and opening and closing it a few times. "Does that happen often?"

"It started a few weeks ago, when I began bringing in the artifacts." He shuffled to the back of the room, stopping a few feet away from her.

"But not before then?" She shrugged out of her jacket and laid it on a table. Her short-sleeved Foo Fighters t-shirt revealed a colorful tattoo sleeve covering her entire left arm. A white rabbit took up most of her bicep, and a pocket watch on a chain wound around her forearm, a blue and gold mosaic pattern filling in the empty spaces.

Blake stepped toward her and brushed a finger down her arm. "This is new."

Her breath hitched as she looked up at him, holding him with her heated gaze. This was the closest he'd been to her since he last saw her in college, and the magnetism that drew him to her back then hadn't weakened a bit.

The muscles in her throat worked as she swallowed, and she gave her head a tiny shake. "I got it five years ago."

Lifting her arm, he turned it gently, admiring the artistry. The detail of the shading made the rabbit look lifelike, and the watch seemed almost metallic. Her skin was soft and warm, and as a hint of her floral shampoo wafted to his nose, he fought the urge to lean in closer. "It's new to me. I like it."

"I wasn't looking for your approval," she whispered as she slipped from his grasp, rubbing her arm where he'd touched her.

He chuckled. "You've never cared what other people think. I always admired you for that." He needed to back off, but the longer he was near her, the hotter the embers grew.

She cut her gaze over his shoulder, reminding him they weren't alone. "We should schedule the investigation. Are you guys free Monday night?"

So much for getting it done sooner. Blake shoved his hands into his pockets and stepped back. He'd been living with the activity for weeks; he could handle a few more days.

"Weekends are crazy busy," Sydney said, as if sensing his disappointment. "We don't run tours on Mondays, so that's the best night to do an investigation, when everyone is fresh."

"Works for me," Eric said.

Jason nodded. "Do you have a manifest of all these artifacts? Something that lists where they came from so we have an idea who we might be dealing with?"

Sydney took her phone from her pocket and smiled at the screen.

"Not yet." Blake couldn't tear his gaze away from the joy on her face as she typed on the device. "I'm working on a database, but at the moment, it's all up here." He tapped the side of his head.

"Can you be here then?" Jason looked at Eric, who nodded. "Without Sean to make direct contact with the spirits, we'll be relying on technology to gather evidence. It's helpful to know the history so we know where to focus our investigation."

"Absolutely." If it meant seeing Sydney in her element, spending more time with her, he'd be there without hesitation.

She looked up from her phone, her grin lighting up her entire face. "Sable Lenore LeBlanc was born at ten fifty-seven this morning. Eight pounds, seven ounces."

"That's awesome," Eric said. "Tell them congrats for us."

"Let Sean know we're doing the investigation on Monday too," Jason added.

"Psh. I'm not telling him that." Sydney typed a message and slipped her phone into her back pocket. "He needs to focus on his wife and baby right now. Anyway, he said I'm in charge while he's gone, remember?" She fisted her hands on her hips.

"I have a feeling you're not going to let us forget." Eric crossed his arms.

"Damn right I'm not." She grinned. "This meeting is adjourned. We'll reconvene Monday night."

"Aye-aye, Captain." Jason tapped Eric on the shoulder and nodded toward the door.

"Thanks, guys." Blake lifted a hand as the guys shuffled out.

Sydney grabbed her jacket and started to follow them.

"Hey, Sydney."

She paused, inhaling a deep breath before turning around and flashing a tight-lipped smile.

"You and I still need to get together to discuss the logistics for the new tour. Sean said that you—"

"I know what Sean said." She let out a breath, her expression softening. "Let's do the investigation first. There's a festival in town this weekend, which is going to make things crazy, and I need…I need a minute to think, okay? One step at a time." She turned for the door, and a flush of panic surged through his chest.

"I'm sorry for the way things ended between us." He clamped his mouth shut and fisted his hands at his sides. He didn't mean to say that out loud, but watching her walk away unearthed a mess of emotions he wasn't ready to deal with. It seemed his ability to keep things professional with her had slipped out the door before she could leave.

She sighed and faced him. "I suppose, since we're working together now, I should apologize too. I'm sorry for ignoring your calls. I thought a clean break would be best."

"It wasn't clean for me. All it did was leave me wondering what I did so wrong to deserve that kind of treatment." An intense ache spread from his chest to his throat, making it hard to breathe. "I was moving away, but I didn't want to break up." *Because you were the one.* He stepped toward her. He shouldn't have, but when she didn't move away, he reached for her face, cupping her cheek in his hand.

She closed her eyes, leaning into his palm, and for a moment, the years they'd spent apart disintegrated. It was just the two of them, together, and nothing else in the world mattered.

"What did I do, Sydney?"

Opening her eyes, she took his hand in hers, squeezing it gently before lowering it to his side. "It's complicated, Blake, I…" Her eyes tightened, and she inhaled quickly. "I need some time to think. Please, just…I need to go."

CHAPTER FIVE

Armed with a bouquet of daisies and a little stuffed rabbit, Sydney navigated the maze of hallways at Trinity Memorial Hospital toward the maternity ward. Her red Chuck Taylors squeaked on the polished tile floor, and the sharp scent of antiseptic overpowered the flowers' sweet perfume. Fluorescent lights cast the entire hospital in a greenish-yellow tinge, and a woman with long, brown braids and a bright smile stood behind the nurses' station.

"Can I help you find someone?"

"I'm looking for Emily LeBlanc." She wiggled the rabbit in her hand. "New baby."

The nurse clicked a few keys on a computer. "She's in two-oh-seven. Right down the hall."

"Thanks." Sydney paced down the corridor and knocked lightly on the door.

"Hey, Sydney." Emily's best friend, Trish, greeted her, stepping aside so she could enter the private room. "Perfect timing. They just brought Sable in from the nursery. Want me to take those?" She gestured to the flowers.

"Sure. Where's Sean?"

"I sent him to the cafeteria. He's hardly slept or eaten since Emily went into labor." Trish carried the bouquet to a table by the window, her blonde hair glinting in the sunlight that spilled in through the glass, and she situated them next to an enormous arrangement of pink roses that made Sydney's offering look like a bundle of weeds.

"Those are from my mother-in-law. She loves to go overboard." Emily sat propped up in bed, a light-blue blanket covering her legs and a sleeping baby bundled in her arms. Her long, red hair was piled in a messy bun on top of her head, and though dark circles rimmed her tired eyes, her contented smile warmed Sydney's heart.

"How are you feeling?" She moved toward Emily and the baby.

"Wait." Trish held up an arm. "Wash your hands first. Doctor's rules."

"Right." Sydney set the rabbit on a table near the bed. "The eyes are just thread, so no choking hazards."

"Thank you."

Sydney shuffled to the sink and washed her hands before returning to the bed and peering at the baby wrapped in Emily's arms. Swaddled in a blue and pink blanket, Sable slept in her mother's embrace, her little squished face a mask of peacefulness, a healthy peach tone flushing her cheeks. A mop of soft, dark hair fell across her forehead, and Sydney reached a hand toward the baby, glancing at Emily.

"You can touch her."

"She's beautiful." Sydney lightly brushed the silky strands on the baby's head.

"Sean says the hair runs in the family. He had a full head of it when he was born too."

Sydney smiled and clasped her hands in front of her. "How are you?"

"Tired. A little sore, but otherwise good." She looked at Trish. "Will you put her in the bassinet? My arms are about to give out."

Trish gently scooped the baby into an embrace and laid her in the plastic bassinet. "She seems like she's going to be a good sleeper."

Emily laughed softly. "We'll see about that when we get her home. How are you doing with the merger, Sydney? Sean said you and Blake might have some history."

She groaned. "Don't get me started." She'd thought what they had was history, but after yesterday, she wasn't so sure. His gentle touch had set off a chemical reaction inside her body, and she hadn't been able to get him out of her mind since.

Emily lifted herself with her hands, wincing as she adjusted her position in the bed. "Are you going to be okay working with him?"

"Yeah. I mean, we dated eight years ago. It's water under the bridge." She bit her lip. That was a lie she couldn't even convince herself to believe anymore. Seeing him again yesterday had stirred up so many unwanted emotions, she'd gone into defensive mode, mouthing off to him as if he'd been an ass, when he'd been nothing but kind. What was wrong with her?

Trish sank into a chair and leaned her elbows on her knees. "C'mon, Syd. You're going to have to do better than that. I'm not the slightest bit convinced." She wiggled her flawless eyebrows. "Is he hot?"

Sydney's lips curved into an involuntary smile. "Smokin'."

"What's the problem then?" Trish asked. "Aside from the fact that you work together, because workplace romances *can* have a happy ending."

Sydney glanced at Emily. "It's complicated."

"Did you see something?" A hint of fear glinted in Emily's eyes.

"Yeah, I did…but I don't know exactly what it means." She chewed the inside of her cheek. Should she share her vision when she hadn't been able to figure out any more details, no matter how many times she meditated on it? Maybe another perspective could help. "I saw a coffin."

Emily's eyes widened. "Who?"

"I don't know. That's the problem." She lifted her hands and dropped them by her sides. "I can't expand this one. The coffin was closed, and I was there with Sean. The second time it came on, Eric was with us, but everyone else is a blur, and I only see the backs of their heads."

"Have you told Sean?"

"No, and I don't plan to. Not until I figure out who is in the coffin, if it's even a person. It might not be." *Please don't let it be a person.*

Emily swallowed hard and gazed at her baby.

"It's not you or Sable. I'm ninety-nine percent sure of that."

"How do you know?"

"Because I saw Sean in the vision. He was upset, but if it were you… He wasn't devastated enough, you know? So, there's no sense in telling him about this, because it will only make him worry like…"

"Like with Courtney." Emily nodded. "You're right not to tell him. We'll keep this between us girls, right, Trish?"

"Absolutely." Trish pursed her lips, furrowing her

brow. "If you aren't sure it's a person, what do you think it means?"

"The first time I had the vision was right before Sean announced the merger. It could signify the death of the company." She wrapped her arms around herself. "And with Blake coming in as his partner…" She locked eyes with Emily. "What if I'm the reason it fails?"

"Why would you be the reason?" Emily shook her head. "Are you even sure it's the company the coffin represents?"

"It's better than it being a person." She lowered her gaze to the floor. Honestly, she had no idea what the damn thing meant.

"I agree with you there, but until you know for sure…" Emily tilted her head. "Sean has spoken very highly of Blake since they reconnected. We had him over for dinner a few weeks ago, and he seems like a great guy. You're both mature adults. I don't think you dating or not dating is going mean the end of Crescent City Ghost Tours."

A weight settled in her chest. Her friend was right; her relationship with Blake—or lack thereof—wouldn't make or break the company. "Then it's going to mean the end of someone's life."

The door creaked open, and Sean slipped inside. His hair was mussed, but his tired eyes lit up when he looked at Emily. "How's our little princess?"

Emily smiled. "Sleeping like a baby."

Sean peered into the bassinet before sinking onto the edge of the bed. "How was the meeting?"

"Great." Sydney plastered on a smile. "We're doing a preliminary investigation Monday night. A door slammed for no apparent reason while we were there yesterday, so the guys are anxious to get started. I'll meet with Blake to discuss the new tour once that's done."

He nodded. "Good. No other issues?"

"Nope. Everything's under control." She forced herself to hold his gaze, and the baby stirred, capturing his attention.

He scooped Sable into his arms and sat next to Emily.

"I have to be at work soon, so I'm heading out." Trish slung her purse over her shoulder. "Call me if you need anything, Em."

"I'll walk you out," Sydney said. "See y'all later."

"Keep me posted on the progress." Sean glanced at her before returning to the baby.

"Will do." She followed Trish out the door and onto the elevator.

Trish's pale pink nail clicked against the plastic as she pressed the button for the parking garage. "What's the story with you and this Blake guy? How long did you date?"

"A few months when I was a freshman in college."

"Wow, so it was pretty serious then?"

Sydney shrugged. "I guess so. I *thought* it was getting serious, anyway."

The elevator doors slid open, wafting the scents of rubber and exhaust into the compartment. They stepped into the garage, and Trish turned to her. "What happened?"

Sydney dug her keys from her pocket. "It's a long story."

"There's a coffee shop next door, and I could use some caffeine. Want to come?" Trish nodded in the direction of the café and headed toward it without waiting for an answer.

"Sure." Sydney shielded her eyes from the midday sun as they stepped out of the garage and onto the sidewalk. A car horn blared, and traffic whizzed past on the busy Central Business District street.

This section of the city, nestled between the quaint French Quarter and the grand homes of the Garden District, boasted modern skyscrapers and freshly paved streets. A Community Coffee House occupied the corner section of the neighboring building's bottom floor, and dry, heated air enveloped Sydney as she passed through the door.

Trish ordered a white chocolate mocha, and Sydney went for a vanilla latte. Heat seeped through the paper cup as she clutched it in both hands and sank into a chair near the floor-to-ceiling window.

"All right." Trish sat next to her. "I haven't had a date in two months, so I'm going to live vicariously through you. Tell me about you and Blake."

Sydney sipped her latte, savoring the taste of the bittersweet liquid on her tongue. As she swallowed, it left a trail of warmth from her throat to her stomach. "We met at a music festival. I punched a drunk guy for groping my friend, and apparently, Blake found that attractive." She shrugged.

Trish's eyes widened. "Did you get arrested?"

"No. We were in a crowd. The guy went down, and I grabbed my friend by the arm and kept walking. Blake followed and told me I had a mean right hook. We went on our first date the next night."

"Wow. He's got balls to hit on you right after you knocked a guy out. Props to Blake." She held up her coffee cup in a toast.

"He's…" Heat crept up her neck as memories of

their relationship danced through her mind. "It was a wild few months. I think what sealed the deal for me was that he just complimented the punch. He didn't qualify it with 'for a girl' or even worse, 'for a little Asian girl.'"

"He saw you for the strong, independent woman you are. So…why did it end? Was he a butt scratcher? Did he pick his nose in front of you?"

Sydney laughed. "No, he was…amazing…for a while. But then…" She shook her head.

"Well, spill the tea, girl. I'm intrigued."

"I had a vision about him. Every time I start dating someone, I see how it's going to end, and Blake was going to stand me up on the night of the Krewe of Horae masquerade ball. It was my induction ceremony. We had matching costumes and everything, but I saw myself sitting on my mom's front porch in my ball gown, mascara streaks running down my cheeks because he never showed."

Trish cringed. "Ouch. What was his excuse?"

Sydney leaned back in her chair and toyed with the plastic lid on her coffee. "I never gave him the chance to make one up. After the premonition, I dumped him via text and then blocked his number. I never spoke to him again."

Her jaw went slack as she blinked. "You dumped him…via text?"

Sydney nodded, her ears burning.

"That's low." Trish set her coffee on a side table and crossed her arms. "As your friend, I feel like I can say this to you honestly… That was a bitch move."

"I know. It was a cowardly thing to do, but I was hurt, and I was only nineteen. He'd just told me he was planning to move to New York for grad school anyway. It's not like the relationship was going anywhere."

"But a text, Sydney?" She grabbed her cup and took a long sip. "And he didn't *actually* stand you up, did he? It was just a vision?"

"My visions are real. It was going to happen."

"How do you know it wasn't symbolic of something else, like you said the coffin could be?" She drummed her nails against the paper cup.

"I suppose I don't, but it felt literal, and everything was in sharp focus, like the universe was certain it was going to happen. This coffin vision feels almost like it's not fully formed. Like maybe the universe isn't sure what's going to happen yet. I don't know." She set her cup on a table and let out an exasperated sigh. Describing how to interpret her premonitions was like explaining string theory to a toddler…impossible because she didn't understand it herself. "I apologized yesterday. It's all good now."

"Is it? Don't you ever wonder if you could have stopped it from happening? If you had talked to him about it, maybe he would have shown up." Trish shrugged.

"First off, he didn't know about my visions. Besides you and Emily, the only other people who know are the guys at work and my mom…and don't even get me started on her. Oh, and *now* Blake, thanks to Eric and Jason, which means Claire will know soon too." She still needed to ream them out for spilling her secret so casually.

"And second, yes, I probably could have stopped him from standing me up. My visions show me what's going to happen if things keep going down the path they're on. I could have changed the path and created a different outcome…but I can't change people. If he has it in him to disregard his girlfriend's feelings and be a self-centered jerk, I can't take it out of him. He would have hurt me later down the road. It was inevitable."

"How do you know that?"

"Because that's what happened with my dad. When I was fourteen, I fell down the rabbit hole and saw my dad cheating on my mom with a woman he was going to meet at a gala my mom wasn't planning to attend. I told her about it; she went to the gala, and he didn't cheat on her that night."

She grabbed her coffee and toyed with the cardboard sleeve. "Then I had another vision. A new woman. A new situation. My mom stopped it from happening too, but the cycle repeated. She told me not to tell her if I saw it happen again—to keep my curse to myself—so the next time, I didn't mention the vision, and sure enough, he cheated."

"Oh, man."

"I could change the situation, but I couldn't change *him*. He's a cheater. My mom wasn't surprised when she found out, and she divorced him. So, when I see how a relationship is going to end, I take it seriously."

Trish took the lid off her cup and swirled the remaining coffee before tipping her head back and finishing the drink. "That really sucks, but Blake's not your dad."

"It happened with two different guys I dated in high school too. I couldn't stop the relationships from ending. All I could do was postpone the inevitable."

"Blake's not your high school boyfriend."

"It doesn't matter."

"Sure it does. Don't you want to find out his side of the story? Maybe he would have had a good reason for what he might have done. You'll never know unless you ask."

"I see your point." Since when was Trish the rational one? She tossed her cup in the bin behind her. "I do have to work with the guy." A pang of guilt stabbed her in the chest, and she sighed. Trish was right. The same thoughts had been running through Sydney's mind since she talked to him, but they were easier to shove aside when no one had said them out loud.

"Yesterday, he asked me what he did wrong, but I couldn't bring myself to answer. I suppose he deserves the truth." Now that Trish had vocalized Sydney's idiocy, she had no choice but to make things right…really right… with Blake.

"And your eyes sparkle every time you talk about him, so…" Trish grinned.

She shook her head. "I'll talk to him. Who knows? Maybe once we clear the air, my funeral vision will change to a party."

"Or a wedding," Trish sang.

Sydney narrowed her eyes. "You're funny. Really funny."

CHAPTER SIX

Blake sat at his desk, chewing on the end of a ballpoint pen and staring blankly at his computer screen. Five full days had passed since he'd asked Sydney for an explanation. Five days for him to roll the demise of their relationship over and over in his mind.

Unless he was remembering it wrong, all he'd done was tell her he'd been accepted at grad school. That wasn't a good reason for her to treat him the way she did.

Now, she'd been avoiding him for days, doing all her work at the old office or from home, not once stopping by the museum to see if she had any work to do there. Sure, they couldn't do much with Sean on leave, but she could have at least made an effort.

Then again, he hadn't made much of an effort to see her either. He could have tagged along on another tour or checked in at the old office. Hell, he was the boss; he could have called her and told her they had work to do, but he wasn't sure he wanted her to answer the question dangling between them. He never should have asked it in the first place.

His phone vibrated on the desk, Sydney's name lighting up the screen, and he tensed. The investigation was scheduled for tonight. Was she canceling that too? He swiped it to open the message: *Do you mind if I stop by early? I'm ready to talk*

No punctuation at the end. What was she ready to talk about? Their failed relationship? The new tour? The weather?

Three dots bounced on the screen as she finished the message, and Blake bit down on the pen, cracking the plastic and sending blue ink dribbling down his chin. "Shit." He tossed it in the trash and wiped his face with a tissue before rushing to the bathroom to examine the damage.

A smear of blue stretched from his lower lip to his jaw, matching the stained tips of his fingers. "Goddammit." He squirted hand soap onto a paper towel and scrubbed his face, thankfully removing the ink before it set.

Returning to his office, he found the rest of Sydney's message on his phone: *about the new tour*

He blew out a hard breath and dropped into his chair. He had his answer. There would be nothing more than a work relationship between them, and that was probably for the better. Maybe they could pretend he never poured his heart out to her. Maybe, one day, the awkwardness would go away. He replied: *Sure. What time?*

Her response came instantly: *20 minutes?*

"Seriously?" Did she expect him to drop everything because she was ready to talk? He typed *ok* and set his phone aside. That woman was his kryptonite.

At least they'd be moving forward with something. He opened his email to pass the time, deleting the junk as he scrolled. When his gaze landed on the name Carmen

Stone, a brick of dread settled in his stomach. Why the hell was his former boss emailing him? She'd already destroyed his career. Wasn't that enough?

He hovered the cursor over the trash can icon, but curiosity won, and he cursed himself as he opened the message.

Hi Blake. I hope this email finds you well.

Finds him well? She couldn't be serious. He continued reading.

I wanted to apologize for everything that happened. What William and I did to you was wrong, but you have to understand that when he found out about our affair, I realized how much he really loves me, and I had to give our marriage another try.

Blake groaned. "You hadn't lived with the man for a year. It wasn't an affair."

I tried and failed, and I left him a few days ago. I'd love to talk to you, to make sure you're okay.

"Oh, hell no." He hit delete and slammed his laptop shut. He wanted nothing more to do with that shit show. His life was here now, in New Orleans, and he would never do anything that stupid again.

Armed with a bag of beignets and two cups of café au lait, Sydney strode toward Blake's museum with purpose. A nauseating swarm of angry wasps spiraled through her stomach, so she wasn't the slightest bit hungry, but Blake had a soft spot for the French doughnuts. Hopefully, they would make her *real* apology go down smoother.

She'd stewed on exactly what to say to the man for days…too many days. She'd left him hanging while she battled the beast of fear and worked up the courage to talk to him, but she wasn't sure which scared her more: that he wouldn't forgive her—because honestly, she didn't deserve his absolution—or that he would, and she'd have to deal with all the old emotions bubbling to the surface, threatening to boil her alive.

The early evening sun had begun its descent behind the buildings, casting long shadows across the potholed pavement. The warm scent of patchouli incense danced in the air as she passed the Voodoo shop on the corner of Bourbon Street, and a crisp breeze kicked up, whipping her hair into her eyes.

She shook her head, using her forearm to brush the strands out of her field of vision as she hurried across the busy street. A cover band belted out a Jimmy Buffet song in the bar to her right, and she picked up her pace, rehearsing her apology in her mind as she trekked the final block toward her destination.

"Hey slot stealer." Damon's weaselly voice grated in her ears, and she turned as he crossed the street toward her. He wore his mousey brown hair gelled straight back and flat against his head, and the patchy scruff on his jaw made him look like an adolescent attempting to pass for an adult.

"Is that the best you can do, dumbass? Surely someone in your krewe can give you an Insults 101 lesson."

He curled his hands into fists and stopped three feet away from her. "You stole our roll time. You're a slot stealer."

Sydney's nostrils flared as she let out a slow breath. She didn't have time for this; she had an apology to make before she chickened out. "When the spot opened, they held a lottery, dimwit. Horae won. No theft was involved."

Damon and his sorry excuse for a Mardi Gras krewe had been pissy ever since they lost the coveted two p.m. parade slot, and their hostility grew as the date approached.

Why Sydney had been singled out to take the brunt of their threats, she had no clue, but she was done with his juvenile nonsense. "Maybe if you worry less about us and more about taking care of your own krewe, you'll be awarded a decent roll time next year." She plastered on a smile. "Have a good day, darling." Turning on her heel, she marched away.

"You better watch your back, slot stealer," he shouted.

"Bite me," she called without turning around. The museum sat three yards away, and she refused to break her stride until she got there. Balancing the cardboard cup holder in her right hand, she reached for the door, but it swung open before she made contact.

"Hey, Sydney. Come on in." Blake stood to the side, his posture stiff, and motioned for her to enter. The wasps in her stomach flitted up to her throat. He wore dark jeans with a light-blue T-shirt that made his eyes pop, and as she stepped past him, she caught a whiff of his aftershave, a deep, musky scent with a hint of pine.

It was the same delicious scent she'd wanted to wrap herself up in eight years ago. A memory of snuggling against his bare chest, falling asleep in his arms, flashed in her mind, and her body warmed at the image.

"Let me help you with that." He locked the door and smiled as he took the drink tray from her hand, but his eyes were tight, guarded. "What's all this?"

"A peace offering. I owe you a better apology." Her pulse thrummed. "And an explanation."

His smile slipped, a look of surprise flashing in his eyes. "I thought you wanted to talk about the tour."

"I…lied." She sucked in a deep breath, trying to calm her quivering insides.

He nodded toward the back of the room. "Let's head to your new office and talk."

"*My* office?" She followed him through a doorway and down a dimly lit hall.

"I know you all shared one at your old building, but we've got a lot of room here. I figured since you do so much behind the scenes, you deserve your own space." He disappeared through a doorway and flipped a switch.

Yellow light spilled out of the opening, and she swallowed the dryness from her mouth before following him inside. A dark wood desk took up nearly half the room, and a high-backed, ergonomic office chair stood behind it, with two more chairs facing it on the opposite side. A brass cup filled with pens and pencils occupied one corner of the desk, along with a stapler and a box of paperclips.

"Nice." She set the bag of beignets on the surface and sank into the chair, her breath catching as she took in the wall opposite the desk.

A framed picture of the white rabbit from *Alice's Adventures in Wonderland* hung in the center of the wall. The drawing, done in a style reminiscent of the original book illustrations, was filled in with vibrant, saturated colors, making the scene seem almost lifelike. The rabbit wore a blue vest, and an oversized pocket watch hung from a thick chain, dragging the ground as the animal darted across the grass.

Blake took the coffees out of the tray and set them on the desk before dragging a chair around to sit cattycorner from her. "I was planning to let you decorate however you want, but when I saw that at a shop on Royal the other day, I couldn't pass it up. I assume you're still into Wonderland stuff, since you got the tattoo."

She drew in a breath to reply, but what could she say? The gesture was so sweet, so typically Blake, her throat thickened. He'd always found little ways to show her he was thinking about her. She hadn't had a single doubt about their relationship in the past, until he told her he was moving away and she had the vision. What had happened for it to have to end that way?

When she didn't respond, he continued, "I've wondered why you loved a rabbit who's always late when you are perpetually early for everything, but I'm guessing the time aspect has something to do with your visions?"

She looked into his eyes, and his gaze held her, a mysterious magnetism drawing the breath from her lungs as her body involuntarily drifted toward him. He'd given her a gift, and a thank you was in order, but her hormones seemed to think the best way to express her gratitude was to lean in and taste those full, kissable lips.

He grinned and cleared his throat.

Oh, crap. She was staring at his mouth. She lifted her gaze to his eyes, and damn it if he wasn't staring at her mouth too. *This is bad. Very, very bad, Syd. Snap out of it.* Grabbing a cup from the desk, she leaned back in the chair and took a sip. "When I was a kid, I always associated my premonitions with Wonderland, because when one would come on unexpectedly, I felt the sensation of falling down a rabbit hole. Tunneled vision, blue and gold sparkles in my peripheral…Wonderland." She shrugged and took another sip.

"That's fascinating." He picked up the other cup and popped off the lid before lifting it to his nose and inhaling deeply. Pausing, he tilted his head and flicked his gaze to hers. "Is there cinnamon in this?"

"Yes. Do you not take it that way anymore? We can switch if you want. Mine's plain."

"This is great. It's…" He looked at the cup and chuckled. "Thank you." Taking a beignet from the bag, he bit into it, and sugar rained from the pastry, covering the desk in white powder. "I forgot how messy these things are. It's been a while."

She wiped a napkin across the mess, trying her best to ignore the flakes of sugar-coating his lips. He slipped out his tongue, swiping it away, and her hands trembled as she tossed the napkin in the trash. Clutching her coffee in both hands, she took another sip, but all she could taste was the imaginary sweetness of his kiss. She would need a cold shower after this meeting ended. *Sheesh.*

"Tell me more about your visions. Do they always come on suddenly with the rabbit hole effect, or can you focus them?" He popped the rest of the beignet into his mouth and brushed his hands on his jeans.

"Both. Sometimes they come from nowhere, drag me under for a few seconds, and when I come up, I've experienced a half-hour glimpse of the future." She set her cup down and drummed her fingers on the desk. "If I meditate on it, sometimes I can get back into the vision. Occasionally, I can expand them, find out more."

"Wow. Why are you giving tours instead of telling fortunes in Jackson Square? Seems like you could make bank with that kind of power." He sipped his coffee and leaned an elbow on the desk.

"It doesn't work that way. I don't have visions about random people. It's always people I know, especially ones I'm close to. If a stranger walked up and offered me fifty bucks to tell her who she's going to marry, I wouldn't be able to. It seems I only get glimpses of things the universe wants me to know, and half the time I don't understand why I'm supposed to know it."

"Maybe so you can affect it? Stop it from happening if it's bad?" She could practically hear the million-dollar question forming in his mind.

"Sometimes that works. A lot of times, it doesn't, no matter how hard I try."

He paused, his intense gaze penetrating her armor, slicing her open and latching on to her soul. "Have you ever had visions about me?"

She couldn't have lied to him if she tried. Clasping her hands in her lap, she lowered her gaze. "That's what I wanted to talk to you about. The reason I broke up with you when I did."

He rested his forearm on the desk and leaned toward her. "I'm listening."

"You were…" She looked into his deep, blue eyes, and ice flooded her veins, freezing her to the spot. Telling him now wasn't any easier than it had been eight years ago, and this time, texting him wasn't an option. Swallowing the frozen lump from her throat, she straightened her spine. "You had just told me you were moving to New York for grad school, and then a few days later, I had a premonition. We were supposed to go to the Krewe of Horae masquerade together."

"I remember. You were going to be inducted that night." His gaze was steady, urging her to continue.

She inclined her chin. "And you were going to stand me up." Her breath came out in a rush, the weight of the accusation she'd carried all these years finally lifting from her chest.

His brow furrowed, and he crossed his arms. "I was not going to stand you up."

"You were, Blake. Maybe you hadn't planned to, but something more important for you was going to come up. I saw myself sitting on my mom's front porch, waiting for you to pick me up, but you never came. I missed the ball because I was so upset. I missed my induction…"

He shook his head. "But that didn't happen."

"No, I didn't let it. I was so hurt, though, I couldn't even talk to you. That's why I texted, and for that, I am deeply sorry. I should have had the decency to break up with you in person, but I was a coward. I was hurt…"

"*You* were hurt?" He leaned back in his chair, gaping. "How do you think I felt?"

"Honestly, I didn't think you'd care at the time. You were moving a thousand miles away, so our relationship was doomed anyway. I figured you standing me up was your way of ending it."

He opened and closed his mouth a few times and laughed, unbelieving. "That's not what happened at all. That's not what was *going* to happen. Sydney, you should have talked to me."

"I know I should have. I'm sorry I didn't, but I'm not sorry I ended it. I went to the Krewe of Horae ball, and I experienced my induction on my own. I'd have missed it otherwise."

He pinched the bridge of his nose and shook his head. "And that's all you saw? You on the front porch crying and deciding not to go to your ball?"

"Yes." What more did he want from her? What did he expect a nineteen-year-old armed with that foreknowledge to do?

He dropped his hands into his lap. "You didn't meditate on it? You didn't try to see any more of the night? To figure out *why* I didn't show?"

"Meditation wasn't in my arsenal at the time. I didn't know how to..." She didn't have to explain this to him. Her curse was her own to bear. "Look, I had dated a few guys before we met, and I've dated a few since. And every time I start seeing someone, I always see how it's going to end. Maybe I can change the circumstances, prolong it, but I can't stop the inevitable. I can't change people."

"Unbelievable." He raked a hand through his hair. "Do you want to know where I went that night?"

"It doesn't matter anymore. Look, you asked what you had done wrong, and I'm telling you. You didn't do anything wrong, because you didn't get the chance to. But you would have."

"No. No, I wouldn't have. I spent the night of your masquerade in the hospital, having an appendectomy."

She blinked. "Wait. What?"

"My appendix ruptured, and I had emergency surgery that evening. You would have been the first person I called when I woke up...in fact, you *were*, but you'd blocked my number. I knew you'd blocked my number, but I called anyway."

Her mouth hung open, her bottom lip trembling before she snapped it shut. Did she hear that right? "You went to the hospital?"

"And you would have known that if you would have talked to me. You never gave me a chance. I spent Spring Break of my senior year of college recovering. I barely made it to class to finish my finals and graduate. I almost died that day." He crossed his arms and looked away.

Her premonition of Blake standing her up wasn't signaling the end of their relationship? Her elbows *thunked* on the desk as her head fell into her hands. She hadn't just been a coward; she'd been stupid. If she would have paid more attention to the details of her vision, talked to Blake about it rather than dumping him at the first sign of trouble, she might have been able to help him. "I am so sorry, Blake."

"I am too, Sydney. I was looking forward to that masquerade. I knew how important it was to you, and I planned on being by your side the whole night. I planned to…" He clamped his mouth shut and shook his head. "You let me spend eight years thinking our breakup was my fault." He shot to his feet and paced in front of the desk.

"I'm sorry." Sydney stood and shuffled toward him, but his rigid posture and jerking movements said he didn't want her sympathy. She clasped her hands together and waited for him to stop pacing. "I was young and really, really dumb. They say your brain doesn't fully develop until you're thirty, so I'm still dumb."

"Is that what you do with your visions? You keep your gift a secret and act on these premonitions without talking to the people involved? Because that's not right. That's messing with people's lives."

"No. I don't…" She sighed. "Seeing the future isn't a gift. I don't want to have this ability. It's messy and complicated, and I don't know why I see what I see, and I just…"

"I thought you were the one I was going to spend the rest of my life with."

She stopped breathing mid-inhale, and as she looked at him, the world ceased to spin. Pain, anguish that she had caused, filled his eyes, shattering her heart into a million pieces. She was a horrible, despicable person. "I was selfish. If I'd known how much it would hurt you… I didn't think it through. I acted rashly without even considering your feelings, and I'm sorry. I could say it a thousand times, and it wouldn't be enough. Can you ever forgive me?"

Pressing his lips together, he searched her eyes for an eternity, and she held her breath. She had hurt him, and she deserved whatever he planned to say. Maybe the coffin in her vision didn't symbolize the end of Crescent City Ghost Tours or the death of someone she loved. Maybe it meant the real end of her relationship with Blake. True closure. If he couldn't forgive her, if they couldn't work together, life as she knew it would end.

"That's asking a lot."

She swallowed hard. "I know. I'm asking for something I don't deserve, and I don't blame you if you can't. I barely have a handle on my visions now, and it was even worse back then. It's no excuse."

"You hurt me."

"I know. I'm sorry."

With a slow exhale, his posture relaxed, and he took a step toward her. "I forgave you a long time ago. I had to in order to keep my sanity."

Cool relief loosened her tension, but her guilt still sat heavy in her stomach. "So, we're okay then? You don't hate me?"

"I grieved when you broke up with me. I was devasted, and then I was angry. Then I let it go. Well, I thought I'd let it go, but seeing you again stirred up all those emotions, bringing them back to the surface. I've been trying to focus on the hurt, but the good memories are stronger. We were good together."

Her chest swelled with so much emotion she couldn't breathe. "We were, until I screwed it up," she whispered.

He rested a hand on her shoulder, and she instinctively moved closer to him. "It was a long time ago. I could have tried harder to contact you, but my pride stopped me. Who knows why young people do what they do?"

"Immature brains."

He chuckled. "I guess so. We're both to blame."

She shook her head. "This is all on me. You didn't deserve to be treated that way."

"Come here, *cher*." He wrapped his arms around her and held her tight. "I forgive you."

She rested her cheek against his chest and closed her eyes, losing herself in the comfort and familiarity of his embrace. His deliciously masculine scent swirled through her senses, and she slipped her arms around his waist, hooking her thumbs in his belt loops.

Having Blake's forgiveness felt like a vise grip releasing its hold on her chest—better than she could have ever imagined. But the knowledge that her vision wasn't meant to signal the end of their relationship burrowed into her mind, blooming into a giant mushroom cloud of *what-ifs*.

If she hadn't seen the end, did that mean there wouldn't have been one?

He kissed the top of her head. "I don't know if—"

The office door slammed shut, the antique wood rattling in the frame, and Sydney jerked her head toward the sound. "Has this one slammed before?"

She let out a breath and tugged from his embrace, striding toward the door. Whether a draft or a ghost was responsible for the distraction, she owed it her thanks. That situation was getting too real way too fast. She'd merely meant to apologize to the man, not end up wrapped in his arms and ready for…who knew what?

Twisting the knob, she pushed the door open, swinging it back and forth to test the hinges.

"I hear doors slamming down here when I'm upstairs, but the door to the front room is the only one I've ever seen shut on its own." He shuffled toward her.

The hinges felt secure, no loose screws to make it off-balance. She examined the frame and opened the door halfway, giving it a gentle push in each direction to see if it would gain momentum, but it only moved a few inches each way. It didn't seem prone to anything but deliberate movement.

Blake watched her as she attempted to debunk the event, a crooked grin tugging up one corner of his mouth, though she couldn't tell if he was amused, impressed, or still thinking about that intense moment they'd shared. "Do you think it—"

She threw up a hand and shushed him. Holding her breath, she listened for any signs of a draft. "Is the heater on?"

"Not at the moment. You can hear it when it's running."

"I can't debunk this. If it's happening a lot, you might have brought in a strong one." She shook her head. "Hopefully he…or she…is just looking for attention and isn't going to be a troublemaker."

"Trouble?" A look of wariness tightened his eyes. "Sean assured me that ghosts can't hurt the living. What kind of trouble are we talking about?"

She leaned against the wall. "Sean has a different perspective on spirits than the rest of us. He sometimes forgets we can't see and hear them like he can."

Blake crossed his arms. "So, ghosts *can* hurt the living?"

"Not directly, but…" She bit the inside of her cheek. They always told clients this line to keep them calm. Spirits seeking attention tended to become more active when they sensed a fear reaction from the living.

"But what?"

Blake wasn't technically a client. He was part of the team now, so he deserved the truth. Especially after everything she'd just confessed. "They're basically people without bodies. If they were ornery in life, they'll be that way in death too."

"Great. And I'm collecting the belongings of a bunch of murderers." He ran a hand through his hair and paced into the hall. "Is what I'm doing…safe? I'm not going to end up possessed by the spirit of The Axeman and go on a killing spree, am I?"

She couldn't fight her smile, but she tried to cover up the laugh that bubbled from her chest with a cough. "Unless The Axeman is really a demon, you don't have to worry about being possessed. Human spirits can't get inside you unless you invite them, and you'd have to be a powerful medium to do it." Nonhuman entities were another story, but she wouldn't elaborate on that unless absolutely necessary.

The tension in his shoulders eased. "That's good to know."

"Human spirits can't physically interact with the living. You may feel a coldness or even a light touch if they try…" She placed her hand on his bicep to demonstrate. "But their forms will pass right through you if they use any pressure."

He glanced at her hand, still resting on his skin. "I see."

Trailing her fingers down his arm, she took his hand in hers, covering his fingers with her other hand. "They can't hurt you *directly*, but if you'd been standing in this threshold when the door slammed, it could have busted your nose."

"Hmm. So if I'm in the way of an axe that gets thrown…"

"It's a solid object. If a ghost can build up enough energy to actually pick it up and throw it, that would be a problem." She squeezed his hand and let it go. "Have you brought in any new artifacts recently?

"Not in the past week."

"If an aggressive entity were here, you'd have had more activity than slamming doors by now. I think you're safe."

"I'll take your word for it. Honestly, I'm a little nervous about tonight. Do you promise not to laugh at me if I squeal like a little girl?" He grinned, but it didn't reach his eyes.

She laughed. "I can't make any promises on that. Everyone's scared their first time. When Sean and I started investigating for the tour, I nearly peed my pants when a chair fell over. I might've squealed too." She winked. "Now, nothing scares me."

He nodded, holding her gaze. "That's not hard to believe."

An ear-splitting buzzing sound reverberated through the building, sending a jolt of adrenaline rushing through her system, making her jump. "What the hell is that?"

Blake laughed. "That's the doorbell."

CHAPTER SEVEN

"Nothing scares you, huh?" Blake winked.

"That wasn't paranormal. It doesn't count."

He couldn't wipe the goofy grin off his face if he tried, and the fact that Sydney's smile was just as big sent a fizzing sensation rushing through his veins. "I'm not judging."

As he stood there, staring into her dark brown eyes, the embers their reunion had ignited grew into a full-blown blaze. He had forgiven her years ago. Finally hearing the true story behind their breakup had taken him aback, but once he recovered from the initial shock, forgiving her again had been the easiest thing in the world. Too easy.

Time had a way of healing wounds. Smoothing over the broken pieces and filling in the cracks. They were both young when it happened, and either one could have handled the situation better. While they had both matured, he had no idea how she'd handle something like that now. Did he want to risk his heart again when she'd so easily smashed it to pieces before?

She still fit in his arms like she belonged there, and the way she'd melted into him, her body conforming to his as he held her tight, accepting her apology, offering his forgiveness... If the universe was offering him a second chance, who was he to waste it?

A memory of his previous failed office romance sliced through his mind, and he bit the inside of his cheek. Opening the exhibit was his last chance in this career. After everything that happened in New York, he'd never find a job in a respectable museum again. His name wasn't just mud in the business; it was dog shit.

When he left, he promised himself he'd never get involved with a coworker again, especially not a boss/employee situation like last time. But this was different. This was Sydney...

The doorbell sounded a second time, the offensive buzz splitting the room before someone banged on the door, and he closed his eyes for a long blink. That could only be one person.

Sydney took a step back. "Are you expecting company?"

"I'm sure it's my cousin. Let me get rid of her." He strode to the front and peeked through a slit in the paper covering the window.

Claire stood on the steps, a paper bag in one hand, a large Styrofoam cup in the other. She held a second cup in the crook of her elbow, and she kicked her leg, missing the resident crow by two feet, causing it to squawk at her. Rolling her eyes, she leaned her shoulder against the doorbell, filling the museum with another offensive buzz.

"Does it have to be so loud?" Sydney stood a few feet behind him, her hands on her hips, her dark hair shining in the museum lights.

He considered ignoring his cousin, taking Sydney in the back so he could spend more time alone with her, figure out what the hell he was going to do about his feelings for her, but the disappointed look on Claire's face tugged at his heart. He couldn't leave her standing out there alone.

"It's a big building." Twisting the lock, he pushed the door open, and Claire's face lit up.

"Were you napping in the back or something?" She moved toward the entrance, but Blake didn't budge from the doorway.

"Now's not the best time."

"I brought dinner." She stood on her toes to peer over his shoulder at Sydney. "Are they about to start the investigation? We can take it to the park to eat."

"No. That doesn't start until later, when the rest of the team gets here." Could she not take a hint?

Claire cocked an eyebrow. "So, you're here alone with Sydney? I hope I'm not interrupting anything…"

Hint taken and ignored. *Typical.* He forced a neutral expression and let out a slow breath, racking his brain to remember why he had agreed to sign on as her babysitter.

"Hey, Claire." Sydney stepped behind him and pushed the door open the rest of the way. "We've been discussing plans for the new tour. Just going over some technical stuff before the investigation."

Claire glanced from Sydney to Blake. "Well, there's plenty here for three. Let's eat, and you can fill me in on the plans."

Angling her shoulders sideways, Claire slid between them, brushing against Blake and glaring at him as she passed. Her knee-high boots thudded on the concrete, and she glanced over her shoulder, making her way through the door into the back of the museum.

Blake sighed and gave Sydney an apologetic look. "I'll have a talk with her."

"It's okay." She pulled the door shut and turned the lock. "We probably should discuss the tour. That is why I came early." Sydney stayed two steps in front of him as he followed her into the back.

Claire strode into Sydney's office and set the cups on the desk. "I see you've decided what this room will be used for." She dropped the bag of food next to the drinks and clasped her hands behind her back as she strolled toward the art on the wall.

Leaning closer, she crinkled her nose. "That's cute. A little juvenile, but cute. Where'd you get it?" she asked Sydney.

"Blake bought that at a shop on Royal." Sydney smiled at Claire and rested a hand on his lower back. "It was my favorite story growing up, and he thought it would help make the transition easier."

Claire put her hands on her hips, shifting her weight to one side. "He's always thoughtful like that, isn't he?"

Sydney cocked her head. "He sure is."

Blake shifted his gaze from his cousin to Sydney. Was this some kind of territorial battle waging between them? Claire had no need for her own office, but the tension in the room grew so thick he could've sliced through it like a stick of butter.

Claire stared at Sydney as if she were sizing her up for a fight. Sydney simply smiled, returning Claire's gaze with a confidence that said she wasn't one to be messed with. Hell, Blake had seen her throw a punch. His money was on Sydney.

What he would have given to have Eric's ability right now so he could figure out exactly what was going on here.

Claire had probably gotten used to being his only employee. It was possible she felt threatened with the new team coming in. He'd have to have a heart-to-heart with her later, reassure her she had a place in the new setup.

"Is everyone getting their own office?" She sank into the chair across from the desk. "Sit. Let's eat." She shuddered, rubbing the back of her neck as she glanced over her shoulder and toward the ceiling. "It's drafty in here."

Sydney looked at him, and he motioned for her to take the big chair. "Just Sean, me, and Sydney for now. If anyone else needs some space later, we'll reevaluate."

He scooted his chair around the corner, closer to Sydney. Siding with her. If his cousin and his maybe-soon-to-be girlfriend were marking their territory, he wanted to be clear where he stood.

"What's this?" Claire opened the pastry bag Sydney had brought and rolled her eyes. "Beignets for dinner, Blake?" She looked at Sydney. "I don't know how he survives without a woman in his life. He'd starve if it weren't for me."

"I'm sure he'd survive." Sydney took a beignet from the bag and bit into it, her gaze never straying from Claire's face.

Claire blinked a few times before lowering her gaze to the desk. Her posture softened, her demeanor shifting in an instant. "You're right. I guess I get protective after everything that's happened. When you lose someone you're close to, you…" She shook her head. "Anyway, do you like boudin balls? I know they're not the healthiest thing to eat, but I can't get enough of them."

"I love them. Thanks for sharing." Sydney smiled and took the Styrofoam container Claire passed to her as if accepting an olive branch.

And just like that, the battle for dominance ended. Sydney had stood her ground and held her own like she always did, and the grip she had on his heart strengthened.

He stood. "I've got some paper plates in the kitchen. Let me grab them."

"If I'd known you had company, I would've brought an extra soda." Claire continued unpacking the food.

"That's okay," Sydney said. "If you have a bottle of water, I'll be fine. I've had enough caffeine to last me a week."

He rushed to the kitchen for the plates. The faster they could eat, the faster he could send his cousin on her way and finish his conversation with Sydney, find out if she was open to rekindling an old flame that had never burned out completely.

If she wasn't, he'd ball up his emotions, shove them into the corner of his heart where they'd been hiding out the past eight years, and get on with his life. Hell, that would probably be best for both of them, but if she was interested…

He closed his eyes and leaned his forehead against a cabinet door. If she felt even half of the fire burning in his heart, he'd crush his rule about not dating coworkers. He shouldn't. His logical mind knew he'd be setting himself up for multiple possibilities of disaster, but his heart was screaming, "This is *Sydney.*"

When he returned to the office, he found Sydney and Claire chatting like their earlier stand-off had never happened.

"I mean, he's cute, but he's so immature." Claire

sipped her soda and swished it around her mouth. "What is it with college guys acting like they've always got something to prove?"

Sydney smiled at Blake as he sank into a chair. "They aren't all like that." She held his gaze a beat longer than necessary, making her statement feel personal. Pinching a piece of breading off the boudin ball, she popped it into her mouth and focused on Claire. "Not that I have any business giving relationship advice. I'm twenty-seven, and I've never dated anyone longer than four months."

He caught her gaze again, and his chest tightened. "Neither have I."

A look of surprise flashed in her eyes. "So, our…?"

"Yeah." He'd dated plenty of women since Sydney, but he'd never connected to anyone on the same level. The longest relationship he'd been in since college had lasted a month, and that was because his girlfriend had gone out of town the last week and a half of it. He'd ended it as soon she returned.

"Well, aren't you guys great role models, then?" Claire teased. "Maybe I should give Austin a chance, so I don't end up like either of you."

Blake chuckled. "If he's a decent guy, I say go for it."

"And if he's not decent, don't be afraid to kick him where it counts." Sydney grinned, and Blake couldn't help but laugh.

"You can definitely take her advice on that. She's got a mean right hook." He angled toward Sydney, and his knee brushed against hers.

She glanced at him and picked up another piece of boudin, popping it into her mouth as she slid her foot toward his beneath the desk until their legs touched from ankle to knee.

His heart thrummed at the innocent intimacy, and for a moment, he felt young again, like a teen hiding his display of affection from the adults in the room. Energy buzzed between them, and he fought the urge to slip his hand beneath the desk to hold hers.

He took a bite of the boudin, closing his eyes as the flavors of the spicy, savory sausage danced on his tongue. "The guys will be here soon. You better head back to the dorm, Claire."

She cut her gaze between them, wariness crossing her expression before she composed herself. "Do you need somewhere to stay during the investigation? I'm sure I can sneak you in. My roommate won't mind. She thinks you're hot."

"I'm good. Thanks." The last thing he needed was a nineteen-year-old fawning over him. He stuffed the trash into the paper bag and rose to his feet.

Claire stood and grabbed the bag. "Where are you going while they investigate? Have a hot date?"

Something like that. "I'm staying here. They thought I could help since they're short one medium."

"Oh." Claire stepped toward the door but paused. "I could—"

"You know what?" Sydney rose and walked her toward the front of the building. "I'm leading a tour at six tomorrow. Why don't you come along and get a feel for how we work? Then we can talk about any ideas you might have for the new one. It would be a big help to have your opinion since you've done so much research on the places we'll be visiting."

Claire's face brightened. "Yeah, okay. I can do that."

"Great. Meet me at the St. Louis Cathedral around five forty-five." Damn, Sydney was good with his cousin.

She had a way with people, holding her ground while keeping everyone happy at the same time. He could learn a lot from a woman like Sydney Park.

"I will." Claire stepped out the door and hesitated. "Hey, Blake? Can I talk to you for a minute?"

He ran a hand down his face. "Excuse me for a second, Syd."

"No problem." Sydney moved deeper into the museum while Blake stepped onto the sidewalk with Claire.

Her smile hardened into a firm line. "What do you think you're doing?"

"What do you mean?"

She tossed the bag into a trash can and fisted her hands on her hips. "I mean, why are you flirting with Sydney? I swear to God, Blake, if you screw up your career over a woman again…" She crossed her arms and shook her head. "Didn't you learn your lesson in New York?"

He stiffened. "First of all, my personal life is none of your business. What happened in New York was none of your business, and it still wouldn't be if you hadn't eavesdropped on my conversations with your dad."

"Step-dad."

He held up a hand. "Second, this situation is completely different. Sydney and I have history. It won't be like that."

"How do you know?"

"Because I know Sydney."

"And what happens when you two break up? She's part of the package with the ghost tour company. You said yourself your partner wouldn't agree to anything unless his whole team was on board. What if she decides she's not on board anymore? Then what?"

He put a hand on her shoulder. "Claire, I appreciate your concern."

She covered his hand with hers. "Someone's got to look out for you."

"I'm supposed to be the one looking out for you, remember? I'm a grown man, and I can make my own decisions. Things are just starting to warm up between us anyway. It may not even go anywhere." God, he hoped it went somewhere.

She nodded. "Just be careful. You've invested a lot of time and money into this, and I'd hate to see you lose it all over a woman. I mean, Sydney's cool. I like her, but you never know what might happen."

"I hear you." It was sage advice, and he should've listened to her. But the pounding of his heart every time he was near Sydney drowned out any logical thoughts his brain tried to throw at him. Was he making a mistake? Possibly. Would it be worth it? Only time would tell.

He tugged from her grasp. "I'll be careful, okay?"

"Okay." She smiled. "I'm jealous you get to do this investigation without me."

"I'll make sure you're included next time. Good night, Claire."

"Bye."

He returned inside to find Sydney sitting on a table, her ankles crossed, legs swinging as she swiped her phone screen. She looked up at him and set her phone down. "Everything okay?"

"Yeah." He raked a hand through his hair and moved toward her, stopping a few inches in front of the table. "I'm sorry about…her. She has these mood swings, and—"

"No need to apologize." She slid off the table to face

him, closing the distance between them. "She's young and still feeling her way around. It's especially hard to find a place in an already established, tight-knit group like ours."

Standing this close to her, all he could think about was taking her in his arms again, holding her tight to his chest and never letting her go. "I'm still trying to figure out where I'm going to fit in."

"I am too." She bit her bottom lip and looked into his eyes.

He held her gaze, and that old familiar magnetism tugged him toward her. Leaning in, he took her hand in his, and she inched a little closer. The floral scent of her shampoo drifted to his senses, and it may have been his memory playing tricks on him, but he detected a faint hint of strawberry, like the lip balm she used to wear. She glanced at his lips and swallowed before returning her gaze to his eyes.

He took her other hand, lacing his fingers through hers. "I know where I want to fit, but I'm not sure if it's a good idea."

Her lips parted as if she were going to speak, but then she pressed them together, a look of longing battling with the confliction in her eyes. "I—"

The damn doorbell buzzer blasted through the room, and she stumbled back, catching herself on the edge of the table and pressing a hand to her heart. "That sound might be the death of me."

This woman might be the death of him. "It has a tendency to ring at the wrong time." He gritted his teeth and turned as the door swung open.

Eric shuffled in, his arms wrapped around a black plastic case, several canvas duffle bags hanging from his shoulders. "Don't worry about picking up any of the equipment on your way here, Syd. Jason and I can handle it all." Sarcasm dripped from his voice as he piled the bags onto a table. "How's it going, Blake?"

"Let me help you with that." Blake grabbed a bag from Eric's shoulder and another one from Jason as he schlepped through the door.

Sydney crossed her arms, opening her mouth for a witty comeback before snapping it shut. That almost-moment with Blake had derailed her, and she scrambled to get her thoughts in order.

Thank you, doorbell.

If it hadn't rung when it did, she'd be wrapped in Blake's enticing embrace again, and heaven help her, she wouldn't have been able to stop herself from kissing him this time. Something about him made her want to say to hell with the ominous vision and dive in head first. Being with Blake again might be worth whatever pain the inevitable end caused, and who knew? That trip to Wonderland might not have been related to him at all.

Her heart sank. Related or not, *someone* she cared about was going to die, and the signs pointed to someone close to the company. *Or the company itself. Don't forget about that possibility.* Either way, until she figured out exactly what the premonition meant, she'd tread carefully. Take things slow. It would be better that way. Taking the time to get to know each other again would get them a lot further than hopping right into bed together, no matter how tempting he was.

"Everything okay?" Eric glanced between them, and Sydney cringed. She may have been immune to his emotional prying, but Eric already knew way too much about her connection to Blake. His emotions were like an open book for an empath to read.

"Yeah. Claire just left. She was upset that she couldn't investigate tonight." Blake locked eyes with her, and heat crept up her neck.

"I'm taking her on a tour with me tomorrow night, so it's all good." She forced a smile, but Eric gave her a knowing look. Damn him and his invasive ability. She gritted her teeth. Damn all their abilities.

"All right then." Jason unzipped a bag and pulled out a camera and tripod. "Let's get this investigation started."

CHAPTER EIGHT

Blake kept busy setting up cameras and running extension cords for the team, while Sydney went into professional mode, barking orders at Eric and Jason and barely sparing a glance for him.

Not that she had much time for flirtatious looks. The amount of equipment involved in hunting ghosts was unnerving. They had night vision cameras with wide-angle lenses set up in two corners of the museum area, another in the hallway leading to the back, and one in Sydney's office.

A once-empty table held an array of devices with buttons, knobs, and lights that would give them clues to the presence of spirits, and Jason set a black, cylindrical object with a silver antenna on the staircase leading to the entresol. He jogged up and down the steps, stopping outside the storage room door, and the contraption lit up, emitting a low-pitched tone each time his foot landed.

"It's a vibration sensor." Sydney's voice close to Blake's ear startled him, and he tried to hide his jumpiness by clearing his throat. She rubbed a hand across his back. "It'll also detect EMF."

Her touch soothed his frazzled nerves, but his heart had decided his blood needed to pump ten times faster. Was it fear kicking his body into overdrive or the woman standing before him? Probably a little of both. Either way, he was done with the startled jumps. If he was going to fit in with this team, he needed to act like he belonged. "What's EMF?"

"Electromagnetic Field. Ghosts emit their own, so if one gets close to it, the device will pick it up." She dropped her arm to her side and stepped away as if she hadn't meant to get that close to him.

"Fascinating. How long have you been doing this?"

She shrugged. "Six years or so. It's easier with a medium present to tell us whom we're talking to—if we're even talking to anyone. But with you knowing the history of the objects, at least we'll know whom to address when we're investigating."

"I'm glad I've got something to offer the team."

She grinned as her gaze swept the length of him. "You've got a lot to offer."

"Do I?"

Her eyes widened. "The team, I mean. You have a lot to offer the team. Your ability will come in handy."

"I am good with my hands." He narrowed his eyes, holding his breath as he awaited her response. Hardcore flirting during a ghost hunt probably wasn't the best idea, but he couldn't help himself. The woman was too damn entrancing.

Her lips parted slightly, her brows lifting quickly in surprise before she composed herself. She slipped out her tongue to moisten her lips, and the blood drained from his head to his nether region, making him dizzy.

Her voice turned sultry. "I remember." She tilted her head, studying him. "But I was talking about your contributions to this investigation."

He chuckled. "I know what you meant."

She narrowed her eyes. "I think things could work out…if we ease into it. Slowly."

"That sounds like a good plan." He inhaled deeply to calm his pounding pulse. Slow was good. It was movement. Forward momentum.

"What are we easing into?" Eric lifted a monitor into his arms. "Can somebody grab that bag?"

"I got it." Blake held Sydney's gaze a moment longer before slinging the strap over his shoulder.

"The investigation." She picked up an audio recorder and fiddled with the controls. "We need to take it one step at a time. Get our preliminary bearings and then decide our next move after we figure out where we stand."

Blake knew exactly where he stood, but his brain and his heart were still battling over what should be the next move. He followed Eric into his office, where he'd set up a sort of mission control center. Eric put the monitor on the desk next to a bigger one already streaming video from the cameras in the museum.

"Grab the cord from the bag, would ya?" Eric nodded toward the satchel on Blake's shoulder.

"Sure thing." He pulled out the power cable and attached it to the monitor. "Anything else you need me to do?"

Eric plugged the cord into the wall and glanced over his shoulder. "Yeah." He stood, dusting off his jeans. "Try to keep your emotions in check tonight. I let down my shields when we investigate, and if you're running high, it can mess with my perception of the supernatural."

Blake nodded. "Got it. Show no fear. I'll do my best."

Eric laughed and continued setting up the monitor. "Not what I was talking about, man."

"Right." He chewed the inside of his cheek. With Eric's extrasensory perception, clearing the air with Sydney right before the investigation wasn't great timing. Reining in his emotions around her wouldn't be easy. "I'll do my best on that too. She's just..." He shook his head.

"She's an incredible woman, whom I'm proud to call my friend. Don't tell her I said that, though." Eric pressed a button, and the monitor flicked on, showing a view of Sydney's office door. "She's also slow to open up. She's got some pretty thick walls because of her whole *seeing how things are going to end* deal."

"Yeah." But this time, things weren't going to end. If they got together, he'd be all in, for good. "Has she ever had any visions about you?"

"If she has, she keeps them to herself." He tapped a few keys on the laptop, and the view on the screen cycled through the different cameras. "I'd rather not know."

Blake leaned against the wall. He tried to focus on what Eric was doing, to learn the tools of the trade, but his mind drifted. "I can't imagine what kind of burden that must be on her. To know things about people and not be able to do anything about it."

"Imagine knowing how everyone around you feels. That's not as fun as it sounds either." He sank into the chair.

"I bet. Sophomore year of college, I found out my girlfriend was cheating on me when I touched her headboard. The energy slammed into me from all three guys. At once."

Eric cringed. "Ouch."

"We all carry burdens."

"I guess we do." He rose and shuffled to the door. "Give Syd some time. I can tell you two have history, and I may not be able to sense her emotions, but I can read body language. There's something there."

"Thanks. I'll try to keep it in check tonight." He followed Eric into the museum to join Sydney and Jason.

She smiled as he approached. "Ready to go lights out?"

"As I'll ever be."

Jason disappeared into a utility closet and flipped the breaker. The hum of electricity faded into heavy silence as darkness swallowed the room. The paper hanging in the windows to block out curious eyes also obscured any light from the streetlamps that otherwise would have cast a silvery glow across the polished concrete.

Blake's pulse thrummed, and sweat slicked his palms. He sucked in a deep breath to calm himself. As long as the ghosts haunting this place weren't murderous, he'd be good.

Sydney turned on a lantern and set it on a table before hitting a button on an audio recorder. "Museum of the Macabre investigation. Ten p.m. Main display room." She turned on another device. "My name is Sydney. This is Jason, Eric, and Blake." She pointed to each man as she said his name. "If there is anyone else here, please make yourself known. You can speak into this device or touch this one, and it will light up."

Blake held his breath, waiting for a door to slam or for

one of the devices to beep. Eerie silence filled the room instead. He ground his teeth as the others asked a series of questions in turn, leaving a span of silence between each one in hopes of receiving an answer.

"Let's play this back and see if we got anything." Sydney pressed play on the recorder and held it to her ear. A few minutes later, she shook her head. "We're not picking anything up. Why don't you tell us about some of the objects? Maybe if the spirits hear their stories, it will bring them out."

"Yeah, or maybe nothing's here. Maybe it's just the residual haunting that was here when I bought the place." His voice sounded way more hopeful than he'd intended.

"Residuals don't slam doors," Jason said.

"Right." *Damn.* "Well, let's start with the worst." He strode across the room and took a hatchet from a box. "This belonged to a man named Antonio. He was one of The Axeman's victims." A shiver ran down Blake's spine. It would be his luck to have brought in the ghost of a serial killer. He set the weapon on top of a display case.

Sydney held a gray device with green, yellow, and red lights up to the hatchet, waving it around the space. "This is a K-II meter. It also measures electromagnetic field. The lights turn on when it picks something up." The device remained dim.

"Is anyone here attached to this thing?" Blake said into the silence. "If so, you can leave. I didn't mean to bring you here." He froze as they all stood motionless, waiting for a response.

"Nothing," Jason said. "Let's move on."

Blake took them through item after item, their faces serious as they examined their machines and adjusted the settings. Nothing seemed to pique their interest. He'd expected to feel relief if they couldn't find any active spirits, but the team's disappointment fueled his own, and his shoulders slumped with the let-down.

"Just because we aren't getting anything now, doesn't mean there's nothing here." Sydney moved next to him, so close he could feel the heat radiating from her bare arm. "There might be something on the cameras or the recording that we'll find later when we go over the evidence."

Her elbow brushed his, and as she dropped her arm to her side, her index finger traced the back of his hand. "Something slammed that door today. We'll find it."

His stomach tightened, and he turned his palm toward her to take her hand. "I'm not worried."

"Good." She searched his eyes, and he fought the overwhelming urge to lean down and take her mouth with his.

"I'm not picking up on any *disembodied* emotions either." Eric leaned an elbow on a tall, cardboard box and gave him a pointed look.

Blake released Sydney's hand as the red lights on the K-II meter flashed.

"Uh-oh." Eric's smile lit up his entire face. "Looks like somebody wants to play."

Sydney rushed toward Eric with her own meter, and Jason picked up a handheld camera, pointing it at them. They worked together like a well-built machine, each person knowing exactly what to do, while all Blake could do was shove his hands in his pockets and watch.

"What's in this box?" Sydney rested a hand on the cardboard, and her eyes widened as her arm hairs stood on end. Excitement danced in her gaze as she glanced at him, and her entire body seemed to radiate with energy.

Seeing her in her element like this sent a zing through his chest, and he decided then and there he couldn't fight it. Screw his no dating coworkers rule. He needed this woman like a flame needed oxygen.

"Blake?"

He shook himself, trying to focus on her words rather than the silky way her voice flowed over his skin like warm honey. "It's…here, let me show you."

They stepped away as he lifted the box covering the sculpture. A papier mâché statue, half-painted in vivid shades of blue, green, and yellow, depicted a floral vine spiraling around a garden gate. The detailed petals and flowing leaves appeared almost lifelike in their rendering, and a spray of brown mottled the unpainted area.

"Wow." Eric raised his eyebrows.

"It's beautiful." Sydney ran a hand over one of the blue-painted petals.

"What is it?" Jason moved around them, panning the camera to take in the entire sculpture.

"It belonged to a woman named Bernadette. It was supposed to go on—"

"A Mardi Gras float," Sydney finished his sentence. "You can tell it's old by the way it warps. My krewe has a couple of these in storage from the first time our parade rolled, and we're going to include them on this year's floats as a tribute to our origins."

"This one never made it to a parade." Blake placed his palm flat against the surface and closed his eyes, allowing the energy the object had absorbed to seep into his senses. He shuffled through the imagery, from the time the materials were first combined to create the sculpture to the moment its fate as a parade decoration ended.

"The artist painting it, Bernadette, was murdered. Her

husband accused her of having an affair with the man who sculpted it, and he stabbed her to death while she was working on it." He pointed to the slash of blue cutting through what should have been green leaves and then to the brown spots marring the surface.

"Is that her blood?" Sydney touched his shoulder.

He nodded and yanked his hand away from the sculpture before the emotions could overwhelm him. "She'd been faithful. His accusations were false, and she felt so much confusion and betrayal at her murder. It wouldn't surprise me if she were still around after that."

The temperature in the room dropped, and goose bumps pricked at his skin. The air around him grew heavy, charged with static, as if a presence was gathering the energy of the atmosphere, trying to manifest.

Sydney smiled. "We may have found our culprit." She switched on the recorder. "Bernadette, is that you? Are you the one who's been slamming doors?" She paused and looked at Blake.

"If it is you, it's okay." He returned Sydney's gaze, and she nodded for him to continue. "We'd just like to know who's doing it."

A spike of adrenaline rushed through Blake's system. No wonder they loved their jobs so much. Actually making contact with a spirit—the non-murderous type—was thrilling.

Eric set his K-II meter on top of the sculpture. "Bernadette, if that's you, will you touch that device I just set down? It will light up to let us know you're here."

The lights on the meter flashed, and Blake's breath came out in a rush. "It's her. Wow."

Sydney gripped his elbow. "Are you the one who's been slamming the doors?"

The lights flickered again.

Relief loosened the tension in his chest. He could handle living with a nonviolent entity.

"Is there something you want us to know? If you speak into this device, we might be able to hear your voice." She set the recorder on the table, and Blake stilled, straining to hear the disembodied voice.

The clank of metal hitting concrete echoed behind them, and a frigid breeze whipped across his face, taking the static charge in the air with it. Blake gasped as the heaviness lifted, the spirit's exodus leaving the air empty and dry.

"Uh, guys?" Jason aimed the camera at the culpable object lying on the floor. "Can we debunk this?"

Blake strode toward the item that fell and stopped cold, his heart lodging in his throat. The hatchet used by The Axeman murderer lay at his feet. *Oh, hell.* This was exactly what he'd been afraid of.

Sydney snatched the weapon from the floor and ran her meter over it, frowning. Eric approached with another device, but no lights or beeping noises sounded. She lay the hatchet in a box and wiped her hand on her jeans. "It probably fell on its own. It was sitting on the edge of the case."

Blake pressed his lips together, hoping to God his face held a neutral expression.

"It wouldn't have been hard for a spirit to knock it off, if it was paranormal." Jason turned off the camera. "Maybe Bernadette was trying to show us how she died."

"I bet that's what it was." Eric turned on a lantern, casting the room in a dim yellow glow. "Syd had just asked her if there was something she wanted us to know. If she couldn't form words, that would be the next best way to get our attention."

Their logic made sense, but Blake couldn't fight the feeling that they were explaining all this for his benefit... trying not to scare him. "Or it could have been The Axeman himself."

"Nah." Eric shook his head. "No way."

"We'd have picked up a lot more energy if the spirit were malevolent." Sydney rubbed Blake's arm.

"Yeah." Jason put the camera on a table. "And ghosts can't hurt the living."

"That's not what Sydney told me."

Sydney shrugged. "He's part of the team now. No use in sugarcoating things for him."

Eric looked at Jason. "Remember the time in the ballroom? Old Mrs. Deveraux went to sit in a chair, and Eli yanked it out from under her. She broke her tailbone."

Jason nodded. "I remember."

"Eli is a ghost that haunts the Maison Des Fleurs," Sydney said. "He gets ornery, but that's the only time he's ever hurt anyone."

"All it takes is once." And if The Axeman were there in the museum, once could be a hatchet to the chest.

"This wasn't The Axeman," Sydney said. "Seriously, I'd be shocked if it were him."

He looked into her eyes, searching for any signs of a lie, but he found complete honesty in her gaze. If a seasoned professional like her didn't think the ghost was a murderer, who was he to contradict her? "Good to know." He raked a hand through his hair and let out a relieved chuckle, dissolving the tension in the room. "That was actually pretty cool, wasn't it?"

Sydney laughed. "It doesn't matter how many times we

do this. Getting a response that we can record is always cool." She pressed play on the recorder and held it to her ear. "We didn't get any audible responses. You got the K-II on camera, right, Jason?"

"Every bit of it."

She nodded. "Good. We can use it in the video presentation. This piece is an eye-catcher. I think it should go right in the middle. It'll draw people in. What do you think, Blake?" Her eyes sparkled in the dim light, and for the first time since he saw her on the ghost tour, she seemed genuinely excited about the project.

"Sounds perfect."

After the investigation, Sydney lay in her bed, staring at the ceiling fan hanging unmoving above her. Though it was three a.m., and she should have been sleeping like a normal person, her mind raced, and her restless legs wouldn't still.

The usual rush from a successful investigation should have worn off by now, but after spending so much time with Blake—especially the time they'd spent alone before the investigation—the adrenaline felt like it would never subside.

She still had feelings for him. Whether the old flames never completely extinguished, or the fire was starting anew, it didn't matter. She couldn't look at the man without melting inside. Every time he caught her gaze during the investigation, she'd wanted to call it. To take him upstairs and erase the eight years they'd spent apart, jumping right back in where they'd left off.

"That's a bad idea, Syd." She dragged her hands down her face.

If she and Blake were going to get back together, they had to take it slow. Get to know each other as friends and coworkers before they moved forward with anything romantic. It was the logical thing to do.

It would be a lot easier if his deep blue eyes didn't pierce her soul every time he looked at her.

That damn premonition was another factor to consider. Something or someone was going to die, whether metaphorically or literally, and she had made zero progress figuring it out.

She closed her eyes and took a deep, cleansing breath, relaxing her muscles and slipping into the meditative state that had become second nature to her. With her mind clear, she focused on what could be, willing the blue and gold kaleidoscope to sparkle in her peripheral.

A quick sinking sensation tugged her under, and the cemetery came into view below her. *Curious.* She'd never floated above the scene in this vision before.

The view gave her a wider angle, but most of the cemetery was blurred or clouded like before. She saw the coffin, the dark brown lid closed, golden handles glinting in the sunlight on the sides of the casket.

She tried to concentrate on the people around the scene, but she couldn't bring their faces into focus. Blurry silhouettes populated this vision, save for Sean and Eric standing off to the side. She pushed forward, rotating the scene in her mind to focus on her friends, and another face came into view: Trish.

Curiouser and Curiouser. Her three friends stood side by side, mourning *something*, but Sydney herself was nowhere to be found. As she panned the scene to search for more details, the familiar sinking sensation pulled her further down, the scenery dissolving into inky darkness. Her feet touched pavement in the vision, and a horn blared behind her. She spun and glimpsed headlights a split second before the kaleidoscope eclipsed her vison, throwing her consciousness back into her bedroom.

CHAPTER NINE

"You're awfully dressed up for a work lunch at a hot dog place." Claire tugged on Blake's sleeve. "I haven't seen you in anything but jeans and t-shirts since I got to New Orleans. Did you iron this?"

He jerked his arm from her grasp and smoothed the material, swiveling in his office chair to face her. "It's a business lunch, and I'm supposed to be the boss. I figured I'd dress the part."

"Really?" She crossed her arms and leaned against the edge of his desk. "Or did you do it to impress a certain employee?"

A week had passed since his heart-to-heart with Sydney. Seven days of low-key flirting, meaningful looks from across the room, *accidentally* brushing against each other when they were close. Hell yeah, he wanted to impress her. "Does it matter?"

"Apparently not. Keeping the workplace professional must not either." She smirked. "But what do I know? I'm just a teenager. If you want to dig your own grave, go for it."

"I'm not…" He inhaled deeply, squaring his gaze on his cousin. "Sydney and I are meant for each other. Don't worry about it."

"Okay. Look, if she really means that much to you, I won't say another word. It's just…" She picked at the hot pink polish on her nails. "I care about you both. You basically rescued me from my inner turmoil, and Sydney's becoming a good friend. I don't want to see either of you get hurt."

"I appreciate your concern, but we'll be fine."

"That's the last you'll hear me say about it." She pretended to zip her lips and throw away the key as she stood and stepped toward the bookcase behind his desk.

"Thank you." While her concern for his well-being was a good sign in her emotional recovery, her interest in his personal life grated on his nerves. Yes, he'd screwed up in the past, but this time was different. Completely different.

He glanced at the clock on his computer screen. Sydney was meeting him in twenty minutes to walk to Dat Dog for the team's weekly lunch meeting. He opened his email and scanned through the messages, his stomach sinking when he found Carmen's name among the senders again.

"What now?" he mumbled as he clicked the message open.

Hi Blake. You never responded to my message, and I wanted to be sure you're okay. I thought I might come to New Orleans for a visit, and I hoped we could talk. Please respond and let me know when a good time would be to meet up. I miss you.

"Jesus, Blake." Claire's voice came from right over his shoulder. "You're trying to hook up with Sydney while you're still involved with your ex-boss?"

He hit delete and slammed the computer shut. "Why are you reading my email?"

She straightened. "You were mumbling to yourself, practically reading it out loud."

A book fell from the shelf behind her, hitting the floor with a *thwack.* Claire squealed and jumped to the side, rubbing the back of her neck. "This ghost is getting annoying. Can't you tell her to stop?"

"She's just trying to get our attention. Sydney doesn't think she's hostile." He could only hope she was right. He wasn't about to let a spirit scare him out of his home.

Claire returned the book to the shelf. "I wonder what Sydney would think about you and your ex-boss still talking?"

He stood and motioned to the door to get his cousin out of his office. "Sydney's not going to think anything because you're not going to tell her. Carmen has emailed me twice, and I've deleted them both. I'm not involved with her, and I never plan to be again."

"Okay, okay." Claire held up her hands as she strutted into the hallway. "I won't tell her. You can have all the rope you want to hang yourself with."

He stepped past her into the museum showroom. "I'm not going to let my past affect my future with Sydney."

"Got it. Mum's the word."

The doorbell buzzer reverberated through the room. "That'll be Sydney. Please keep your mouth shut."

Claire rubbed her lower belly. "I need to use the little girls' room before we go. I'll meet you outside in a minute."

"Make it fast." He stepped through the door, and despite his annoyance with his cousin, as he greeted Sydney on the sidewalk, he couldn't help but smile.

She wore faded jeans and red Converse, and her leather jacket, zipped halfway up, concealed most of her dark gray t-shirt. A gust of wind whipped her dark hair across her face, and as she ran her fingers through it, he glimpsed pale yellow polish on her short nails.

"You're early." His heart pounded as she stepped beside him, and he fought the urge to wrap his arms around her and plant a kiss on those delicious mulberry lips.

"I'm always early; you know that. Where's Claire?"

"In the restroom. She'll be out in a minute." The resident crow flapped onto the stairs leading to Blake's apartment. It dropped a crushed aluminum can on the top step and puffed out its feathers, cawing at them.

"More trash?" He shooed the bird away and grabbed the can before walking down the sidewalk to drop it in the bin near the street.

Sydney followed, her eyes tightening with wariness. "Does it do that often?"

"Nearly every day now."

"Here I am." Claire beamed a smile as she trotted out of the museum. "Sydney, I have an idea for the new tour I can't wait to tell you about."

Sydney returned the smile and stood on the edge of the sidewalk, preparing to cross the street. "All of your suggestions have been stellar so far, so I can't wait to hear it."

"Hold on." Blake moved next to her, motioning toward the museum. "I need to lock up."

Tires squealed and a horn blared as a black sedan barreled around the corner. Blake grabbed Sydney's arm, yanking her back against the building as the car lurched onto the sidewalk, knocking over the trash can before bumping back onto the pavement.

"Are you okay?" He clutched Sydney's shoulders, ignoring the car as it skidded to a stop a few yards away.

"Yeah." Her brows drew together, confusion clouding her eyes for a moment before her lips parted on a gasp.

The car door opened, and Claire raced toward it. "Hey! What the hell? You almost killed my friends."

The driver slammed the door and sped away.

"Sydney?" Blake searched her eyes.

"I'm fine. Are you okay?" The corners of her lips twitched.

"I'm good." He'd nearly had a heart attack and peed his pants, but he'd survive.

Sydney smiled, a look of relief smoothing her features. "That was a close one."

"What a jerk." Claire strutted toward them. "He drove off without even apologizing. I saw his face, though, so I'll kick his ass if I see him again."

Blake released Sydney's shoulders, dropping his arms to his sides. "Did you get the license plate?"

Claire pressed her lips together and lowered her gaze. "I didn't think about it. I'm sorry."

Sydney tugged on the hem of her shirt, straightening her clothes. "It was probably a drunk driver. We're close to Bourbon Street." She nodded in the direction of the restaurant. "We better head out, or we'll be late."

"Right." Blake locked the museum and walked next to Sydney. She was quiet, chewing on her lip and gazing at her surroundings as they trekked through the Quarter toward Frenchman Street. Thankfully, Claire remained silent too.

His heart finally slowed to a normal pace as they approached Dat Dog, and he peered at the two-story building with its bright blue façade and line of double doors with twin windows sporting cartoon caricatures of franks in various comic poses. The restaurant wasn't much more than a hot dog stand when he'd left for New York, and now it was a culinary icon with multiple locations in Louisiana. A lot had changed in eight years, but his feelings for Sydney were as strong as ever. They'd simply been put on hold.

Sydney paused on the sidewalk outside the restaurant. "I stopped by the office early this morning on my way to the warehouse, and a box of old bank ledgers nearly fell on top of me. I think our resident ghost wants to talk."

"Are you okay?" First a ghost attack and then nearly getting run over by a car? The urge to protect her overwhelmed him, but he didn't know what she needed protection from. Bad luck?

"Oh, yeah." She waved off his concern, but it didn't stop him from worrying.

Claire looked at her incredulously. "You're not afraid at all? Even after the hatchet fell?"

"Nah. She hasn't been aggressive, so there's nothing to worry about." She looked at Blake as if reassuring him.

"A book flew off the shelf and almost hit me today." Claire put her hands on her hips. "I'd call that aggressive."

"It fell like something knocked it off, but I wouldn't say it flew." He'd been quick to write it off as a grab for attention when it was Claire, but now that he knew Sydney had been affected too, he didn't know whether to call the act aggressive or not.

"Still." Claire shook her head.

"The activity always seems to pick up when y'all are around," he said. "When I'm there alone, I don't hear anything but the residual sounds and the occasional slamming door."

"I wonder why that is." Claire tilted her head.

"The ghost is a woman, and so are we," Sydney said. "She probably feels like we'll be the easiest ones to talk to. I'll have to start carrying a recorder with me in case it happens again. If she's gathering strength, she may work up enough energy to be heard."

"What would it take to make you scared of a ghost?" Claire asked.

Sydney shrugged. "I don't know. We've dealt with a lot worse than Bernadette the painter. Maybe if she became aggressive. Started throwing stuff at me rather than knocking things over." She glanced at Blake.

"Is that possible?" Claire's eyes widened, but he couldn't tell if it was out of fear or curiosity.

"I suppose. I talked to Sean this morning. He's going to stop by and check it out next week." Her dark eyes held his. "Emily and the baby are doing great."

"That's good to hear."

They slipped inside the restaurant and placed their orders before settling into a bright blue wooden booth in the corner. Claire sat across from Blake, and Sydney slid onto the bench next to him, close but not nearly as close as he wanted to be.

The undeniable chemistry building between them was about to make him boil over in anticipation. Every moment he spent with her added fuel to the fire until he had no doubt in his mind she was the one for him.

He had to know if she felt the same.

The rest of the team arrived, and Eric sat on the bench next to Sydney. She scooted closer to Blake, her knee resting against his, as was now commonplace when they were together. If that wasn't a sign she was interested, he didn't know what was.

They discussed the week's schedule and tossed around new ideas for the crime tour, he and Claire fitting into their machine as if they'd always been a part of it. It was a dream come true. Now if he could work his way into Sydney's life after hours, he'd be set.

When they finished eating, Eric cleared the trash from the table and sauntered back, rubbing his hands together. "Tomorrow night is our monthly laser tag face-off. Are you two in?" He glanced from Blake to Claire.

His cousin straightened her spine. "Sounds like fun."

"Actually…" Sydney drummed her nails on the table. "I canceled that right before Sable was born. I didn't know our team was going to be growing by two at the time."

"Aw, man." Eric dropped onto the bench with a dramatic sigh. "I've been looking forward to kicking your ass all month."

"Let me see if they still have availability." She pulled out her phone and tapped the screen before looking at Blake. "That's if you're interested. We've been doing this once a month for a couple of years now."

A slow smile curved his lips as he looked into Sydney's eyes. Was he interested in spending time with her outside of work? Hell yeah, he was. "I'm in."

"Good." She lowered her gaze to her phone, her expression drooping with her shoulders. "They're completely booked tomorrow."

"Damn." Eric crossed his arms.

Damn, indeed. Well, he'd just have to ask Sydney out on a date. If she shot him down, so be it, but her knee had been pressed against his leg the entire time they'd been sitting there, the energy between them charging so high he could practically hear it crackling. This taking it slow business was killing him.

"Do you guys ever play paintball?" Claire glanced up from her phone. "Some of my friends from class play at this place called Gulf Coast Gunslingers. It's not too far from here, and they have an opening tomorrow afternoon at one."

A conspiratorial look passed between Jason and Eric.

"She won't have Emily to tip the scales," Jason said.

Eric raised his eyebrows. "I'm down."

Sydney smiled at Claire. "I think we can give these boys a run for their money. Let's do it."

Eric laughed. "You won't stand a chance without your secret weapon. And you'll be outnumbered. Prepare for the worst defeat you've ever experienced, Syd."

She rolled her eyes. "Emily is good, but she's also taught me a thing or two."

"I see." Blake stretched his arm across the back of the bench seat. "So, we're teaming up boys against girls?"

Sydney leaned into his side. "Yep."

"You know, my dad used to take me to the shooting range when I was a kid. Are you sure you want to go against me?"

"Because shooting a piece of paper is exactly the same as a moving, human target." She grinned. "I'm shaking in my boots."

He laughed. "You should be."

"He is a pretty good shot," Claire said. "My step-dad used to shoot with him."

Sydney let out a dramatic sigh. "All right. So you guys don't get too cocky, I'll call in reinforcements to even out the team. Three on three, tomorrow at one."

Blake smiled. "I can't wait."

CHAPTER TEN

"It can't be that different from laser tag, can it?" Sydney strapped on her chest protector and eyed the black plastic mask lying on the bench.

"The concept is the same." Trish tightened one of the straps, cinching her gear in place. "Except now you're actually being hit when you get shot. It stings."

"I should've worn long sleeves."

The midday sun hung high in the cloudless sky, warming the field to a comfortable seventy degrees. Sydney wore an ancient pair of jeans, a worn-out Eric Clapton t-shirt, and her old Adidas shoes.

"I should've rethought my entire outfit." Claire wore pale yellow cotton pants and a crisp, white sleeveless button-up. She'd curled her brown hair and put enough contour in her makeup to make her look more like she was headed for a runway than a paintball field.

"You'll be fine." Trish shoved up the sleeves of her appropriately long-sleeved t-shirt. "It doesn't hurt *that* bad."

Massive, bright yellow inflatables dotted the field, and

a line of trees created a U-shaped ring of forest around the area. A heron squawked from somewhere in the distance, and gravel crunched beneath tires as Blake's silver Audi A4 rolled into the parking lot.

Sydney's stomach fluttered, and she clenched her teeth. The man hadn't even stepped out of his car, and she was already giddy as a school girl. *Get a grip.*

"Y'all lucked out with the weather." The lone attendant handed Sydney a rifle. "Winter's a slow time here."

"I bet." She smiled at the attendant before locking her gaze on the driver's side door swinging open.

Blake stepped out, rising to his full six-feet two-inch height and raking a hand through his light brown hair. He wore faded jeans and a loose-fitting black shirt with long sleeves that blocked her view of his muscular arms, but it didn't matter. Blake would look good in a potato sack... Even better in nothing at all.

As he shut the door and met her gaze, his thousand-watt smile sent a jolt of lightning straight to her heart, solidifying her decision to move forward with their relationship.

After her strange vision had tumbled into a head-on collision with a car, and then the near-miss on the sidewalk yesterday, she was convinced they were in the clear. That the vision had been warning her about the drunk driver, and Blake's quick action thwarted the impending death.

But as she'd stepped out of the shower this morning, she was pulled under again, finding her friends in the same damn cemetery, Jason joining the crowd now. The options for who occupied the coffin were narrowing, and her hope that the funeral was symbolic diminished with every trip to Wonderland. The most recent adventure down the rabbit hole ended with her floating in darkness again, a Mardi Gras float shattering in front of her, and a Cheshire cat head, carved from ice, tumbling through space.

She couldn't decipher the confounding vision if her life depended on it—and someone's obviously did—but one thing was certain. The path she was on wasn't going to stop the funeral. It was time she changed direction.

Eric parked his Toyota next to Blake's car, and he and Jason clambered out in jeans and long-sleeved t-shirts. It seemed Sydney and Claire were the only ones who didn't consider what getting blasted with a stream of paint would feel like on bare skin.

Trish let out a low whistle. "If he were ten years older, I'd be all over that."

"Which one?" Claire curled her lip, glancing between the guys as if she wasn't impressed with any of them.

"Eric. He's a hottie." Trish shoved the chamber of paintballs into her gun and cocked it.

Sydney's heart pounded as the guys approached, but she straightened her spine, playing it cool despite the urge to grab a handful of Blake's shirt and plant her lips on his. Was it getting warmer outside?

Eric crossed his arms and cocked an eyebrow. "You didn't tell me Trish was coming."

"And ruin the surprise?" Trish picked up her face mask and balanced it on her head. "What fun would that be?"

A crooked grin split Eric's face, and an awkward silence hung between them until the attendant arrived with their gear. He gave them a rundown on the rules and how to operate the guns before turning them loose to start their hour-long session of aggressive team-building.

Trish had obviously gotten some pointers from their sharp-shooter friend, Emily, before they arrived. She proved a valuable asset on their team, landing shot after shot square in the guy's chests, though she reserved most of her firepower for Eric.

Poor guy didn't know what he was getting into, but as he ducked away from Trish's assault, he hit Sydney in the back before she could slip behind the inflatable she ran toward.

"That was a cheap shot, asshole." She spun, grinning, and fired back, hitting him just above the belt.

"I take 'em when I can get 'em. Ow!" He clutched his arm where a splash of red paint from Trish's gun exploded across his sleeve.

Claire fired at Blake, clipping him in the shoulder, and he sprinted between the inflatables, out of sight.

Breathless, Sydney slid behind a barricade on the outskirts of the arena, leaning against the unfinished wood and pressing a hand to her chest to slow her breathing. Something moved in the brush, and Blake's face appeared from behind a trunk before disappearing into the trees.

"The woods are out of bounds." She slinked to the tree line, her gun at the ready in case this was some kind of trap. She wouldn't put it past Eric to plan an ambush using Blake as the bait. "Blake?"

When he didn't respond, she crept deeper into the thicket, her pulse pounding in her ears. A branch snapped, and she spun to find Blake standing to her right, holding his gun vertically by the barrel, his face mask in his other hand.

"Don't shoot. We're out of bounds."

She lifted her mask onto the top of her head. "What are you doing out here?"

"Getting you alone." The intensity in his gaze stole the

breath from her lungs, and she couldn't stop the whimper from escaping her throat.

Recovering, she swallowed and strutted toward him. "And what do you need me alone for?"

His eyebrow arched, and a deep chuckle rumbled in his chest, making heat pool below her navel. His laugh had always had that effect on her. She stopped by a tree and dropped her mask on the ground before wiping the sweat from her brow.

Blake closed the distance between them, leaning his rifle against the thick trunk behind her. A bead of sweat dripped from his hairline to his eyebrow, and he flicked it away with his index finger. "I needed you alone because I want to ask you to dinner without the rest of the crew wanting to tag along."

"You want to ask me to dinner?" She feigned surprise. If he hadn't stepped up to the plate, she'd have taken the lead. She was tired of skirting around the edges of their desire.

"I do."

"Like a dinner *date*?" She tried to fight her smile, but the curve of her lips was too strong.

"Would that be all right with you, *cher*?" He inched a little closer, and the masculine scents of sweat and aftershave mixed with the earth and arbor, making her head spin.

It was more than all right, but if she was going to change her path, he needed to be on the same one with her. "There's something I need to tell you before I answer that."

He pulled away slightly, wariness drawing out his words. "I'm listening."

"I had a vision."

He held up his hands. "Whatever I'm going to do, I'm sure there's a logical explanation. I have no intentions of hurting you."

"You're not going to do anything." She leaned her back against the tree. "I'm seeing a funeral." She explained the visions and the psychedelic scenes they'd ended with. "Sean's always there, and now he's with Eric, Jason, and Trish. And the ends of the premonitions are just crazy. They've never been so abstract."

His mouth screwed up on one side as he processed her words. "I can think of a thousand different scenarios that could lead to a funeral. I don't think our feelings for each other are going to kill anyone...do you?"

"I honestly don't know. I've run those thousand scenarios through my mind hundreds of times, and I can't figure it out." She chewed her bottom lip, her frustration gnawing in the back of her mind. Now he knew, but would that change anything?

He set his jaw and nodded once. "Have you told anyone about this?"

"Trish and Emily know, but I haven't told Sean. I saw his first wife's death, and I don't want to put him through that again."

He cringed. "I don't blame you. I won't say anything to him until we figure it out."

"Don't tell Eric either. He has a habit of blabbing. Jason might let it slip too. Just...please don't tell anyone."

"We'll keep it between us."

"At least until Emily is in the clear. Someone new seems to come into focus every time, and if it is a person in the coffin, it could be..."

"It could be me."

"Or Claire or Emily or one of our family members...

or even me. I don't know. I shouldn't have told *anyone* about this, but I just don't know what to do." Other than pray that telling Blake about the vision would be enough to change the outcome.

"Hey." He glided his fingers across her forehead, tucking a strand of hair behind her ear. "Thank you for trusting me."

She closed her eyes for a long blink, his tender touch sending warm shivers down her spine. "Given our history, if we're going to start dating again, I thought you should know. If I slam on the brakes or start acting weird, you'll know why."

He smiled, his gaze dancing between her eyes and her lips. "Are we going to start dating again?"

"You did say you wanted to ask me to dinner."

"I did, and you still owe me an answer. So…"

She licked her lips, soaking in the deep blue of his eyes. "I would love to have dinner with you. This is my night off."

He leaned toward her, his right hand reaching behind her, and she couldn't help herself. She closed her eyes and pressed her lips to his.

He froze on a quick intake of breath. Then she froze, the realization that he was not kissing her back causing her ears to burn. She pulled away, covering her mouth as he straightened, gripping the gun in his hand.

Oh, dear lord, what had she done? The heat from her ears crept across her cheeks toward the bridge of her nose, and she squeezed her eyes shut, hoping when she opened them she'd realize this had been a trip to Wonderland, and she hadn't actually committed the worst faux pas she could think of.

Alas, when she lifted her lids, Blake stood in front of

her, chewing his bottom lip.

Way to go, Syd. "You weren't leaning in to kiss me, were you?"

He opened his mouth but paused before speaking. "I was planning to see how things went tonight before I laid one on you like that." He lifted the gun, showing her what he'd actually leaned in for…not her lips.

Oh, the humiliation. Her face felt tight, her forced smile making her cheeks ache. "You know me. Perpetually early for everything."

He chuckled. "That's not a bad thing. Maybe I was just late. Let me put this back, and we'll try that again."

His eyes locked with hers, and he rested the gun against the tree trunk, taking her face in his hand, stroking her cheek with his thumb. "I've been wanting to do this since I went on your ghost tour."

He leaned in and took her mouth in a kiss. Gentle at first, he brushed his lips against hers, pausing with his bottom lip barely grazing her top. His chest rose and fell twice before an *mmm* emanated from his throat, making her limbs tingle.

Sliding her hands to his shoulders, she leaned into him, parting her lips and continuing the kiss. He responded this time, opening for her as he placed a gentle hand on her hip.

As his tongue slipped out to tangle with hers, the world stopped spinning for a moment. He tasted like a wintergreen breath mint…like she remembered…and though his shoulders had filled out with muscle since she last kissed him eight years ago, the familiarity of his mouth, the softness of his kiss, and the tender way he touched her erased the time they'd spent apart.

The rustle in the trees barely registered in her mind as

she lost herself in his enticing kiss, but the pop of an air rifle and the sting ripping across her bicep yanked her out of the clouds and into the present. "Ouch!"

"Sorry, Sydney." Claire grimaced. "I have terrible aim." She turned her gun to Blake and popped him in the chest. "There. That's what I was shooting for. One point for the girls' team."

Blake lowered his brow. "That doesn't count. We're out of bounds."

Claire cut her gaze between the two of them. "Yes, you are. That's okay though." A branch above her rustled, and a pine cone dropped onto her head. "Ouch." She rubbed her scalp and glared at the tree. "Let's finish the game." She jogged back to the arena.

"Are you okay?" Blake ran a finger over Sydney's arm, wiping away the paint.

An angry, red welt formed on her skin, but the sting had already subsided. "I'll be fine. We better get back in there." She grabbed her gun and returned to the game.

Half an hour later, sweaty and breathless, they piled into their cars and headed home. Sydney pulled into the parking lot of Claire's dorm and hit the button to unlock the door.

Claire hesitated with her fingers on the latch. "So… you and Blake, huh?"

"We're going to have dinner tonight. See how it goes."

Claire nodded absently. "You don't have any jealous exes or anything, do you? You've never dated any of the other guys in the group?"

She furrowed her brow. "Goodness, no."

"Did Blake ever tell you how he lost his job at the museum in New York?"

"He mentioned they fired him because he refused to

acquire an artifact that was a forgery. They didn't believe him that it was fake." An image of his jaw clenching as he told her and the guys formed in her mind. He'd been short when Eric asked him why he left New York, not wanting to elaborate.

Claire laughed, but there wasn't any humor in it. "That's the official story. The truth is, he was sleeping with his married boss."

"Oh?" Her stomach soured. That didn't sound at all like the Blake she knew in college, but time could change a person.

"Her husband was on the board of directors, and when he found out about the affair…" She made a cutting motion across her neck. "He dragged him in front of the entire board and made a mockery of him. Told them about his ability, calling him a fraud and questioning his character. I'd hate for something like that to happen to him again. He's made some bad decisions, but he's still a great guy."

"Umm… No need to worry. I'm completely single."

"Good to know. He still talks to her sometimes, but I'm sure it's nothing to worry about. Thanks for the ride, Sydney. I'll see you around." Claire slid out of the car and slammed the door.

Sydney gripped the steering wheel, chewing the inside of her cheek as she mulled over Claire's words. Having an affair with a married woman was unacceptable behavior. She'd seen firsthand what infidelity could do to a family, and she wanted nothing to do with a man who was willing to sever someone's sacred bond.

But Blake didn't seem the kind of man who would do something like that. Not now and certainly not when she knew him before.

CHAPTER ELEVEN

If Blake's heart didn't stop pounding, it might burst right out of his chest. His knee bounced incessantly as he perched on the edge of the couch, waiting for Sydney to arrive, and he picked at a brown thread that had come loose on the seam of the soft fabric. He'd been a ball of excitement since she agreed to go out with him, and now his cheeks hurt from the goofy smile that had been plastered on his face since that kiss.

And what a kiss it was.

He'd almost blown it. Shock that she went for it had frozen him, and it took a full thirty seconds for his brain to comprehend what was happening. He needed to figure out her definition of taking it slow. Better yet, from now on, he'd let her set the pace.

The chatter of the television didn't provide the distraction he'd hoped, so he turned it off and rose to his feet. Silence engulfed the room, and he stood motionless, listening for signs of his disembodied roommate. Laughter drifted in from the sidewalk below, and a car door slammed before an engine purred to life, the sounds of the living drowning out any evidence of the dead.

That was fine with him. While he'd gotten used to the residual bumps and footsteps in his apartment at night, the activity below unnerved him. Thankfully, the active ghost seemed to be contained in the museum, most likely attached to the artwork she'd been painting when she died.

That was the theory, anyway.

He tried to ignore the feeling that the air in his apartment grew heavier by the day. The occasional static charge in the atmosphere and the way his arm hairs liked to stand on end every now and then were purely symptoms of his nervousness. Between the ghost downstairs and Sydney coming back into his life, he'd been on an emotional rollercoaster for weeks.

He glanced at the clock on the wall. Six fifty-five. Sydney said she'd meet him at seven, but she was usually at least ten minutes early to everything.

He'd offered to pick her up, but she insisted it made more sense for her to drive into the Quarter since her house was across the river. He knew better than to argue when she had a logical reason for doing something. Her fierce independence was one of the things that drew him to her, and while she may not have needed a knight in shining armor, she deserved to be treated like a queen.

Hopefully the activities he planned for tonight would be the final crack in her own armor, and her walls would crumble. If she thought about him half as often as he'd thought about her since they reunited, they would be a couple by the end of the night. He couldn't get enough of her.

The doorbell rang, a gentle *ding-dong* as opposed to

the ear-splitting buzzer from below, and he trotted down the stairs to open the door.

Sydney stood on the front steps, wearing a knee-length black skirt that hugged her hips and thighs, flaring at the hem in a delicate ruffle. The top two buttons of her long-sleeved, deep blue shirt were undone, revealing a teardrop-shaped sapphire pendant, and a pair of black ankle boots completed the look. *Gorgeous.*

As he caught her gaze, her eyes brightened briefly with her smile before they tightened, uncertainty hardening her features.

Uh oh. Something had changed between the paintball game and now.

He joined her on the narrow front steps. "You look stunning."

She adjusted her purse strap and glanced into his eyes before looking away. "Thanks." Her mouth closed with an audible click. She had something to say, and the defiant set of her jaw said it wasn't that she was happy to see him.

"We've got about half an hour before we have to leave. Do you want to come up?"

She looked over his shoulder at the stairway leading to his apartment and took a deep breath. "I'd rather not. Let's take a walk or something."

As he stepped back into the doorway, a brick settled in his stomach along with the feeling she was ready to end things before they even began. "Let me run up to grab my keys and turn off the light. I'll be right back."

She nodded and descended two steps to the sidewalk.

He hesitated, smiling to lighten his words. "Are you going to be here when I come down?" Because her tense posture and guarded expression said she was ready to bolt.

"Yes. We need to talk about something."

And there it was. *We need to talk.* Next it would be *It's not you, it's me.* Well, it had been a fun four hours thinking he and Sydney had a chance at happiness together. *Goddammit.*

He took the steps two at a time, flipped the light switch, and grabbed his keys from the bowl by the door. When he reached the sidewalk, Sydney stood, grimacing and rubbing her shoulder.

"What happened?"

She glanced down the empty street. "Some asshole rammed into me as he walked past. I'm fine." Her brow pinched, confliction clouding her eyes as she gave Blake a once-over. "You look nice."

He smoothed his black button-up down his stomach. "Is something wrong? What did you want to talk about?"

"I spoke to Claire when I dropped her off at the dorm. Or, rather, she talked to me." She paused, blinking at him as if gauging his reaction.

Oh, hell. "Claire has issues with coworkers dating. She's been warning me about pursuing you since she first noticed the chemistry between us."

"I wonder why that is." She inclined her chin.

"Her best friend, the one who was murdered, had just started dating the manager of the restaurant where she was waitressing. Claire blames him for her death."

Sydney's eyes softened. "She didn't tell me that. Was he responsible?"

"He's a suspect. What did she tell you?"

"You lied about why you were fired."

"Sydney, I didn't lie." He reached for her, but she took a step back.

"You weren't dating your married boss? And her

board-member husband didn't fire you when he found out?"

His nostrils flared as he blew out a long breath. Emotionally damaged or not, his cousin needed to learn to mind her own business. No doubt she'd spun the tale, making Blake look like the bad guy in that career-ending train wreck. He sat on the steps and pinched the bridge of his nose.

"Is that what happened, Blake, or isn't it? Because if that's the type of man you've become…"

"Sydney, no." He stood and dropped his arms to his sides. "You know me, okay? I haven't changed. I would never…" *Goddammit, Claire.* "Yes, that's what happened, but please let me explain."

Her eyebrows rose, and she angled her body toward him. "I'm listening."

"She had filed for a divorce. I saw the paperwork on her desk, and she confided in me. We started talking, having lunch together, then we had dinner a couple of times. I…" He lifted his hands and dropped them. "I thought it was a done deal. Now, I think she was using me to make her husband jealous. They called off the divorce, and yes, he is on the museum board, but I wasn't lying when I told you I was fired for not acquiring the artifact they wanted."

He moved toward her, and she uncrossed her arms. "The *priceless* fifteenth-century samurai sword was truly worthless. It was an exquisite forgery, but it was still a fake, manufactured in a twenty-first-century forge. They acquired it anyway and used it as an excuse to drag me over the coals."

He took another step closer, and she didn't move away. "Their court date was a week off when it happened. I swear, Sydney, I wouldn't have dated her if I'd known they weren't through. I made a mistake, and it cost me my job. I can't stand to lose you too."

Her jaw ticked, and she swallowed hard. "Claire is afraid you're making the same mistake again."

"She's afraid, but I'm not. The way I feel about you… it would be a mistake to fight it. I'm willing to take a chance."

"She also said you still talk to her."

"She's messaged me a couple of times, but I haven't responded. I'll show you my email account if you don't believe me." He reached for his phone, but Sydney shook her head.

"I believe you." She searched his eyes, narrowing her own as if trying to decide whether she truly did. "Why didn't you tell me the whole story before?"

"Before? When you were barely speaking to me or when we finally started connecting? I'm not sure which would have been a better time to bring up my previous relationships."

Her lips twitched before tugging into a hesitant smile. "I see your point."

"Are we good, then? My past isn't too haunted for you?"

She closed the distance between them, placing a hand on his shoulder. "You know I love a good haunting."

Rising to her toes, she pressed a kiss to his mouth, and this time, he didn't hesitate. He slid his arms around her waist and pulled her closer, coaxing her lips apart with his tongue. She leaned into him, the feel of her soft curves against his body and her sweet, feminine scent making his head spin.

Relief flushed through his chest as she gripped the

back of his neck, deepening the kiss. For a moment there, he almost thought he'd lost her. As long as they kept the lines of communication open, though, they could make this work. Hell, this was *meant* to work. Why else would it feel so right?

As the kiss slowed, she stepped back, cupping his cheek in her hand. Her gaze flicked upward, and she cocked her head. "I thought you were turning off the lights?" She nodded toward his upstairs apartment, where the living room light burned bright in the window.

"I thought I did." Though he'd been in such a rush to get back downstairs, it was possible he'd missed the switch.

"Maybe the ghosts like the lights on. Are you starting to have activity upstairs?" Her eyes sparkled at the mention of paranormal happenings.

"No, thank God." He pulled out his phone to check the time. Seven twenty-five. "Let me run up and turn it off. Our ride will be here any minute."

"Our ride? Where are we going?"

He smiled. "You'll see." No way was he ruining the surprise.

He darted up the stairs…again…and did a sweep of the living room. Everything seemed in place. He hadn't even made the connection that the light turning back on —if he had indeed turned it off to begin with—could have a paranormal source.

Great. Another thing to make him jumpy in his own home. He was just starting to get used to the residual stuff.

He turned for the door, but a carving knife sitting on the kitchen counter caught his eye. He'd done the dishes this afternoon and put everything away. At least, he *thought* he'd put everything away. His mind had been so preoccupied with Sydney he could have left it out accidentally. That was the only logical explanation. He crossed the living room and shoved the knife into the block, turned off the light switch—for sure this time—and headed down the stairs.

Sydney smiled as he closed the door and locked it before taking her hand. "You are grinning from ear to ear," she said. "What's going on?"

The clip-clop of hooves on the pavement grew louder as a mule pulling a white buggy rounded the corner. Sydney's eyes widened, and she pressed a hand to her heart as she looked at the carriage and then at Blake.

The driver tugged on the reins, stopping the mule near the sidewalk.

Sydney's mouth hung open for a second before she spoke. "Is this for real? Did you…? Are we…?" She was speechless. Just the reaction he was hoping for.

He gestured toward the carriage and bowed. "Your chariot, m'lady."

Sydney could barely breathe as she climbed into the white wooden carriage. A dark blue blanket sat folded on the corner of the red velvet seat, and Blake tossed it on the bench across from them as he slid in next to her.

The driver turned toward them. A splash of gray accented his curly, black hair at the temples, and deep creases lined his forehead, crinkling around his eyes as he smiled. "Evening, Mr. Beaumont."

"Hi, Jack. Thanks again for doing this last minute."

"My pleasure." Jack nodded and shifted his gaze to her. "How are you, Miss Sydney? It's good to see you again."

"I'm good." She blinked at the man before looking at Blake. "Is he…?"

Blake chuckled. "Jack's an old friend of the family."

"But he's the same…" Her brain hadn't caught up with what Blake had managed to pull off in a matter of hours. "This is exactly like our very first date."

"It worked so well the first time around, I figured, why not try it again?"

It had worked well. At the end of their first date eight years ago, Sydney had been convinced Blake was *the one*. A carriage ride through the French Quarter, snuggling under a blanket while looking at Christmas lights. Dinner at Tableau on the balcony overlooking Jackson Square. He'd even made sure a heater was situated next to their table, though the fire he'd lit inside her had kept her plenty warm that night.

He tugged the blanket from the bench and unfolded it, laying it across their laps. "Am I correct to assume that, by the smile on your face, it's working this time too?"

She slipped her hand into his. "It's unexpected and familiar at the same time. Good call."

"Hm." He searched her eyes, a crooked smile tugging one corner of his mouth. "We'll have to settle for looking at Mardi Gras decorations this time, though. I hope you don't mind."

She leaned into his side and rested her head on his shoulder. "Like the first time we did this, I'm more interested in the company than the scenery."

"Ditto." He wrapped an arm around her, holding her close as the carriage traveled up St. Ann toward the Mississippi, her stomach fluttering the entire way.

They talked about their lives, filling each other in on what they'd missed the past eight years, and by the time they reached Tableau, she felt as if the years had compressed, their time apart becoming insignificant compared to what might lay ahead of them.

Thoughts of the cemetery vision tried to wriggle into her mind, but she pushed them away, staying in the moment, in the carriage with Blake. If the premonition changed after tonight, giving her more information about its meaning, she'd deal with it then. The future could wait.

Tonight, she was all about the present.

They settled at a quiet table on the balcony. Though the starry night sky spanned cloudless above them, the chill in the air kept most patrons inside the dining room, making their dinner almost private.

The restaurant, situated above Le Petit Theatre on the corner of St. Peter and Chartres, featured authentic Creole cuisine and a stunning view of Jackson Square. Though the central park area closed at dusk, the bustle of the pedestrian plaza rarely died down until well after midnight.

Tonight a street performer balanced a bicycle wheel on his head and juggled a set of five flaming batons while a trio of musicians played a jazzy tune on their horns. A crowd gathered across the walk from the St. Louis Cathedral, preparing for a haunted history tour, and Sydney let out a contented sigh, thankful her night off happened to be tonight.

She scanned the menu and glanced up to find Blake watching her, his full lips bowing up at the corners, crinkling his eyes. Folding the menu, she set it on the table. "What?"

"Nothing." His smile widened. "Thank you for talking to me earlier. I'm glad we could clear the air."

"If this is going to work, we have to talk to each other. I learned my lesson."

He reached across the table, taking her hand. "This is going to work."

His voice held so much conviction she believed it without a second thought. "It sure feels like it is. But…I have a confession."

He arched a brow. "Do tell."

"I know this is supposed to be a reenactment of our first date, but…" She leaned forward, lowering her voice. "I don't remember what I ordered that night."

He let out a breath and pretended to wipe his brow as he leaned back in his chair. "Good. I don't either. I guess we can't expect everything to be the same, can we?"

"No, I guess not." Nor did she want it to be. Past Blake may have made her blood hum, but the man sitting before her now lit up every nerve in her body, making them all fire on overdrive.

Sydney's barbecue shrimp and grits was a divinely savory sensation, and the bite of Blake's steak he fed to her melted on her tongue like butter. They shared a bottle of pinot grigio with their meal—something they hadn't done when she was nineteen—and split a serving of crème brûlée for dessert.

After dinner, they strolled along the bank of the Mississippi and cuddled on a bench overlooking the water. He slipped an arm around her shoulders, tucking her into his side, where she fit like a jigsaw puzzle piece clicking into place. Their conversation lulled to a comfortable silence as they watched the boats drifting on the water, the lights twinkling on the surface like jewels.

His heart beat against her fingers resting on his chest, the steady rhythm comforting her as she laid her head on his shoulder. She could have sat there with Blake all night, but the tiny hairs on the back of her neck stood on end, and she jerked her head around, peering into the shadows.

"Everything okay?" Blake rubbed her shoulder.

No sound had drawn her attention, no movement from the corner of her eye, but… "I keep thinking someone's watching us. You know that sensation when you can feel someone's eyes on you?" She shifted on the bench to look behind them, but nothing appeared out of sorts. No monsters lurking in the shadows.

That she could see.

"I get this feeling during investigations sometimes, and the activity always picks up right after." She rubbed at the goose bumps on her arms. "I'm sure it's nothing. Could be a ghost we introduce on the tour wondering why I'm not talking about him tonight." She laughed, but she couldn't shake the uneasy feeling churning in her stomach.

Blake checked the time on his phone. "We should head back anyway. I promised Jack we'd be done by eleven."

"Is it already that late? Time seems to speed up when I'm with you."

He rose and tugged her to her feet, catching her in his arms. "I know the feeling."

Her paranoia dissipated as the carriage drove them back to Blake's apartment, but as they pulled in front of the museum, light cut through the cracks in the window coverings, creating a spooky glow around the storefront.

"I swear I turned those lights off too." Blake thanked Jack for the ride and took Sydney's hand as she stepped out of the carriage.

"I'd say it's either an electrical problem, which is possible in old buildings like this, or our ghost friend has learned a new trick." Her heart rate sped at the idea of new paranormal activity.

"I love the way your eyes light up when the supernatural is mentioned. You're really passionate about this, aren't you?"

"It's that obvious?"

He grinned. "I think we should check it out, don't you?" He fished in his pocket and pulled out a set of keys. Without waiting for her answer—because, really, was it even a question?—he unlocked the door and held it open. "Shall I be a gentleman and say, 'ladies first,' or a macho man and make you wait out here while I see if the coast is clear?"

She laughed. "Just be yourself."

"We'll go in together then." He offered her his hand, and she accepted.

She still stepped through the door before him, but only because they wouldn't fit side by side. As Blake shut the door behind them, the main lights in the gallery clicked off, washing the room in darkness.

"Well, that's creepy." He tightened his grip on her hand and nodded to the back wall.

Light from the office area seeped under the door, and something solid moved in the hallway, blocking the illumination from left to right before a *thud* echoed from the back.

Blake swallowed audibly, his palm slicking with sweat. "Tell me you saw that too."

"I did. Has it ever happened before?" Her breaths growing shallow, she moved toward the door, tugging him behind her.

"No, but how can something without a body block out the light?"

"I don't know how, but I do know they can." She released Blake's hand and gripped the knob, slowly twisting it and cracking the door open. Her pulse thrummed, and she braced herself for a rush of cold air or an electrical buzzing to shimmy across her skin.

She held her breath, tensing her muscles. Nothing happened.

Opening the door fully, she stepped through the threshold and peered into the first office. Empty. Blake followed her as she tiptoed down the hall, checking each room for anomalies. Aside from the light being on, nothing seemed out of place.

"Do you think it was Bernadette?" Blake flipped off a light switch in one of the offices.

"It's possible. She's been noticed, so she may be trying to communicate."

"Do you want to break out the equipment? See what she has to say?" He raised his eyebrows, trying his best to look excited about the prospect, but Sydney knew better.

While a spirit rarely ever scared her, she wouldn't be keen on dealing with unknown ghosts in her house either. "You said you don't get this kind of activity upstairs, right?" She moved toward him, sliding her hands up his chest.

His heart pounded beneath her palm. "Aside from what happened earlier, which was probably my own fault, no."

"I don't think we should stir up any more activity tonight then. She probably used up all her energy playing with the light switches anyway." She rose onto her toes to press a kiss to his lips. "I'd love to see your apartment."

His breath came out in a rush of relief before he smiled. "I'd love to show it to you." He pulled his phone from his pocket and turned on the flashlight feature before flipping off the hall light.

The thin beam cut across the exhibition area, reflecting off the plexiglass containers as they made their way to the exit. Before they reached the door, movement in the air like a chilly breath brushed across Sydney's skin, rustling her hair.

She swiped at her neck, swiveling her head to see if an insect had buzzed by, but the room sat still, the air stagnant. Not even the heater was blowing.

Sydney.

She froze, the whisper of her name seeming to come from everywhere and nowhere at the same time.

"Having second thoughts?" Blake stood in the doorway, concern tightening his eyes. "We can call it a night if…"

"No. No second thoughts." He must not have had the same experience, nor heard her name being whispered. Maybe she'd imagined it. She followed him out the door.

Blake put on a brave front, but as the activity picked up, she could tell his unease increased. No need to worry him. Not yet anyway.

CHAPTER TWELVE

Blake led Sydney up the stairs to his apartment, silently cursing himself for acting like a scared little kid in the museum. When something moved behind the door, Sydney had headed straight for it, literally tugging him along because he couldn't make his feet move.

She was fearless, and he'd been a fool. Even when he'd attempted to act nonchalant about a spirit that could turn on and off light switches—which, to be honest, freaked him out—she'd seen right through his mask. At least she'd been the one to suggest they leave, though she didn't look the slightest bit shaken by the activity until the very end when she'd paused before reaching the door.

Even then, she'd brushed it off and put on a smile. Hopefully ghosts would become second nature to him after a while too.

He'd think twice about going down there alone after dark, though.

They reached the top of the stairs and turned into his apartment. "Here we are. My living room."

Sydney released his hand and shuffled to the center,

turning a circle as she took in the surroundings. He hadn't done much to decorate the place. A tan sofa sat against one wall with a flat-screen mounted on the adjacent one. A potted aloe vera rested on a small table near the window, and a round table with four wooden chairs took up most of the open dining area.

She padded to the window and peered outside. "Nice view." Turning toward him, she smiled. "I like it. It's cozy. Is your bedroom upstairs?"

Something about the way she looked at him as she asked that question made him want to scoop her into his arms and carry her to the room in question, dropping her clothes on the floor along the way. "It's in the back. The staircase to the third floor is outside. They're two separate apartments."

"Does anyone live up there?" She leaned to the side, peering down the darkened hallway.

"Not at the moment. I was thinking about having it remodeled to make my living area bigger. The idea of having upstairs neighbors doesn't thrill me."

"That's understandable." She slinked toward him, gliding her fingers across his chest as she brushed past him. "So, your bedroom is this way?"

He caught her hand, tugging her toward him and wrapping his arms around her waist. "It is."

She rested her hands on his shoulders and leaned back, her gaze drifting from his eyes to his lips. "Will you show it to me?"

His knees nearly buckled at the breathy sound of her voice, and with her hips pressed tightly against his, she must have *felt* his real answer. "Are you sure you're ready to see it? It's only our first date."

"My notch is already in your bedpost, Blake. We'll

simply be whittling it deeper." She kissed him, and a flush of heat unfurled in his core, weakening his knees even more. Cupping his face in her hands, she pressed her forehead to his. "Are you up for a little woodwork?"

"The notch you carved was in my heart, not my bedpost, *cher*. You've always meant more than that to me."

"I know. Me too." She held his gaze as he tightened his grip on her waist. The intensity in her eyes bore into his soul, deepening the hold she had on him.

She couldn't possibly understand how much she meant to him after all these years, and he planned to take his time showing her, proving to her that he was worth whatever consequence her visions predicted.

"Right this way then, m'lady." He gestured grandly to the short hall and followed her toward the bedroom. Pushing the door open, he slipped in behind her and spread his arms. "To the left, you'll notice my dresser, the drawers filled with my casual apparel. Straight ahead is the closet, where you'll find my unnecessary collection of suits and other semi-formal attire I may never wear again."

"Hmm." She feigned a haughty attitude. "Moving to New Orleans and opening a macabre museum must have been a step down on the social ladder for you."

"Down or up, depending on your perspective. Personally, I enjoy the casual nature of the new work environment." He rested his hands on her hips, tugging her closer.

"Do you now?"

"I do. And, if you'll look to your right, you'll notice the main attraction, the bed I bought when I moved here. This one is notch-free and ready to be broken in."

She laughed. "Six months and no notches?

"You'll be the first and hopefully only."

She blinked, her lips parting on a quick intake of air.

Dammit. He shouldn't have said that. *Way to go, man.* "Too much too soon?"

She opened her mouth to respond, but something on the dresser caught her eye. "Is that…"

He followed her gaze. "Your necklace. Yeah."

She stepped toward it, tracing her fingers across the surface of the dresser, hesitating to touch the pendant. Her hand hovered above it, her fingers trembling, before she scooped it up and laid it flat in her palm. "I can't believe you still have this."

"I have a box in the closet where I keep things that were…are…important to me."

Her eyes glistened as she looked at him. "After I gave this to you, you always had it on when we were together."

"I never took it off."

"And you could read my energy in it? See things I'd done?"

With two strides, he closed the distance between them. Cupping his hand beneath hers, he traced a finger across the top of the sundial. The bumpy metal felt cool against his skin, and as he dropped his shields, the memories soaked in. "I could see the shop you bought it in. A witch-themed store on Dumaine. I got glimpses of you studying, doing normal teenager stuff, but I also felt lots of emotion, which is unusual. I suppose it's because you wore it a lot, so it absorbed your feelings."

"I rarely took it off until I gave it to you."

"I could sense your feelings for me at the time, and that's why I was so confused when you broke up with me." He laughed dryly. "I never saw it coming. Of course, now the predominant emotions attached to it are mine after you left me."

She closed her fingers around the pendant. "I want to

make new memories." Undoing the clasp, she slid the necklace around his neck, hooking it before resting her hands on his shoulders. "Let's replace the negative with something positive."

"I think that's an excellent idea. How should we start?"

With her hands on the back of his neck, she pulled his face to hers. Their lips met, and she kissed him with a fierceness that shot fire through his veins. Blood pooled in his groin as she leaned into him, her hands roaming along his shoulders, down to his stomach to untuck his shirt.

Holy crap, this was happening. The one that got away was back in his arms and about to be in his bed.

She broke the kiss to unfasten the buttons and jerk the fabric off his shoulders. Her soft fingers trailed down his chest, turning his skin to gooseflesh as her pupils dilated, and she slipped out her tongue to moisten her lips.

"Look at you, all grown up now." She gripped his sides, running her thumbs over his abs. "Time has been good to you."

"It led me back to you."

"Took long enough."

"Better late than never."

Her breath hitched as her thumb traced the pale, diagonal scar on the right side of his lower abdomen. "Is this…?"

He took her hand, bringing her fingers to his lips. "It's in the past."

"I'm so sorry." She cast her gaze downward.

"Don't be." He hooked a finger under her chin, gently lifting her head. "Stay in the present with me, *cher*. Now is what matters."

"You're right." Her gaze slid down to the bulge in his jeans as she undid the buttons on her shirt and slipped it over her shoulders. "It's the only thing that matters, and right now, I want you."

"And I want to give you what you want." He traced the lacy edge of her light pink bra before cupping her breasts in his hands, teasing her nipples through the fabric.

She leaned into his touch, closing her eyes and finding his mouth with hers once more. A faint hint of peppermint lingered on her tongue, and the softness of her lips felt both familiar and brand new at the same time.

He slid his hands to her back, unhooking her bra and tossing it aside before pulling her to his chest. It had been way too long since he'd held her in his arms like this, skin to skin, heart to heart. They belonged together...then and now...and he would never let her get away again.

She kissed his jaw, trailing her lips along his neck and pressing them to his ear. "Make love to me."

Her words were like a jolt of lightning to his heart, unleashing an urgency he refused to fight. He needed her. To be with her. In her. A part of her.

They finished undressing, tossing their clothes aside before falling to the bed together. With Sydney on her back, he lay on his side next to her, exploring her mouth with his tongue, her exquisite body with his hand.

She was all warm skin and soft curves, and as he dipped his fingers into her wet folds, his mouth watered to taste her. Rising onto his hands and knees, he moved down, pressing a kiss between her breasts, to her navel, to her inner thigh, before settling between her legs.

As he flicked out his tongue to lap at her clit, she gasped, and he couldn't stop the moan rising from his throat. She tasted better than he remembered. He licked her again, circling his tongue around her sensitive nub and slipping a finger inside her.

"Oh my God, Blake." Her breathless voice sent a shiver down his spine, and she tangled her fingers in his hair. "Yes."

He slid a second finger inside her, and she arched her back, an erotic mewling sound emanating from her throat as she writhed beneath his tongue. She was a goddess, the sexiest woman on the planet, and he would gladly spend the rest of his life pleasuring her like this.

She cried out as she climaxed, her hips bucking as he continued his pursuit. "I need you, Blake. Inside me. Now."

With a deep inhale, he rose to his knees and took a condom from the nightstand drawer. He rolled it on and lay on top of her, pressing his tip against her folds. She trembled beneath him, and as he gently thrust his hips, filling her completely, she cried out again.

The beautiful sounds she made and the warmth of her body against his...the feel of her wrapped around him, squeezing him... It was almost more than he could bear.

Lying with her, making love to her, the piece of his heart she'd taken when she left mended, and though his heart was now whole, it was beating inside her. He gave himself to her—his whole self. Damn the consequences. Whatever ending her ominous vision portended, he'd deal with it when it came. Being with Sydney was all that mattered.

He pumped his hips as she clung to his shoulders, his orgasm coiling tight like a spring before unfurling in his core, lighting every nerve on fire. He moaned and pressed into her, burying his face in her neck and riding the wave until it subsided.

Her chest rose and fell with her heavy breaths beneath him, their hearts beating in time as they held each other. Passion-drunk and light-headed, he rose onto his elbows to look at her, and her smile took his breath away.

"That was even better than I remembered." She glided her fingers along his back, raising goose bumps on his skin.

"No kidding. My memory did not do that justice. Wow." He rolled off her, tossing the condom in the trash before snuggling beneath the sheets with her.

She nestled against his side, her cheek resting on his pec, one leg draped across his hips, and a comfortable silence stretched between them. He felt no need to fill the calm with chatter; instead, he tightened his arms around her, letting the perfect way they fit together explain why they were meant to be.

He lost track of how long they lay there, basking in the afterglow, but the sound of footsteps on the staircase broke the quietness of the night. He closed his eyes and listened as the sound grew louder and then faded to silence.

Sydney propped her head on her hand. "I'm guessing, since you didn't react, that's the sound of your residual haunting?"

"Happens every night. I only hear it if I'm already awake, so I'm getting used to it." He rolled on his side to face her. "What got you interested in ghost hunting? It's an unusual hobby…or job, in your case. What is it that you like so much?"

"Honestly? It makes me feel less alone. I don't know anyone who has premonitions like I do. I didn't even know Sean could see ghosts until I was twenty years old, and I've known him all my life."

He trailed his fingers across her forehead, brushing her

hair aside. "I guess all us weirdos tend to keep our quirks to ourselves."

"For good reason. If I could get rid of this ability, I'd gladly give it up. I hate knowing what's going to happen, especially when I can't do anything to change it."

"I can imagine what a burden it is. When did you start hunting ghosts with Sean?"

"When he decided to open Crescent City Ghost Tours, he asked me to help. I thought I was just going to be developing the presentation for him and guiding the tours, but he asked me to help him gather evidence too. He can talk 'til he runs out of breath about all the ghosts he sees, but people don't believe it until they see hard evidence. That's where I came in."

She took his hand, kissing the back of it casually, and his chest gave a squeeze. Did she feel the perfection of this setting like he did?

"Since I was majoring in Media Studies, I had experience with camera and audio equipment. We started investigating the places he'd seen ghosts, gathering evidence, and the company was born. I didn't know I'd end up loving it so much."

"Wow. You've been with him from day one." He added her dedication and commitment to her passion to the list of attributes that drew him to her. She was confident, kind, funny, and insanely gorgeous on top of it all.

"I'm invested in it. That's why this vision worries me so much. The first time I had it was right before Sean announced he was joining forces with you, so I can't help but think that this…the joint venture, us being together again, something…is the catalyst for the funeral."

"We'll figure it out. This…" He ran a hand down her

side. "All of this, especially you and me together, feels too right for it to be the cause of something so wrong."

She opened her mouth to respond when a thud sounded from the closet. "More residual stuff?"

"I've never heard that before." He sat up and listened, and the faint sound of footsteps receding down the stairs thudded on the other side of the wall—in the staircase that led to the third floor. Rising to his feet, he pulled on his underwear and padded to the closet.

Sydney slipped her shirt on, clutching it at her chest as she followed him. "Could something have fallen off a shelf?"

"It's possible." He yanked the cord to turn on the light and scanned the floor. Nothing was out of place.

Sydney peeked inside and nodded at a three-foot-high door in the back corner. "What's behind that?"

"It's a crawl space." He twisted the knob and pushed it open, bracing himself for a raccoon or an opossum to come barreling out. When nothing happened, he let out his breath. "There's no light in there."

Sydney stepped out and returned with her phone, shining the flashlight into the space. Dust motes hung stagnant in the dank, musty air, glistening in the beam as it cut across the small room.

She shined it toward the back wall and on the sides, but the room was as empty as it had been the day he bought the building. "This is creepy. Do you know what it was used for?"

"No clue. This building is nearly two hundred years old. The inside has been redone so many times, it could be anything. Only the outside hasn't changed."

Buildings in the French Quarter were required by law to maintain their original outward appearance. It was one of the reasons this part of the city had retained its charm. Remodeling the inside was fair game, though, and many buildings that had started out as single-family mansions had been converted into apartment buildings, Blake's home included.

"What's on the other side of the back wall?" She fastened the buttons on her shirt and slipped on the rest of her clothes. So much for his dream of falling asleep with her naked body pressed against him.

"The staircase to the third floor. The only access is through the back, and the property gate is locked, as well as the door. The alarm would have gone off if it opened." He turned off the closet light and shut the door. "It's an old building. I'm sure it was nothing."

"We should check it out anyway. An animal might have gotten trapped in there, or someone could have disarmed the alarm." She pulled on her shoes and straightened, fisting her hands on her hips.

"You're right." With a sigh, he snatched his pants from the floor and dressed. Investigating a possibly haunted staircase in the middle of the night wasn't how he planned on ending this date, but she did have a point. The security system was outdated, and he hadn't installed cameras yet.

She followed him downstairs to the front door, where he opened the alarm panel. "Everything's set. I haven't messed with the back door alarm in weeks."

Resting a hand on his shoulder, she rose onto her toes and peered at the lights on the panel. "Probably an animal then. We should check it out."

He chuckled as he disarmed the system and stepped out the door.

"What's funny?" She followed him around the side

and through the gate blocking the narrow alley that led to the courtyard in back.

He paused at the corner and turned to her. "You're not afraid of anything, are you?"

She grinned. "Does my implied bravery threaten your manhood? Would you rather I play the damsel in distress?" She tilted her head toward the sky, resting the back of her hand on her forehead, and thickened her Louisiana accent. "Help me, Mr. Beaumont. I heard a scary noise."

He grabbed her ass and pulled her to him. "My manhood has never been in question, *cher*. You be as brave as you want."

Her breath caught, her lips curving into a seductive smile as her gaze flowed down to his mouth. The fiery look in her eyes tempted him to pick her up and carry her back upstairs to the bedroom, but he didn't get dressed and traipse out into the frigid night for nothing. They were investigating that staircase.

He released her and motioned toward the dark courtyard. "Ladies first."

She hesitated. "Are there any lights out here?"

He flipped the switch mounted to the wall, flooding the courtyard in warm white light. A cobblestone walkway led to an old, broken fountain in the center of the yard. The stone statue had to be at least a hundred years old, and it featured an ornate cylindrical pillar with three pedestals surrounding it in layers. A platform sat empty at the top of the column, whatever figure had occupied it long since gone. A ring of bricks encircling the structure should have served as a reservoir for the falling water, but all it contained now was a layer of dried leaves.

Sydney made her way toward the back door, but her

gaze trained on the fountain. "That's beautiful. Do you ever turn it on?"

He stepped past her toward the door and turned the key in the lock. "It's broken. I haven't gotten around to fixing it."

"You should. It'll be nice to sit out here in the spring if you can get it flowing. Ready?"

"For spring?" He mentally moved having the fountain repaired to the top of his to-do list. Whatever this woman wanted, he would give it to her.

She laughed. "To see what kind of animal has gotten trapped in your building. My money is on raccoons."

She moved to open the door, but he stepped inside first. His manhood might have needed a little defending around a tough-as-nails woman like her.

He fumbled his hands along the wall until he found the switch and flipped on the lights. Cold and slightly damp, the air in the corridor hung heavy and stale. He stilled, listening for sounds of phantom footsteps or tiny claws scurrying through walls. Sydney stepped inside, and the door clicked shut behind her. Silence engulfed them.

"A rodent would have tucked tail and run to its hidey hole the moment the lights flicked on." Her chest brushed against his arm as she squeezed past him and ascended the stairs. "Keep an eye out for droppings."

"Droppings." How the hell did he go from making love to the sexiest woman on the planet to searching a staircase for animal shit?

"The size can help us figure out what it is." She reached the landing and made the 180-degree turn to head up the next flight when she paused, cocking her head. "What's down there?"

Blake stopped on the landing and followed her gaze.

A narrow passage, barely wide enough for a person to fit through sideways, extended past the stairs toward a small, shuttered window. "Just space they didn't use wisely when they turned the top floors into separate apartments."

"There's something down there. Look." She shimmied between the staircase and the sheetrock and knelt on the floor, running her hands along the cream-colored wall.

"Shit." He wiggled through, emerging beneath the stairs next to Sydney as she picked at a seam in the peeling paint.

"This is a doorway. It was painted over, but it's been pried open. Look." She slipped her finger into a slit in the drywall and tugged. The panel swung outward, the squeak of the hinges echoing in the empty corridor like they were smack in the middle of a horror movie. "What do you think is in there?" She pulled out her phone and shined the flashlight inside.

"Body parts? Booby traps? A pack of rabid raccoons? Don't go in there, Syd." He reached for her hand, but she ducked inside the tiny room before he could grab her.

"Goddammit." He hit the flashlight button on his own phone and bent down, peering inside. "Are you okay?"

"I think this is the crawlspace to your closet." Hunched over, she inched forward, shining the light across the floor. "There are your droppings. Probably opossums."

"Fantastic." It couldn't be something cute and fluffy like a raccoon. No, his building had to be infested with beady-eyed, oversized rats.

"Don't knock 'em just because they're ugly. They're harmless, and they eat roaches. At least you won't have a bug problem while they're here."

That was nice, but he still wanted them out of his building.

She ran her hand along the wall as she shuffled forward. "Found the knob."

His palms slicked with sweat. "Don't…"

She pushed open the door and disappeared.

"What are you doing, Sydney?" He followed her through the opening and found himself standing inside his own closet.

Sydney pulled the string to turn on the light and grinned. "Told you."

"Jesus, are you crazy? There could have been an axe murderer hiding in there."

She rolled her eyes. "Don't be so dramatic. The back door is the only other way into that stairwell, right?"

"Yeah, but that doesn't—"

"And it was locked, and the alarm had been set. It couldn't have been a person. The scariest thing I might have encountered in there was a rodent, and it would have been more afraid of me than I was of it."

"Still." He opened the closet door and marched into his bedroom. She had a point, but he cared about the woman, dammit. It was his right to be concerned for her safety.

She stood before him and rested her hands on her hips. "I'm sorry if I scared you."

"You didn't scare me." He grinned. "Your fearlessness is actually a turn on."

She arched a brow. "That's good to know."

"I guess I should call an exterminator. If opossums got in, who knows what else is living in the walls."

"I didn't see signs of anything else."

"You're an animal expert too?"

"I'm a paranormal investigator. We always look for signs of pests to debunk claims of strange noises. I didn't find any more. Whatever made that noise was either an opossum or a ghost."

"I don't think an opossum would make footstep noises on the staircase." He plopped onto the bed and lay on his back.

Sydney bit her lip as she sank onto the edge of the mattress. "I wonder if I brought the activity upstairs. Most of the commotion in the museum happens when I'm there, right? Or Claire?"

He nodded.

"Maybe Bernadette followed me up here."

"Do you think she would do that?"

"She has been trying awfully hard to get my attention."

"Fantastic." He dragged his hands down his face.

"Do you want me to leave? See if the noises stop?"

The ghost would have eventually made her way up here sooner or later. This was bound to happen whether Sydney came to his apartment or not. He sat up and wrapped an arm around her shoulder. "I want you to stay the night. I ain't afraid of ghosts."

She laughed. "Are you trying to quote *Ghostbusters* now? Next you'll be asking to use the proton packs and ghost traps."

"As long as the Stay Puft Marshmallow Man doesn't descend on the city, I think we'll be fine. Will you stay?"

"I think that can be arranged."

CHAPTER THIRTEEN

Sydney set the web page to demo mode and used her phone to scan the six-foot-tall QR code painted on the Styrofoam wall. This Mardi Gras float would be the first of its kind for their krewe, with the massive code spanning the entire width of the trailer and the words *Scan Me* in a style reminiscent of Wonderland scrawled across the top.

She smiled as a colorful prize wheel lit up her screen. *Spin me for your chance to win!* was emblazoned across the top, and beneath the wheel, a bulleted list displayed the prizes available, including the big one: a chance to ride with the Krewe of Horae in next year's parade.

When her suggestion for this year's theme had been selected, she'd been beyond thrilled. Now, seeing it come to life in the massive warehouse storing the thirty floats for their parade, giddy excitement bubbled in her chest.

It took months to build the fifty-foot-long floats from planning to building the frames on the trailers to the papier mâché-covered Styrofoam to painting and finally adding the lights and finishing touches. While a few of the krewe members had the skills to help with the process, they hired out most of the work to professional artists and carpenters, and for good reason.

The result was a set of gorgeous, lavishly decorated floats dripping with colorful flowers and dotted with whimsical creatures like caterpillars, butterflies, and even a Cheshire cat.

Sydney clicked the wheel on her screen, and a slew of digital beaded necklaces rained down as it rolled to a stop on her prize: a buy-one-get-one-free hurricane coupon at Bayou Daiquiris in the Quarter. Most of the patrons would win a coupon for a freebie of some sort at one of the local establishments, but they were also offering a few cash prizes in addition to the grand prize to heighten the excitement.

She hopped off the float and jogged a few yards away to get a view of what it would look like to the crowds lining St. Charles Avenue. Bright yellow flowers trimmed with gold glitter to catch the sunlight accented the area where the krewe members would stand, and green, leafy vines wound around the entire structure. A *Drink Me* tag accented a giant corked bottle on the left, and a massive slice of pink teacake sported an *Eat Me* tag on the right.

It was perfect. Everything was coming together…for the parade and in her life. Her date with Blake had been better than she could have imagined, and making love to him was… She shivered.

His body had changed. He obviously hit the gym in his spare time, resulting in a delectable six pack and pecs she could bounce a quarter off of. He'd filled out in all the right places, turning the lanky young college boy she remembered into a mouthwatering man.

But his attention to detail…to *her*…felt so familiar.

He remembered how she liked to be touched, and he was responsive. He listened to the sounds she made, the way she moved, and he adjusted his position and pressure accordingly to give her a thrilling ride. *That* hadn't changed a bit.

Most men went into sex with one thing in mind: their own orgasms. Blake tended to her like a precious flower growing in a garden, giving her exactly what she needed to bloom.

She crossed her arms to rub at the goose bumps rising on her skin. She'd be a fool to fight this anymore.

"Congratulations, Sydney." Erin, this year's krewe queen, sashayed past on her way to her team's float. "Lucky you."

"Thanks? What did I do?"

Erin paused, resting a hand on her hip. "You won the raffle. Check your email. Great job on the prize wheel thingy, by the way. I love it. As long as Damon's krewe doesn't screw anything up for us, this'll be our best roll yet."

"Yeah, I ran into him the other day, and he said I should watch my back." She lifted one shoulder in a dismissive shrug. "I told him to bite me."

Erin scowled. "I won't be surprised if they try to sabotage us so they can take our place."

"Let them try. We can take 'em."

"Damn right. Love your float, by the way. That yellow pops."

"Thanks." She tugged her phone from her pocket as Erin continued on her way. The email in question sat at the top of her inbox, and she tapped it open.

Congratulations, Sydney. You've won the grand prize: six tickets to the Wonderland Masquerade. Please reply with the names of your guests ASAP so we can add them to the list.

"Wow." She hit reply and typed Blake's name immediately. She'd planned on him being the one guest krewe members were normally allowed to invite to their exclusive event. With six tickets, she could invite the whole team. Eric would love it, and while Jason wasn't the most social person, he wouldn't want to miss a party like this. She added their names beneath Blake's and hesitated.

The ball was next week. Would Sean and Emily be ready to venture out without their baby? She swiped over to her messaging app and texted Emily. Her reply came in a few seconds later: *Thank you, but we'll pass this year.* A pause and then: *Trish says she'd love to go.*

Not surprising that Emily wanted to sit this one out. She typed Trish's name in the email and chewed her bottom lip. One ticket left. Well, there was always Claire. It would be good for her to get out and socialize. She added her name and pressed send before shoving the phone into her pocket.

What a night this was going to be.

She climbed onto the float and grabbed her jacket from the railing. Everything was ready to go for the parade next week. Almost all her friends would be at the masquerade with her. She hadn't had a single vision of her relationship with Blake ending anytime soon. Things were falling perfectly into place.

She should have known better than to have a thought like that, though. As soon as it passed through her mind, the familiar blue and gold kaleidoscope pattern sparkled in her peripheral.

A sinking sensation dragged her under, and her vision flashed bright white before a new scene came into view.

This time, the cemetery felt real. Her peripheral shimmered in the colors of Wonderland, but the rest of her surroundings appeared crisp, saturated in lifelike color.

Row after row of above-ground tombs and mausoleums lined the graveyard, making the walled-in space look like a true city of the dead. White plaster covered many of the towering graves, gleaming in the early morning sunlight, while other tombs appeared abandoned, decades of weather wearing away the paint to reveal the brick and mortar beneath.

To her left, a weeping angel statue sat atop a massive family vault, and a crowd gathered around an open tomb directly in front of her. A thin layer of morning fog hovered on the grass, giving the peaceful cemetery an eerie, unsettling ambiance.

No, no, no. Not now. Not this.

The mourners were in crisp focus, and through the crowd, she peered at the coffin…the same one from her original vision, only this time, the lid was open. Her stomach soured, and she tried to pull herself out of Wonderland. She didn't want to see who was in that coffin, but her premonition held her, urging her forward.

A crow hopped toward her through the grass, and it laid a string of shiny plastic beads at her feet. She ignored the animal, her gaze fixed on the scene before her.

She scanned the backs of people's heads as she slowly made her way toward the casket. Emily's bright red hair was pulled back in a twist, and she patted Sean's shoulder as he stood between her and Sydney in the front row.

Sydney allowed herself half a second of relief that her friend wouldn't have to endure the loss of yet another loved one, but her heart sank at the other possibilities seeing Emily alive left behind.

An icy fist of dread clenched in her chest, and the pressure in the air increased, pushing down, threatening to crumble her. This premonition was too sharp, too detailed to be a metaphor. A deep sob bubbled from her stomach, hitching in her throat as she moved forward in her mind and peered into the coffin.

No.

Nestled in the blue satin, his eyes closed peacefully, his hands folded on his stomach, lay the man who held her heart. Blake.

"This is my fault." The sound of her own voice whispered from behind her.

She turned her vision toward the crowd and saw herself leaning into Sean's side. *"I did this to him. I should have known."*

"There's no way you could have known." Sean wrapped an arm around her shoulders. *"No one saw this coming."*

"I'm a fucking clairvoyant, Sean. I should have."

"Sydney?" Erin's voice drifted in the air, and cold fingers tapped Sydney's cheek. "Someone, call an ambulance."

Sydney pried her eyes open, blinking against the bright, fluorescent lights as she tried to focus on her surroundings. No blue and gold trimmed her peripheral. She was back in the real world. "No, don't. I'm okay."

She pushed to sitting, and her head spun. Pressing her hand against her throbbing temple, she leaned forward, closing her eyes until the room stilled. She sat on the cold concrete of the warehouse and peered up at the float she'd been working on.

"Here's some water." A member of the krewe handed her a cold bottle and knelt in front of her. "Are you okay?"

"Yeah." She took a long pull from the bottle and recapped it. Her shoulder ached, and a purple bruise was forming across her bicep, but nothing felt broken.

"What happened? Did you pass out?"

The last thing she remembered was seeing Blake in her vision, her entire world shattering in an instant, before she woke up on the floor. "I guess I shouldn't have skipped lunch."

Clutching Erin's hand, she rose to her feet and rotated her arm. It was going to be sore for a while.

"Here." Someone handed Erin a granola bar, which she passed to Sydney. "Maybe your blood sugar dropped. Are you diabetic?"

Sydney accepted the bar and shook her head. "I'm fine. Sorry to scare everyone. I think I'm going to head home." She had eaten lunch, but she wasn't about to divulge the real reason she'd fallen off the float.

The cemetery vision may have started out not fully formed, and perhaps the universe hadn't known who would occupy the coffin when it began, only that *someone* would. But now…

Blake was going to die, and Sydney would be the one to blame.

"Thanks for coming out." Blake shook Sean's hand as he stepped through the door. "How's the wife and baby?"

"Good. Loud." Sean strode to the middle of the room and turned a circle. "The baby. Not the wife." He chuckled. "I didn't know the definition of tired until now, though."

"I won't keep you long."

"It's good to get out of the house. Your email updates are helpful, but I'm excited to be coming back to work next week." He eyed the Mardi Gras float sculpture. "What's going on? Sydney said it was urgent when she called."

The office door swung open, and Claire strutted into the exhibit area. "Hi there. You must be Sean." She shook his hand. "I'm Blake's friend, Claire."

"This is my cousin's kid I told you about. Syd's training her to be a guide for the new tour."

Claire cast him a sideways glance. "Speaking of Sydney. Isn't she coming?"

"She's on her way." He looked at Sean. "I'm not sure why she said it was urgent. We had some new activity upstairs last night, but she assumed it was because the ghost seems attracted to her."

"Too many things going bump in the night up there?" Claire crossed her arms and arched a brow.

His jaw ticked with irritation, but he ignored her jibe.

"She's here," Claire sang as the front door opened.

Sydney stepped in, her eyes rimmed red, and she scowled as she strode straight into Blake's arms. With hers wrapped tightly around his waist, she pressed her face into his chest and inhaled deeply. Her back was rigid, her shoulders stiff, and as she let out her breath, she held him tighter.

"Hey." He kissed the top of her head. A faint hint of sweat mixed with the floral scent of her shampoo. "What's wrong?"

She squeezed him so hard, his breath came out in a

wheeze. Then, she let him go, stepping back and wiping tears from her cheeks. Her bottom lip trembled, fear widening her eyes, and Blake's heart tumbled into his stomach.

"Did you see something?"

"Syd?" Sean touched her tattooed arm, and she nodded.

"I don't want to say anything yet, in case someone here…" She blew out a breath. "See what you can pick up on first, Sean. Then we'll talk."

Sean paled. "Emily…"

"No." Sydney shook her head. "She's fine. Sable too."

Sean's shoulders dropped in relief, and he nodded, but tension drew Blake's toward his ears. His heart ached to see Sydney upset like this, and his mind spun with all the possible scenarios that could have her this distraught.

"All right." Sean took a deep breath and rolled his neck. "If there are any spirits here, my name is Sean, and I can probably see you if you want to show yourself. I might be able to hear you too, so…I'm here if you want to talk."

Claire perched on the edge of a table, her gaze flicking between Sydney and Blake before settling on Sean.

Sydney's jaw clenched, her muscles working as she ground her teeth. She fisted her hands, crossing and uncrossing her arms impatiently.

Blake put his hand on the small of Sydney's back and looked at Sean. "Are you getting anything?"

"Sometimes it takes a bit for the spirits to warm up. Are there any specific artifacts that seem to cause activity?"

"The sculpture you were looking at earlier." Blake nodded at the giant floral statue.

"I felt some energy coming off of it." Sean shuffled toward it. "What's the story?"

Blake explained the woman's untimely death at the hands of a jealous husband. "According to the people I got it from, her name was Bernadette."

"Names are good." Sean rested a hand on a flower. "Bernadette, if you're here, I'd love to talk to you." He paused, his breath coming out in a rush before he swallowed. "She's here…in her death state, but…here."

Sydney clutched Blake's arm, and his heart raced. It was one thing to see little blips on an electronic device and occasionally witness things fall, but for a real psychic medium to actually *see* the ghost haunting his building… that was another thing entirely.

"Parade?" Sean's brow furrowed. "She's asking when the parade is. I don't think she understands what happened."

"You mean she doesn't know she's dead? Does that happen to people?" Claire gripped the edge of the table.

"Sometimes." Sean tilted his head as if he were listening to something. "Especially when the death is tragic… She said your name, Syd. You know about the parade?"

"I'm sure I've talked about ours. It's next week." Her voice sounded strained, like she was holding back tears.

"I don't think she'll hurt anyone," Sean said. "She's strong, so she's capable of shutting doors, knocking things down, but she doesn't seem to have any sinister motives. She just wants to be in the parade."

Blake let out a breath of relief. "So we're safe here? I didn't bring in any murderous ghosts?"

"None that I can see at the moment. Give me a second." Sean closed his eyes and took several slow, deep breaths. "Hold on." He opened his eyes and squinted at something off to the right. "There's another spirit trying to come through, but I can barely make out her form.

He stepped toward the empty space he'd been staring at. "Take your time. Try to gather some energy from the atmosphere."

The temperature in the room dropped a few degrees, and a static buzzing in the air raised the hairs on the back of Blake's neck. "Who are you talking to, Sean?"

He grimaced. "Christ. I think you've brought in another victim." He tilted his head, standing silently as everyone in the room seemed to hold a collective breath. "She's gone."

"Did she say anything?" Sydney gripped Blake's hand so tightly his fingers ached.

Sean's brow pinched. "She tried. It sounded like she might have said, 'air,' but I can't say for sure. Her throat was slit."

Claire leaned toward him. "What did she look like?"

"It was hard to see her clearly. I think she had short, blonde hair. Early twenties maybe."

"Do you think she was one of The Axeman's victims?" Claire asked, her voice thin.

Sean shrugged. "It's possible."

"Is there anything we need to be worried about?" Blake rubbed the back of his neck to chase away the chill.

"Both of the ghosts were victims," Sean said. "I don't sense anything malicious from them, so I don't think you need to worry. Messing with the lights and moving things is probably an attempt to get your attention."

Blake laughed dryly. "It worked."

"I'm not sensing anything else, but spirits can hide from the living. If they aren't attached to the building or an object, they could just not be here right now. But most ghosts are harmless."

"Well, that's a relief, right, guys?" Claire smiled.

Sydney cast her gaze to the floor.

Blake stood in front of her, hooking a finger under her chin to gently raise her head. "Hey. Tell me what you saw."

She shook her head, clamping her mouth shut.

"You promised, remember? We can work it out whatever it is."

Her jaw trembled as her lips parted. "I saw who was in the coffin. It's you."

His breath hitched, and it took a moment before his body allowed him to drag in any more air. "But it's a metaphor, right? You said sometimes your visions aren't literal."

She sank into a chair. "This one was literal." She described what she'd seen. "It's going to be my fault."

"No." He knelt in front of her, resting his hands on her thighs. "C'mon, let's be reasonable. How could it possibly be your fault?"

"I don't know." She inhaled a shaky breath. "But I heard myself talking to Sean, and I said it was my fault."

"Well, your visions don't always come true, right? You can change what's going to happen."

"Only if I can figure out exactly what needs to happen to elicit the change. And sometimes, even when I know, I can't affect the outcome, no matter how hard I…or anyone else…tries." She glanced at Blake before looking over his shoulder.

He followed her gaze and found Sean standing rigid, the tendons in his neck protruding as he clenched his jaw.

Something silent passed between them, a grief so palpable it thickened the air.

Sean dragged a hand down his face. "Did you try to backtrack to when it's going to happen?"

"I did, but you know I can't force visions like that. They show me what they want to."

His expression hardened. "You need to learn control so you can see how it's going to happen. You need to get help and learn to harness your power."

She shook her head. "I saw everything with Courtney, and it didn't matter. I'm the shittiest clairvoyant ever."

"Only because you're afraid of your gift." Sean slid a chair next to hers and sank into it.

"I'm not afraid of it. Maybe I was when I was younger, but now I know it's just a part of who I am. A curse I have to live with. I've done everything I can to embrace it, but it's hard enough with the ability I have. If I get help, if I unlock any more of this power…I'm not sure I could handle it."

Blake took her hand. "Why do you say that? If it's part of who you are, why couldn't you handle it?"

She blew out a hard breath. "I was nine years old when I figured out the premonitions weren't normal. I talked to my mom about it, and she called my grandma in a panic. After she got off the phone, she told me never to tell anyone about my ability, that it was a family curse, and I should only confide in her when I saw something."

Her hand trembled in Blake's palm. "So, yeah, I was afraid of it when I was a kid, but it didn't go away. I handle it better now, and I know other people have the ability, but I've never sought anyone out. My mom and my closest friends are the only ones who know. It's not like they have clairvoyant schools or anything."

"I know someone who can help you," Sean said.

"No one can help me." The despair in her voice made Blake ache for her.

Sean's hands curled into fists. "Look, I don't think there was anything you could have done differently to change what happened to Courtney, because you saw it all. You did all you could. But, Syd, guilt's a bitch, believe me. If you don't try to figure out what's going to happen to Blake, how will you live with yourself?"

She dropped her head in her hands, sobbing, and Blake's heart wrenched. He glared at Sean. "Not cool, man."

"No, he's right." She sniffled and raised her head. "He knows exactly what it feels like to lose someone you care about."

Sean's posture softened. "It took me years to get over the guilt that I should have done more to save her."

"And I put that guilt on you by telling you about it." Sydney sobbed again.

"I'm sorry I let you believe that. I'd have felt the guilt whether I knew her death was coming or not. In my grief, I was angry with you for telling me. Hell, I was angry at the world, but knowing…it gave me the chance to appreciate her while she was alive. Now, looking back, I know that I—that *we*—did everything we could to stop it from happening. Don't you want to do everything you can to save Blake?"

Sydney nodded, and Claire, who had been silent during the entire exchange, finally spoke. "Let's think logically about this. You said you're to blame in the vision, right? And the paranormal activity here picked up when you did the investigation. Bernadette was killed by a jealous lover, so maybe she's going to take revenge on Blake, since you two are a couple now."

"That's a stretch." Blake appreciated her attempt to defuse the situation, but killed by a ghost? He looked at Sean. "Is that even possible?"

Sean stared across the room. "The ghost looks appalled at the suggestion. She's shaking her head."

Claire crossed her arms. "Well, would you admit to a murder before you even committed it?"

The overhead lights flickered, and a rush of cold air blasted past Blake before a box cutter on the table next to Claire clattered on the floor. She raised her hands. "That wasn't me."

"Maybe we should move this conversation outside," Sean said.

"Right. Come on, Sydney. We'll figure this out." Blake tugged her to her feet and wrapped his arm around her, guiding her out the door. As they exited onto the sidewalk, he locked the museum and nodded at a building across the street. "There's a coffee shop. Let's grab a table."

Sydney clung to his side as they crossed the street and entered through a dark blue wooden door. The rich aromas of coffee and cinnamon tickled his nose as he settled into a chair next to her. Black and white photos of famous French Quarter buildings decorated the walls, and he stared at an image of Lafitte's Blacksmith Shop, the oldest bar in the country, until his vision blurred.

They sat in silence, a sinking sensation forming in his stomach as he thought about what could have happened if someone had been in the way of that box cutter. "Last night, when I went upstairs to turn out the lights, I found a knife on the kitchen counter. I don't remember leaving it there."

Claire's eyes widened.

Sydney straightened. "You didn't tell me that."

"I didn't think anything of it at the time, but it was out of the block again this morning when you left." He took her hand beneath the table. "Could Bernadette's ghost gather enough strength to hurl something like that with enough force to…" He swallowed, unable to finish his sentence.

Sean rubbed his forehead. "Most of the time, spirits just want to be heard. Her life ended tragically, and while she does seem confused, I don't…" He let out a hard exhale. "It's possible. Yes."

"What about the other one you saw?" Claire asked.

"Bernadette disappeared right before the box cutter fell. I assume she focused her energy on moving the object, and that's why I couldn't see her when it happened. It's always possible the other ghost did it, but…" Sean pursed his lips and stared at the ceiling for a moment. "She was weak, but there was something off about her. Like she didn't belong. She may have drifted in, attracted by Bernadette's energy. I'm not worried about her."

That was easy for Sean to say. He wasn't the one Sydney saw lying in a coffin. "What are my options here? I've got a ghost who likes to move sharp objects and a clairvoyant who's seen me dead. They must go together, so we've got to do something about the ghost."

Sean nodded. "It's your space, so the dead have to do what you say. You can order them to leave and salt the entire building. If all the spirits in there are human, that would force them out."

"If the ghosts are physically attached to the artifacts, he wouldn't be able to order them out, would he?" Sydney put her hand on his thigh beneath the table. "How would that work with the salt?"

"They'd be forced out of the building, but not very far. And the salt wouldn't keep them out for long." Sean raked a hand through his hair. "I don't see either of the ghosts I encountered today hurting you on purpose, but I suppose accidents do happen."

"If I get rid of the artifact she came with, will Bernadette go away?" It made sense. The ghost came into his building with the Mardi Gras sculpture. If he returned it to the owner, or burned the damn thing, the problem would be solved. If the other ghost really had drifted in, attracted to Bernadette's energy, maybe she'd leave too.

"She might." Sydney's voice was strained. "It depends on if her attachment to the object is physical or emotional. If it's physical, she'll have to move with it. If it's emotional, she can find something—or someone—else to attach herself to. Could you tell when you talked to her?"

Sean shook his head. "She didn't follow us here, so that's a good indication it's physical. It's impossible to tell, though, unless she leaves the building."

"Okay." Blake squared his shoulders. "Problem solved. I'll get rid of the artifact."

"If you could somehow put it in a parade, I think the ghost might move on. Her main focus was the parade," Sean said.

"I can take it. It's whimsical enough to fit with my krewe's theme. I'll stick it in between some of our flowers, and it will blend right in, but..." Sydney's eyes tightened. "Blake, I had this vision after we slept together."

"Maybe the ghost watched you, and she's jealous." Claire raised her brow.

Sydney shook her head. "I can't shake the feeling that

us being together is the catalyst. I had the first vision a few minutes before Sean broke the news that you'd be joining us. It's too convenient to be a coincidence."

"That's ridiculous." He refused to let her think the best thing that ever happened to him was the thing that would lead to his death.

"Yeah, Sydney," Claire said. "How could sleeping with him cause his death? Unless you've got a jealous ex who's planning to murder him?"

Sydney sighed, resigned. "I already told you I don't."

"Getting the sculpture out of the museum is a good first step." Sean typed something on his phone, and Sydney's buzzed. "I sent you the number for my friend Natasha. She's a Voodoo priestess, and she might be able to help you develop your gift."

"Sean…" Sydney shook her head.

"At the very least, she can give you a reading. She doesn't have visions of the future like you do, but she might be able to help you with the here and now."

"I think that's a fantastic idea." Blake would try anything at this point. "I'll go with you, let her do a reading for me too. Maybe my death has nothing to do with you. Or maybe it's another metaphor."

"It's not a metaphor. I can tell. Everything was crystal clear."

He squeezed her hand. "I'm not going down without a fight."

She looked into his eyes, chewing the inside of her cheek before she nodded. "Then let's fight."

CHAPTER FOURTEEN

*S*ydney inhaled a breath of chilly air, trying to quell the churning in her gut as she and Blake strolled up Dumaine toward Mambo Voodoo, a combination tourist shop and Voodoo temple. But nothing could relieve the ominous sense of dread pressing on her shoulders, squeezing her chest.

Claire had been her only savior last night on the tours. Sydney could recite the words without a second thought, but she couldn't muster the energy to put on the kind of show required to hold the audience's attention. Claire had stepped up and guided the groups, Sydney only tagging along to give occasional reminders of things she'd forgotten.

The vision of Blake's funeral played through her mind on a constant loop all night, and now, with the afternoon sun dipping toward the horizon, she resolved to do whatever it took to stop the premonition from coming true, no matter the cost.

"Have you met Natasha before?" Blake's deep voice pulled her from her thoughts.

"Sean has called her for help once or twice when he sensed danger with a spirit, but when that happens, he moves us out. I've never met her in person."

"I guess you've never had much need for having your cards read."

"Not really, no." She didn't need a reading now either. Blake's death wasn't a metaphor, and though all she could see was the funeral, she knew, deep in her bones, that she was directly involved. She'd take the sculpture and the ghost out of the museum, but keeping him safe would require so much more.

"Here we are." Blake stopped outside the shop and pulled her into a hug. "Everything's going to be okay, *cher*. We've got this."

She leaned into him, letting his masculine scent and the feel of his strong arms embracing her take her away for a moment. Her throat thickened as she held him, and she squeezed her eyes shut, willing her tears not to fall.

Why in heaven's name would the universe bring this man back to her, only to rip him away when she'd finally opened her heart to him?

He kissed the top of her head. "Are you ready?"

"Not really." She slipped from his embrace, wiping the moisture from her eyes before he could see. "Let's hear what the Voodoo priestess has to say."

"After you." He tugged the green wooden door open and motioned for her to go inside.

Incense burned near the entrance, and the calming, woody scents of sandalwood and lotus greeted her senses as she stepped into the store. An assortment of colorful handmade dolls lined one wall, and a rack filled with small bottles of essential oils sat in the corner. She scanned the labels, finding blends meant for good luck, money, and love, but nothing for warding off impending death. If she could just figure out *how* Blake was going to die, then maybe she'd stand a chance at stopping it.

A woman with cropped blue hair smiled from behind a cash register. "Hi there. How can I help you?"

"We have an appointment with Natasha." Sydney attempted to return the smile, but the corners of her mouth merely twitched.

The woman ran her finger down the page of an appointment book. "You must be Sydney and Blake?"

"That's us." Blake rested a hand on Sydney's back.

"Through the altar room." The woman pointed to the right. "You'll find a set of orange stringed beads hanging in a doorway. Head that way. Natasha is ready for you."

"Thank you." Sydney shuffled through the first doorway into a room filled with altars to the various loa or Voodoo spirits. Each one had a colorful flag draped across the dais with an image representing the loa, and an assortment of offerings lay on the altars. Believers had left everything from flowers to rum and tobacco in hopes that the spirits would answer their prayers.

"Are we supposed to make an offering to one of these on our way through?" Blake's voice was hushed.

"I wouldn't know which one to honor, would you?" She took his hand and tugged him toward the beaded curtain. "Let's get this over with."

Blake held the beads aside and followed Sydney through the door. "Natasha?"

A woman in a long brown skirt and orange tunic rose and drifted toward them. Her black hair was woven into long braids, and her eyes crinkled with her smile. "Come on in, you two. Blake and Sydney, right?"

She nodded.

"Have a seat." Natasha motioned toward a small, wooden table with three matching chairs. A stack of worn tarot cards lay in the center, and Sydney's throat tightened.

Coming here was a bad idea. She'd only agreed to do this to appease Blake and Sean, to show them she was doing everything possible to prevent her lover's impending death. The only thing this session with the priestess would accomplish would be confirming Sydney's vision…and she didn't need confirmation. She needed answers.

She sank into a chair next to Blake, and Natasha reached a hand, palm up, toward each of them. Blake rested his palm in Natasha's hand, but Sydney hesitated. "What did Sean tell you about us?"

"Just that you need some help." She wiggled her fingers, urging Sydney to put her hand in hers.

Natasha's palm was warm, and as she closed her fingers around theirs, a chill ran down Sydney's spine. The priestess shut her eyes and swayed slightly, nodding as if receiving messages from the other side.

"What kind of ability do you have?" Sydney asked.

Natasha shook her head, squeezing her eyes tighter. "You both have the gift of sight. The past and the future blend together well with you, but your present is in turmoil." She opened her eyes and released their hands, picking up the deck of cards and shuffling them.

"Did Sean tell you that?" Sydney glanced around the spacious room. A set of antique wooden cabinets filled with herb jars stood against one wall, and a line of small burlap dolls occupied the top shelf. Her stomach roiled, and another shiver racked her body. Something about this place gave her the willies. It felt oddly familiar, yet completely foreign at the same time.

Natasha pushed the cards toward Sydney, pausing

before passing them to Blake instead. "Sean ain't told me nothing. Shuffle those."

Blake mixed up the cards before handing them to Natasha. "Should we tell you what our problem is?"

The priestess turned over three cards, frowning at them. "Let's see what my spirit guides have to say first. Sometimes the problem ain't what you think it is." She dealt two more cards and looked at Sydney. "Your visions have been muddy. Plenty of signs for you to decipher, but you don't know how. One thing is clear, though…" She looked at Blake and shook her head.

Sydney's heart sank. This was exactly what she thought would happen. Confirmation that Blake was meant to die. "I know what's going to happen to him. We need help to stop it."

"I'm sensing trouble with your relationship. External forces are at play, but also emotions. Jealousy is a tricky beast. There's uncertainty. A wavering decision dependent on many factors." She scooped up the cards and stacked them on the table. "Does this make sense to either of you?"

Sydney chewed the inside of her cheek.

"A little bit," Blake said. "Sydney saw my funeral and heard herself saying my death was her fault."

Natasha nodded and looked at her. "You need to delve into your vision. Back it up until you see what will end his life. It's the only way to stop it from happening."

Sydney blew out a breath and slumped in her chair. "I wish it were that easy. I've tried to get more details about the premonition, but I don't have that kind of control."

"You never developed your gift. Why?"

She laughed but couldn't force any humor into it. "It's a family curse."

The priestess glowered, holding out her hand again. "You ain't cursed, child. Give me your hand."

Sydney cut Blake a sideways glance, and he nodded, encouraging her to comply. She sighed and rested her hand in Natasha's. "Both my mother and my grandmother were afraid of it. They told me not to—"

"Shh…" Natasha held up a finger. "Give me a minute." She squeezed her eyes shut, nodding as if receiving another message from the Great Beyond.

Must be nice to have spirit guides telling you what to do. Sydney was clueless.

"You got Creole in your veins. Your ability comes from your Voodoo roots."

Blake raised his brow, blinking at her, and mouthed the word *Voodoo*.

"My great-grandfather was Haitian Creole. He died before my grandma was born."

Natasha tightened her grip on Sydney's hand. "My guides tell me he was murdered."

Sydney yanked from her grasp and rubbed her hand on her pants. "Which is why we don't talk about it." Her sordid ancestry was nobody's business.

"What happened?" Blake rested a hand on her leg.

She closed her eyes and let out a slow breath. Her family's history was a dark spot on her lineage she'd prefer to erase. "My mother's side is a long line of old money. Very prominent New Orleanians who ran several plantations. Her grandmother fell in love and got pregnant when she was sixteen. Her grandfather, who worked on the plantation, disappeared shortly after that."

"Oh." Blake cringed.

"It was the thirties; she wasn't married. It was a huge scandal at the time. Her older sister adopted the baby, my grandma, claiming they got her from an orphanage to explain the mixed race." Sydney swallowed the lump from her throat. "No one ever talked about it, until I started having premonitions. Then I found out my great-grandfather had psychic abilities, and my great-grandmother's family was terrified of him. They said he was cursed, and she was forbidden from having contact with him. She didn't obey, and he died for it."

Natasha steepled her fingers. "Your great-grandfather wasn't cursed, and neither are you. You have a gift, and you need to learn how to use it."

"I don't want to see the future." She slammed her hand on the table. "It sucks knowing how things are going to end before they even get started, and when someone is going to die …" She shook her head. "I've seen someone's death once, and I couldn't stop it from happening. All I could do was warn her."

The priestess cocked her head, studying Sydney as if she could figure it all out by simply looking at her. "Maybe that's all you were meant to do."

"Maybe, but why?" She lifted her hands in the air and dropped them in her lap. "Why put this burden on me?"

"The spirits wouldn't have blessed you with a gift if there weren't no purpose. You're meant to help people. To give 'em the opportunity to help themselves."

"How can I help Blake? I don't even know how he's going to die." A sob rolled up from her chest when she said the words out loud, and he wrapped an arm around her shoulders.

"You're the only one who can help him, child. You have the gift of foresight. Use it." Natasha rose and sashayed toward the antique cabinets.

"How? Tell me what to do, and I'll do it." Sydney turned in her chair to face the priestess. "I've tried meditating on it. Nothing works."

"Where did you learn to meditate?" Natasha opened a cabinet door and ran her fingers over the assortment of jars.

Sydney leaned into Blake's side. "The Internet." Her ears burned from the embarrassment of telling this woman, who probably wrote the book on meditation, that she learned the skill from a couple of YouTube videos. "The first time I saw someone's death, I did a little bit of research."

"Why did you stop?"

"Because she died anyway."

Taking a white candle from a shelf, the priestess pinned her with a pointed gaze. "Do you really want to help him?"

"Of course I do. I don't want him to die." How could she even ask such a thing?

Natasha scooped a bunch of dried leaves into a plastic bag and set it and the candle on the table in front of Sydney. "Developing a gift like yours takes time…more than you have. It's gonna require commitment to do a rush job like this, and even then, you might not break down your walls in time to save him."

"I'm going to be the reason he dies." Another sob threatened to bubble from her chest, but she caught it in her throat. "I'll do whatever it takes to stop it from happening."

He squeezed her shoulder gently. "We'll do it together. How can I help?"

Natasha leveled a heavy gaze on him, pausing and

nodding thoughtfully. "You're the target. Caught in the crossfires of something sinister."

"Is it a ghost? I deal in haunted artifacts, and I'm getting rid of one of them that has an attachment. I can liquidate my assets if need be. Anything to ensure Sydney and I have a long, happy life together."

The priestess smiled sadly. "Try to stay out of trouble. My guides can't tell me the cause. Too much uncertainty surrounds you."

"Blake…" They couldn't have any kind of life together. Not when his was on the line, and she'd be to blame.

"Drink the tea tonight and in the morning," Natasha said, "and meditate on this candle for thirty minutes each time. Then, I want you to stop by tomorrow at ten for a guided meditation, and we'll see if we can't strip away some of your blocks."

"Thank you. I will." And in the meantime, she'd take care of the problem the only way she knew how.

"This is good news, right?" Blake zipped his jacket against the chilly air as they stepped onto the sidewalk. A homeless woman sat on a ratty piece of cardboard on the corner, her mangy golden retriever huddled next to her as she shook a jar of coins. Blake dropped a five-dollar bill into the container as they passed before taking Sydney's hand, stopping her out of the woman's earshot.

"Hey. Talk to me."

Her eyes glistened as she glanced at him and looked away. "I can't. I don't… I need a minute." She continued pacing away.

"Sydney." He jogged to catch up. "Why are you upset? This is good news. If you can unblock your ability or develop it or…whatever…you'll be able to see what's supposed to happen and stop it. We should be celebrating."

"No, Blake." She whirled to face him. "You don't get it. Even if I can figure out a way to see what's going to happen to you, that doesn't mean I'll be able to stop it from happening. Maybe I'll figure out how to see it, and maybe I'll be able to warn you before it happens, but I can't actually change the future. You heard Natasha. All I'm meant to do is give you a heads up."

"And once you do, I'll take it from there. If you tell me I'm going to choke on a piece of bacon, then I'll never eat pork again. If I'm going to be run over by a streetcar, I'll steer clear of the tracks."

"It's going to be my fault."

"I don't believe that for a minute, but whatever I have to do, I'll do it."

She jabbed her fingers into her hair and pulled it at the roots. "Do you mean that? You'll do whatever I say needs to be done? Because I can't live another day in this world if you aren't in it."

His chest ached at her confession, but when he reached for her, she stepped back. "Of course, Syd. Anything."

"I'm going to work on my visions. I'll do what Natasha tells me to do, but in the meantime, the only way I know to keep you alive is for us not to see each other. If we're not together, I can't cause your death."

"No. That's… No." He just got her back. He wasn't about to lose her all over again. "You said it was spring in your vision. Remember? It was warm outside, so it's not like I'm going to die tomorrow. We have time to figure it out."

She pressed her lips together, shaking her head. "It was cooler this time, and a different time of day. Maybe it was originally going to happen in the spring, but something changed, speeding up the timeline. Our being together has sped it up, so we need to be apart."

His heart wrenched in his chest. She couldn't actually think this was a good idea. "If I'm destined to die, I want to spend what little time I have left with you. Don't let me leave this world brokenhearted."

Tears welled in her eyes. "I won't let you leave this world at all. Let me do this my way. Give me a week to work on my visions and see if I can figure out what's going to cause your death. I can't be with you knowing I'm somehow going to kill you."

"Sydney, you're not going to kill me. Survivor's guilt made you say that to Sean, nothing more." He took her hand, but she pulled from his grasp.

She set her jaw, a mask of resolve falling over her features. "I'm not taking any chances. I'll call you when I figure it out." Turning on her heel, she strode away.

Blake stood alone on the sidewalk until she disappeared around the corner. His legs felt heavy, and he couldn't force them to move. A mule-drawn buggy stopped on the street in front of him, the driver turning toward the Voodoo shop and weaving an eerie tale about the dark magic intertwined with the mysterious religion.

Nothing about that temple had felt dark or ominous to Blake. The priestess inside had been kind and helpful, her advice promising, whether Sydney believed it or not. As the buggy rolled past, he forced himself to move in the opposite direction.

He knew that stubborn look on Sydney's face, and he knew better than to argue with her when she'd made up her mind about something. If she wanted space, he'd give it to her.

For a while.

CHAPTER FIFTEEN

*S*ydney spent the next two days thinking of nothing but her vision, drinking Natasha's bitter tea, meditating, and doing everything the priestess instructed her to do…to no avail. She felt *something* happen in her mind when she did the exercises, and the tea did help to bring the vision into sharper focus, allowing her to move around in the scene and pick up more details.

She'd gained the ability to travel easily through space within the vision, but not through time. Backtracking to the events that would inevitably lead to the funeral seemed an impossible task, which wasn't surprising. Her ability was a curse, no matter what the others wanted her to believe, and nothing good ever came from a curse.

Sitting cross-legged on the carpet in the center of her living room, she lit the candle and stared at the flame, holding Blake in her thoughts and concentrating on the flickering light until her vision tunneled into the kaleidoscope of Wonderland.

Every time she meditated on the man, she was

dropped into his funeral at the exact same moment she heard herself telling Sean that she was to blame. Frustration gnawed in her gut, and she squeezed her eyes shut tighter, as if scrunching up her face might somehow allow her to move backward through time.

She tried backing out of the cemetery, infusing her thoughts with *how?* and attempting to open her mind to more of Blake's life…to his death. Like every time she'd tried to manipulate the goddamn vision, it threw her out, sending her into a void of darkness before she pulled herself back to the present.

She blew out the candle and flopped onto her back, dragging her hands down her face and screaming at the ceiling, "Why the hell would you show me he's going to die if you aren't going to give me any hints as to how?"

As usual, the universe didn't provide an answer.

Two more days went by with the same routine. She had the haunted Mardi Gras sculpture moved into the warehouse with her krewe's floats. Whether or not the activity in the museum had decreased didn't matter. Her damn premonition hadn't changed a bit, so all the worry over the ghosts had been for nothing.

Blake's life depended on her, so she isolated herself, avoiding the museum—and the man who owned it—as much as possible. She did her scheduled tours, but Claire tagged along on most of them, her casual mentions of Blake cutting into Sydney's heart until a bloodied pulp was all that remained.

She skipped the weekly lunch meeting to avoid contact with him. At this point, a thousand different scenarios of his death had played through her mind, and she couldn't chance a single one of them coming true. What if it was something as simple as her distracting him, so he stepped into the street and got hit by a car? It had almost happened before.

Anything was possible, and forcing her will on her visions wasn't doing a lick of good.

After days of avoiding Blake, yet thinking of him constantly, her true feelings for him had solidified in what was left of her heart. She couldn't go on like this. Even though she hadn't laid eyes on the man, his essence was everywhere...on the tips of her friends' tongues, in the paths she took to avoid running into him, on her tours. She had to try harder.

"This isn't working." She dropped into a chair in Natasha's office and squared her shoulders. "Teach me how to read the cards. My visions aren't getting me anywhere."

"Reading tarot ain't your gift, child. You are making progress." Natasha handed her another bag of tea leaves and sat across from her.

"I'm not making it fast enough. Blake's still going to die, and the universe isn't giving me any more signs to figure out why."

"What about the crow laying the necklace at your feet? You mentioned that last time you were here. Are there any other signs like that in your life or in the visions?"

"There's a crow that hangs around Blake's house. It leaves shiny trash on his doorstep, so I assume it's reinforcing the literalness of the vision. Other than that, it's a normal cemetery. There's some fog on the ground, which isn't unusual in the morning." She shrugged. "Every time I try to back out of it, I end up floating in darkness, like I'm not meant to see more, and I come back to the present."

Natasha leaned forward, resting her elbows on the table. "Has that ever happened before?"

"The darkness? A couple of times."

"Did you see anything in it?"

"Once I saw a float falling apart and a decapitated ice sculpture rolling by, but I'm sure that was because I've been so caught up in the madness of Mardi Gras."

The priestess cocked her head. "Anything else?"

Sydney's eyes grew wide. "I saw headlights and heard a blaring horn. The next day, Blake and I were almost hit by a drunk driver." Her pulse thrummed. "Should I be focusing on the darkness?"

"It sounds like the darkness is the recesses of your mind. Places you haven't tapped yet." Natasha closed her eyes, swaying slightly as she shook her head. "You may find answers there, or you may only find confusion in your haste."

"I'll try anything at this point." Sydney went home and lit the meditation candle, slipping into her vision with ease. As soon as the casket came into view, she attempted to pull back, and once again, she was thrown into darkness.

She held still in her mind, focusing on the blank canvas and willing something to appear. *Come on, universe, show me what you've got.* In the distance, a wavering image came into view. As it drifted closer, she made out the shape of a giant rabbit with long, white ears.

A pocket watch appeared in its paw, and it turned its head toward her. "You're late."

A gunshot exploded to her right, and the rabbit clutched its chest before dissolving into the darkness.

Her eyes flew open, and she gasped, blinking the room into focus. *What the hell was that supposed to mean?* Sydney was never late for anything, and apparently, if she was, a rabbit was going to get shot.

Could the rabbit symbolize Blake? Was he going to be shot because Sydney was late? But late to what?

She groaned and cast her gaze to the ceiling. "Why do you have to be so goddamn cryptic?"

She spent three more days in isolation, trying her damnedest to decipher that scene, but she couldn't bring the rabbit through the darkness again. Her vision went back to the same scene in the cemetery, and it grew more and more stagnant the harder she tried.

Could her mind have been playing tricks on her? Did the rabbit scene mean nothing more than the rolling Cheshire Cat head she'd seen before? Natasha wasn't kidding when she'd said Sydney may only find confusion in the darkness. She was going insane. She needed to talk to Blake, but was it worth the risk?

Sydney wrapped up the Friday night tour and handed her iPad to Claire. "Would you mind taking that to the office? My charger at home is busted, and we'll need it for tomorrow night."

"Sure. No problem." Claire slipped the device into her backpack. "Are you okay? You seem down tonight. Well… more down than usual. Did you figure out your premonition?"

"No." She sank onto a step in front of the St. Louis Cathedral and dropped her head in her hands. "I'm frustrated. Things are getting weird, and I'm not making any progress, but that's not new."

"What is it then?" Claire sat next to her, wrapping her arms around her knees. "Stress?"

She raked her fingers through her hair and stared up at the sky. A thick band of clouds stretched across the moon, dimming its soft light until it barely filtered through. "Honestly? I miss Blake. Spending all this time away from him has made me realize how much I care for him."

"Yeah, but you're staying away from him *because* you care for him, right?" She smiled and bumped Sydney's shoulder with her own. "You're doing the right thing."

"How can staying away from the person you love be the right thing to do? It feels…wrong." And there it was. Though she'd tried to deny it, refusing to let the word venture into her thoughts over the past week, she couldn't avoid it anymore. She was in love with Blake.

The corners of her mouth tugged upward, and a brief bout of happiness tingled in her chest in spite of everything. She loved him…and he was going to die. The tiny spark of elation blinked out like a candle reaching the end of its wick.

Claire pursed her lips, nodding and gazing up at the Andrew Jackson statue in the park across the walkway. "Falling in love is the wrong thing to do. I will never let myself care that deeply for anyone, because the people you love are always taken away."

"That sounds like a lonely life." Lonely, but perhaps less painful than the alternative. Whoever said *it's better to have loved and lost* had probably never lost anyone they truly loved.

Claire picked at the seam of her jacket sleeve, her gaze losing focus. "My dad was everything to me. He was a superhero, and I idolized him." She linked her fingers together, squeezing until the tips turned red. "To call me daddy's little girl was an understatement. We were inseparable. Then, when I was ten years old, he had a heart attack. I was playing in my bedroom, and when I came into the living room to show him something I'd made with my building blocks, I found him slouched in the recliner. He wasn't breathing."

"I'm so sorry, Claire. That must have been hard."

She laughed dryly. "You have no idea. It messed me up pretty bad. I never really got along with my mom after that, and my step-dad, Blake's cousin, well…he's a pretty cool guy, but I refused to let myself get close to him." She shrugged. "He's only been with my mom for two years anyway."

Claire wrapped her arms around herself. "Then Brooklyn… She was living with me because her own home life was shit. I let myself love her, you know? She was my best friend. We did everything together. Right before we graduated, she got a job waitressing and started dating one of the managers. Then she moved in with him, and I hardly saw her after that. She abandoned me for that worthless piece of…" She blew a hard breath through her nose.

"Blake told me what happened. I can't imagine."

"I can. I'm the one who found her. I went over there because she hadn't called me in days. The front door was unlocked, so I let myself in, and…" Her body shuddered. "I knew she had gotten herself into trouble. Her boyfriend dealt drugs, you know?" She shook her head. "Anyway, love isn't worth the loss, believe me. You're better off without Blake."

What a sad view on life for a nineteen-year-old to have. Of course, if Sydney had been through all that Claire had, she'd probably feel the same way. She would gladly give up her "gift of sight," as Natasha called it, to get rid of the pressure and guilt she carried around because of it.

Sydney took a deep breath and blew it out hard. "I don't think staying away from him is helping. It's been a week, and he's still in the coffin."

Claire cast her a sideways glance. "You're not thinking about calling him, are you?"

She drew her shoulders toward her ears. "I might. It hurts too much to be away from him."

"You can't do that. He deserves a long, happy life, and you'll just cut it short if you're together."

"Even if we're not a couple, there are still hundreds of ways I could be the cause of his death." She'd never forgive herself if he died, but staying away from him obviously wasn't the change that needed to be made.

"You're willing to risk his life just to be with him?"

She opened her mouth to respond, but Claire had a point. Sydney's emotions didn't matter when Blake's life was on the line. It wasn't worth the risk. "I don't know what to do."

Claire stood and slung her bag over her shoulder. "Please don't kill Blake."

"I'm not—"

Claire turned on her heel and marched away.

A sour sensation churned in Sydney's stomach as she climbed out of her car and trekked up the front steps. Her hands trembled, and she cursed as she fumbled with the key. It jammed into the lock on the fourth try, and she pushed open the door, marching into her living room.

The damn meditation candle, nearly out of wax, sat on

her coffee table. She plopped onto the sofa, heaving in a ragged breath as she snatched the lighter and set the wick ablaze.

Not having Blake in her life was nothing short of torture. She couldn't live another day without him, and until she talked to Claire, she'd made up her mind to call him. Now, she wasn't sure.

Straightening her spine, she took a deep breath and focused on the candle, clearing her thoughts and tumbling back into Wonderland. Her heart sank as she eyed the open coffin across the grassy path. Nothing had changed.

She started to pull out of the vision, but she felt a tug toward the casket. Was it morbid curiosity? She certainly didn't want to see Blake in his death state again. Once had been one time too many, but she couldn't ignore the urge, like an electricity humming around the coffin. She had to look inside.

Pushing forward in the scene, she approached the casket and peered into it. Ice ran through her veins, and she spun to see the faces in the crowd. She should have been standing next to Sean, screaming about it being her fault, but she wasn't there. Instead, Sydney lay silent, nestled in the satin lining of the coffin.

CHAPTER SIXTEEN

*B*lake sat on the sofa in his living room, staring at the phone in his hand. A reporter on the ten o'clock news chattered in the background, and colorful scenes of a parade in Metairie filled the screen. Sydney's parade would be happening soon, and then her krewe's masquerade.

With a huff, he tossed the phone on the coffee table and leaned back on the couch. He'd given her a week. A whole goddamn week of zero contact, and for what? Even with Bernadette's sculpture out of the museum, the haunting activity hadn't stopped. He'd found the same damn kitchen knife sitting on his counter three more times before he got frustrated and shoved them all into a drawer. According to Sean's last update, the funeral premonition hadn't changed at all, and the only progress Sydney had made was to see some psychedelic scene of a rabbit getting shot. Maybe that meant Blake would be shot too, or maybe it didn't. No one knew.

Obviously, the guilt Sydney would express at the funeral was nothing more than survivor's guilt. She was too close to the situation to see that though, and it was his job to open her eyes. He refused to spend another day away from her when it would have no effect on whether he lived or died.

He snatched the phone off the table and swiped the screen, but a simple call wouldn't do. He needed to see her, face to face, so he could convince her they belonged together. She didn't need to take all the responsibility for her visions.

Rising to his feet, he grabbed his keys and trotted down the steps. As he yanked open the door, Claire nearly fell through the threshold, her hand held up to knock. He caught her by the hips, stumbling back as she threw all her weight into him and wrapped her arms around his neck.

"There you are." She turned and spoke over her shoulder to a dark-haired woman stumbling down the sidewalk. "Here he is. See?"

She reeked of cigarettes, beer, and cheap bourbon. Clutching her shoulders, he gently pushed her back. "Are you drunk?"

She giggled and straightened, swinging her hand toward the door jamb but missing it by half a foot. Her ankle twisted, and she toppled, but he caught her by the arm before she hit the concrete.

"Here. Sit down before you hurt yourself." He guided her down onto the front steps.

"Your boss is hot." The other woman plopped onto the sidewalk cross-legged and dug through her purse to pull out a pack of cigarettes. "That picture didn't do him justice."

Blake scowled and sank down next to Claire. What had she gotten herself into? "I'm her cousin."

"Only by marriage." Claire waved an arm, swaying.

Her eyes were bloodshot, puffy like she'd been crying, but it could have been the alcohol. "This is my roommate, Samantha."

"You can call me Sam." She passed a cigarette to Claire, her arm swinging from side to side a few times before their hands met.

"You don't smoke." He snatched the cigarette from Claire.

She grabbed his arm, nearly falling into his lap as she took it back. "I do now."

He set her upright and scooted to the opposite end of the step. "Where did you get the alcohol?"

"On Bourbon Street, of course." She flicked the lighter over and over, but it failed to ignite.

"You're nineteen. You're not supposed to be served."

Claire laughed, dropping the cigarette and lighter to clutch her chest, lifting her breasts and pressing them together. "Look at these. I be served whatever I want."

"Me too." Sam grabbed her own breasts, and both women cackled with laughter. "And we didn't spend a penny."

He groaned. His cousin was smarter than this. "Do you realize how dangerous it is to accept drinks from strangers? Someone could have drugged you."

Claire wiggled her fingers in front of his face. "Not if I test the drinks first."

He grabbed her hand and peered at the swirling designs on her nails. "I didn't think the drug-testing nail polish ever hit the market."

"It didn't, but test strips did. Caitlin makes them into nail polish stickers. Aren't they cool?"

He released her hand and rubbed his forehead. "Who's Caitlin?"

"She's our neighbor in the dorm." Sam giggled. "Keep up."

"You still shouldn't be drinking in public. You could get arrested, even in New Orleans."

Sam made a *pshh* sound and waved off his warning. "Claire was sad, so we had to go out."

"That's right." Claire crossed her arms. "I'm sad. Sydney is going to kill you."

"What?" A chill rushed through his veins. "Did she see something?"

"No." Claire leaned back against the door and closed her eyes.

He looked at Sam. "Do you know what she's talking about?"

Sam shrugged and took a drag of her cigarette. "I dunno." She motioned with her head toward Claire. "Hey, she's asleep. Do you wanna make out?"

"No. No, I do not." He shook Claire's shoulder, and her eyes fluttered open.

"Blake!" She sat up, blinking.

"What did Sydney tell you?"

"Oh." She glared at him. "She's thinking about calling you."

"Calling me? You said she was going to kill me." What the hell was she talking about? He needed to get her some coffee or food…something to sober her up. He couldn't decipher the ravings of a drunk teenager.

"She said she misses you. If you get back together, you'll die." Tears pooled in her eyes. "You're all I have left in the world now."

"What am I? Canned dog food?" Sam crushed her smoke on the sidewalk and stumbled to her feet. Standing with her legs wide apart, she held out her arms as if catching her balance. "Whoa. Why is the street spinning?"

Blake jumped up and held her arm, guiding her down to the pavement. Sam leaned against the steps and squeezed her eyes shut.

Claire started to lean against the door again, but he set her up straight and knelt in front of her. "When did she tell you this?"

"Tonight, after the tour." She paused, studying him. "You don't have to answer when she calls. You have me now."

Leaning forward, she threw her arms around his neck and crushed her mouth to his. Faster than his mind could form the words *oh shit,* he shot to his feet, wiping his lips with the back of his hand. "What the hell, Claire?"

"I thought… You were looking at me like… Like you cared." Her bottom lip trembled.

"I do care, but not like that. I'm eleven years older than you." He parked his hands on his hips. "For Christ's sake, we're family."

She shrugged, lowering her head and flicking her gaze up at him. "Only by—"

"Don't." He held up his hands. "This is not okay." *Shit.* What the fuck was he supposed to do with two drunk teenagers on his doorstep? "We need to get you back to your dorm. How did you get to the Quarter?"

"Uber." She shrank in on herself, pulling her knees to her chest like a little girl. She *was* a little girl. This situation had gotten way out of hand, and he needed to put an end to it before he got blamed for something he would never do.

"I'll order one." Sam dug in her purse. "If I can find my phone."

"No driver with half a brain is going to let you into his car in this condition." He paced four steps away before turning on his heel and marching back. *Goddammit.*

"Sure he will," Sam slurred. "We have boobs."

"No." No way was he putting them in a position like that. "I'll take you."

"Oh, yay." Sam moved up to the second step and rested her hands on her thighs. "A ride with Claire's hot boss. I'm game."

Claire snored softly with her forehead on her knees.

This is not happening. Careful not to tip her over, Blake maneuvered Claire's purse out of her lap and grabbed her phone. He found Sydney's number in her contacts and pressed the call button.

She answered on the third ring. "Hey, Claire." She sounded resigned. Tired. Like the past week had taken a toll on her.

He tried to speak, but the words got stuck on the lump in his throat. None of this…not coming home, not the museum…none of it would mean anything to him without Sydney to share it with.

"Claire?"

He cleared his throat. "Hey. It's Blake."

Silence answered him.

"I know you don't want to talk to me, but—"

"So you decided to use Claire's phone to call me?"

"Would you have answered if I'd called from my own?"

She let out a heavy sigh. "Yes, Blake. I would have. I was thinking about calling you."

"You were?"

Claire moved, and her head slammed against the door jamb. Her eyes opened briefly before fluttering shut.

He groaned. "Claire is drunk, sleeping on my front steps as we speak. I need to get her back to her dorm."

"Why don't you put her on your couch?"

"Her roommate is with her. I don't know this girl, and I'm not taking two nineteen-year-olds up to my apartment overnight." He could imagine the headlines if Sam's parents flipped out.

"What about a cab or an Uber?"

"They're in bad shape. If I stuck them in a car with a stranger, and then something happened to them…"

"No, I guess that's not a good idea either." She paused. "What do you need me to do?"

"Come over. Help me get them home, so I don't look like some thirty-year-old pervert carrying two drunk girls back to their dorm after who knows what."

Sydney chuckled. "You're her cousin. You won't look like a pervert."

"You know she insists we aren't related, and anyway…" He ran a hand over his mouth, covering it to muffle the sound. "She tried to kiss me."

"She tried to kiss you?" She sounded incredulous.

He looked at his cousin's kid leaning against the doorjamb, a line of drool dripping from the corner of her mouth. How the hell did he get himself into a situation like this? "She didn't try. She *did* kiss me."

"Seriously?" Jealousy laced her voice, and if he hadn't been so disgusted by the thought of kissing Claire, he might have been flattered.

"I need your help, Syd." God, he needed *her*.

"Hang tight. I'm on my way."

Claire lay passed out in Blake's lap as Sydney rolled to a stop in front of the museum. The other girl sat on a lower step, leaning back and resting her head on Claire's hip.

Sydney had been mulling over her new premonition and her situation with Blake for two hours, and her insides were tied tighter than a sailor's knot. She'd briefly considered telling Blake he was on his own, so she could continue working out her issues by herself. But if something happened to him while he was trying to get these girls safely home, she'd never forgive herself.

So, here she was, sitting in her car in front of his house while he attempted to wrangle two drunk teenagers to their feet. Shoving her emotions aside, she climbed out of her seat and met him on the sidewalk, slipping Claire's arm over her shoulder as they guided her to the car. The musty scents of stale cigarettes and cheap alcohol assaulted her senses, making her eyes water.

"Sydney, you came back." Claire let go of Blake, throwing her other arm around Sydney's neck.

She stumbled, but Blake opened the car door and pried Claire's arms apart, lowering her into the back seat.

"How much did they drink?" Sydney straightened her shirt and stepped toward the other girl.

"Not *that* much, and before you lecture me too, I have special nail polish." Claire wiggled her fingers. "Nobody drugged my drinks." She scooted across the seat, making room for her friend. "Sam, get your ass in the car," she yelled before dropping her head back on the headrest, her mussed dark hair falling across her face as she turned sideways.

"I'm coming." Sam clambered to her feet, and Blake took her elbow, guiding her in before shutting the door.

He turned to Sydney. "Thank you for doing this." Five

words left his lips, but the pain in his eyes could have filled a novel.

A lump formed in Sydney's throat as he held her gaze, her chest tightening to the point she could hardly breathe. She'd hurt him. Again. All he'd wanted was to be with her, and she'd shoved him away under the guise that it was for his protection, when in reality, she'd been protecting herself.

She was scared, terrified of losing him again, and it had taken her conversation with Claire earlier that evening to make her realize it. People went away. They moved out, moved on, made mistakes…died. It was a fact of life, and it would happen whether Sydney could see it coming or not. She couldn't continue pushing people away when she knew they might not be in her life forever.

She'd stopped talking to her dad when she'd first discovered he was going to cheat. When she'd learned of Courtney's impending death, she'd distanced herself from one of her closest friends, hoping to make the end less painful. It didn't work. Breaking up with Blake in college, before he had the chance to stand her up, hadn't made losing him any less painful either.

The window slid down, and Sam stuck her head through. "I don't feel very good."

Blake nodded toward the car. "We better get them home."

"Yeah, I'd rather not have to clean vomit out of my back seat." She gave his arm a squeeze and hurried around to the driver's side.

They were silent on the short drive to the university dorms, and Sydney clutched the steering wheel tightly, fighting the urge to reach for Blake and tell him how sorry she was. It seemed like all she did was apologize to this man.

She pulled up next to the sidewalk in front of Claire's building and turned around to look over the seat. "Can you ladies walk in? If we have to carry you, you might get into trouble with your resident advisor."

"Yeah, we're fine. Thanks for the ride." Claire fumbled with the latch before pushing the door open.

"I'll walk up with you." Sydney slid out of the car and helped Sam to her feet, holding her arm until she was steady. "I'll be right back," she said to Blake before shutting the door.

She walked between them, occasionally placing her hand on their backs to remind them to at least pretend they had this under control. Sam used her student ID to open the front doors, and a flight of stairs loomed directly in front of them as they entered the drab beige building.

"What floor are you on?" Sydney tensed, expecting them to say the third and wondering how in hell she'd get them both up without causing a scene.

"Right down this hall." Claire stumbled ahead and threw open the third door on the right. Sydney and Sam followed her inside.

In typical freshman dorm fashion, two twin-size beds sat against opposing walls, with not much more than a walkway running between them. A desk and small closet stood at the end of each bed, and a bathroom, shared with the neighboring room, sat off to the right.

Claire plopped onto her bed and grabbed a handful of pink beads from her desk. "Somebody broke my necklace." She frowned at the mess. "Blake gave this to me. They're dicks."

Sydney eyed the beads still on the table, which were, in fact, tiny pink dicks. "That was…nice of him."

"But now it's broken."

"Thanks for bringing us home." Sam face-planted on her bed and started snoring.

"Right. Well, get some sleep. Good night, Claire."

Claire waved, and Sydney slipped into the hallway, closing the door behind her before making her way to the parking lot.

As she slid into the driver's seat, Blake turned to face her, his deep, blue eyes saying so much more than his words. "They made it to their room?"

She fought a smile. "You gave Claire a dick necklace, and then you wondered why she kissed you?"

His eyes widened, his mouth opening and closing a few times before he answered, "A bachelorette party stopped me on the street a while back and put it on me. Claire saw it and wanted it, so I gave it to her." He held up his hands. "I swear to God nothing has or ever will happen between me and Claire. She's my cousin's kid, for Christ's sake."

Sydney laughed, more at herself for the ridiculous stab of jealousy she felt. She didn't *actually* believe Blake had any interest in Claire, but the fact that she'd kissed him, even in a drunken stupor, had woken Sydney up to how stupid she was for pushing Blake away. If she pushed any harder, she might send him into someone else's arms, and she obviously wouldn't handle that very well.

"I know." She shifted into drive and pulled out of the parking lot.

They didn't talk on the drive back to Blake's apartment either, but a static charge seemed to build between them, waiting for one of them to light the match and set everything ablaze. She glanced at him, and he inhaled a quick breath like he wanted to speak, but he merely smiled and shook his head.

As she turned onto St. Ann Street and approached his building, he finally broke the silence. "Do you want to come in?"

"Yeah." Her answer came without thought. Yes, she wanted to come in. Yes, she wanted to be with him. Yes, she wanted it all.

She parked behind the building and followed him up the stairs to his living room. As he dropped his keys into a bowl by the door, he gestured to the couch before sitting on the edge.

Sinking down next to him, she angled her body toward his. "Blake."

He said her name at the same time, and they laughed awkwardly. "Let me go first." He took her hand. "I know about the rabbit vision and the possibility of me getting shot."

"Blake, I…"

"Let me finish, please." He sandwiched her hand between both of his, and comforting warmth permeated her skin. "I don't care what your visions are telling you about how long my life is going to be or who will be to blame if it ends. I don't want to live another minute without you. I know what it feels like to lose you, and I can feel it happening again, and I just can't…I *won't* allow it to happen this time."

He searched her eyes as the electric charge building between them intensified. "I want to be with you for however long forever happens to be for us. Whether it's two more days or fifty more years, I want to spend every second of it with you. I love you, Sydney."

Tears welled in her eyes, and a sob bubbled up from somewhere deep inside her. Those were exactly the words she wanted to hear. Words that reached into her heart, wrapping around her soul and putting in roots. "I love you too, Blake. I'm sorry for pushing you away." She lowered her gaze to their entwined hands.

"It's okay. Hey, look at me." He lifted her chin. "I get it, okay? You're used to handling things by yourself. You've carried the burden of your premonitions all your life, with no one to talk to, but you don't have to bear it alone anymore. You have me now."

"Thank you," she whispered.

"Whatever you see, good or bad, we'll tackle it together." He wiped the tear from her cheek with his thumb. "All I ask is that you promise to keep me in the loop. Let me help you with your visions. For real this time."

Her bottom lip trembled. She needed to tell him about the new one. That now it seemed her own life would be cut short too. Instead, she pressed her lips to his.

Talking could wait. Right now, she needed to be with him. To show him how much she appreciated his understanding, his compassion, his love. She coaxed his lips apart with her tongue, and he moaned, leaning into her and wrapping his arms around her.

The end-of-the-day scruff around his mouth was coarse, contrasting with the softness of his lips, and as he kissed along her jaw and down her neck, she reveled in the masculine, scratchy, tickling sensation on her skin. He nipped at her earlobe, sending goose bumps running down her arms. The warmth of his breath made her shiver, and as she slipped her hands beneath his shirt, the juxtaposition of soft skin and hard muscles made heat pool below her navel.

He pulled away to look at her, his intense blue eyes stripping her bare, penetrating into her soul. Blake *got* her. He understood what it was like to have an ability nobody could comprehend. He sensed the burden she carried on her shoulders, and he lifted it, taking some of the weight onto his own back, giving her a sense of reprieve she'd never experienced before.

There couldn't be a more perfect match for her. He was kind, gentle, and hotter than hellfire on a flaming baton.

"I want you, Blake. I want to be with you now and always, and I promise not to push you away again."

"You have no idea how happy I am to hear that." His chest rumbled, his voice thick with need.

She kissed him again, grabbing at his shirt and tugging it over his head before removing her own. Then she climbed into his lap, straddling him, exploring his mouth with her tongue as she removed her bra and tossed it aside.

His dick hardened beneath her, and she ground against him, her hands roaming over his body, memorizing the way he felt beneath her fingertips. Scooting back, she popped the button on his jeans and slid down the zipper before slipping her hand into the denim and rubbing the stiff mound through his boxer-briefs.

He groaned, pulling her mouth to his for another kiss. God, this man was irresistible. She'd been an idiot to try and stay away from him. She needed him like she needed air to breathe.

Sliding off his lap, she dropped to her knees and worked his clothes over his hips. As she got him completely naked, she sat back on her heels, admiring the cuts and dips of his muscles, the smoothness of his skin, and the sprinkling of hair across his chest. The thin, white scar from his appendectomy shone in the light, and her chest tightened with regret. She would never leave him again. She gripped his dick, giving it two firm strokes that made his eyelids flutter before letting go and shimmying out of her clothes.

His eyes smoldered as he watched her, his gaze caressing her body as he swept it down her form. "I am a lucky man."

"You're about to get luckier." She dropped to her knees and ran her hands up his thighs to his stomach. As she grazed her lips along his length, he inhaled a deep breath and held it, his muscles tightening in anticipation.

She licked his tip, and his breath came out in a hiss, sending tingles down her spine. Parting her lips, she took him in, gliding her mouth up and down his cock as he gripped her shoulders.

He moaned and dropped his head back on the couch as she sucked him, his breathing growing heavy, his hands roaming over her arms, her shoulders, her neck. As her teeth grazed his sensitive flesh, he sucked in a sharp breath and whispered, "Oh, Sydney."

She shivered.

Releasing his dick, she climbed into his lap, taking his mouth with hers. She moved against him, and he held her hips, rocking his own to increase the friction. An electric sensation zipped through her abdomen, and a lustful moan escaped her throat.

"Condoms are in the bedroom," he whispered.

"I'm on birth control." She leaned back, looking into his eyes. "I need you, Blake."

"I'm yours."

Lifting her hips, she guided him to her folds and lowered onto his cock. A pleasurable ache spread through her core as their bodies met, and she paused, memorizing the moment, the way they fit together, his delicious, musky scent, the feel of his hands on her body.

She loved him, and he loved her. The realness of it sank in as she looked into his eyes, and tears welled in her own. Her visions be damned, in this moment, she was tearing down her walls and giving herself to this man...*for however long forever happens to be.* Love was about the journey. Screw the destination.

Cupping his face in her hands, she kissed him hard, pouring her emotions into their lovemaking as she moved her hips, sliding up and down his dick and creating a sensuous friction that drove her closer and closer to the edge.

He stroked her clit with his thumb, thrusting into her with urgency, claiming her as his own.

And she was his for the taking.

Her climax built in her core, the pressure intensifying like a river behind a dam. As the levee broke, she cried out, her orgasm rolling through her body, setting her nerves on fire. She buried her face in his neck as he gripped her hips, thrusting until he found his release.

His body shuddered, and she leaned into him, closing her eyes and reveling in the feel of his arms wrapped around her, their bodies still joined in an intimate union she wasn't ready to break.

"God, I missed you." He tightened his arms around her, strengthening his hold on her heart. "Never leave me again."

Thoughts of her vision invaded her mind, tightening her throat. "I might not have a choice."

CHAPTER SEVENTEEN

"I had another vision. A new one."

Blake's stomach soured as he slid beneath the sheets next to Sydney. Lying on her side, her head propped on her hand, she picked at the seam of the pillowcase, refusing to make eye contact.

"What, umm…" He swallowed hard, dread forming a tight knot in his throat. "Did you see how it's going to happen? How I'm going to die?"

She gave her head a tiny shake. "It was another funeral. This time, I was in the coffin."

"No." A spark of anger ignited in his chest. No way in hell would he let the woman he loved wind up in a coffin. "Unless you saw yourself at eighty years old, that's not going to happen. I won't allow it."

She pressed her lips together, her brow knitting as she lifted her gaze to his. "I wasn't eighty."

He scooted closer to her, entwining his legs with hers and clutching her hand. "What can I do to help? Do you need more sessions with Natasha? I'll pay for them if you do. Or do you need time off to meditate more? I can rearrange the tour schedule. Whatever you need, name it, and it's done."

She sighed. "I'm not sure there's anything either of us can do. I've meditated myself into a stupor, done all the exercises the priestess gave me. It would take years to develop this ability the way I would need to in order to have that kind of control." She sounded resigned to her fate, as if she'd accepted that both their lives were coming to an end, and there was nothing she could do to stop it.

But Blake was just getting started. "I'm not going to let you die."

"I don't want to die. I don't want either of us to."

"Okay. Let's think about this rationally. Chronologically, where are we? Which premonition is supposed to happen first?"

"I don't know. I guess you would go first, because I saw myself at your funeral. When I saw mine, you weren't there, but…" She raked a hand through her hair. "I'm frustrated to no end. I don't know which way is up anymore, and I…"

"Is this what your life is like? Are you constantly seeing people's deaths?" He couldn't imagine living with this kind of ability. It would have driven him insane a long time ago.

"I've seen one other death. Just one. I don't know why I'm seeing so much now. Before all this started, I could go weeks without having a premonition, and the ones I did have—aside from Courtney's death—were happy or at least easy to solve."

She took his hand, lacing her fingers through his. "All I know is that my visions show me what will happen if things continue on the track they're running. I thought by us being apart that I could change it. That we could avoid the death the universe is predicting. But all it's done is added my own death to the formula."

He chewed the inside of his cheek, rolling her words around in his mind. "Our being together must not be the track that needs changing."

"Ugh." She flopped onto her back. "What are we going to do?"

His heart warmed at her words. Sure, they were discussing both of their impending deaths, but they were doing it *together*.

She rolled onto her side to face him again. "Why are you smiling?"

"You said 'we.'" He pressed a kiss to her lips. "'What are *we* going to do?' I think that in itself is a start, don't you?"

She smiled. "Yes, it is. So, what are *we* going to do? I hope you have some ideas, because I'm stumped."

"What's changed in the past week?" He sucked in a breath. "I know. We moved the haunted Mardi Gras sculpture out of the museum and into your krewe's warehouse. Do you think it could be related to that? The activity here hasn't stopped, so maybe Bernadette isn't physically attached to it. Maybe she's angry with you?"

"It's possible. I can ask Sean to come to the warehouse and talk to the ghost again. I'll have to sneak him in, because our floats are top secret until the parade."

"Which is only two days away."

"Jeez, you're right. Where has the time gone?"

"We've wasted far too much of it." He reached for her hip, tracing his fingers along her soft curves.

She rested a hand on his chest. "We sure have. I'll call him first thing in the morning."

He gazed into her dark brown eyes, and his chest swelled with hope. They could beat this. Whatever ending the universe had planned for them, they'd chart a new course for their lives and win. "We have a plan now." He glided his hand up her side and over her shoulder, reveling in the softness of her skin as he slid his fingers into her hair. "We're doing all we can, so we might as well enjoy the moment."

"I suppose we are." She slipped her hand beneath the sheets to grip his dick.

He gasped at the feel of her fingers wrapped around his rock-hard cock. God, he loved this woman.

She grinned. "Seems we're thinking the same thing."

He rolled on top of her and made love to her slowly, gently, showing her how much he treasured her. With their needs satiated, he lay on his back, Sydney snuggled into his side, and he drifted into a contented slumber.

Soft morning sunlight filtered into the room, painting the backs of Blake's eyelids red. He hesitated to open them, fearing last night had been nothing more than a dream, but as his senses awakened, the feel of Sydney's soft, warm skin on his was unmistakable.

He opened his eyes and kissed the top of her head, his lips lingering on her hair as he wrapped himself up in her feminine scent. She stirred, snuggling deeper into his embrace and letting out a contented sigh.

"I like waking up with you." She brushed her lips to

his chest before lifting her head and smiling at him sleepily.

"It's something I'd like to get used to."

"Me too." She traced a finger from his nose to his lips, tugging the bottom one down before leaning in for a quick kiss. "You're on the guest list for my krewe's masquerade, if you're interested."

He arched a brow. "Am I?"

She nodded, biting her lower lip.

"Are you asking me to be your date?"

"I am."

"Hmm…" He feigned deep thought. Hell yes, he wanted to go to the ball with her. He'd have given anything to undo the mess their relationship devolved into when he missed the first one. This was his do-over. His second chance.

She drew a shoulder toward her ear. "I should have asked you sooner, but I was busy being an idiot. If it's too weird…"

"As long as you promise not to dump me before it happens, I would love to be your date to the masquerade."

She pulled back, looking him square in the eyes. "I have no plans of dumping you ever again. I promise."

Not a shred of doubt entered his mind. Sydney was finally his, and he could have leapt to his feet and bounced on the bed with excitement. Instead, he simply smiled. "Okay then. What are we going to wear?"

She grinned. "The theme is Wonderland."

"How perfect." The doorbell chimed, and he glanced at the clock. Eight a.m. "Who the hell?"

Sydney sat up, and the sheet fell away from her body, exposing her breasts and the delicate curve of her waist. Her hair was mussed on one side, and she had a crease across her cheek from the fabric of the pillowcase. She was the sexiest woman alive. "Were you expecting any deliveries at the museum?"

Blood rushed to his groin, and every fiber of his being urged him to tug her down and make love to her again. To hell with whoever was at the door. They could come back later. "Not that I recall."

The bell rang again, followed by three knocks. *Oh, for Christ's sake.* He rolled out of bed and pulled on a pair of sweatpants. "Let me go see what they want." He leaned down and kissed her temple. "I'll be right back."

"I'll be here."

He hurried down the steps, mentally willing his hard-on to retreat, as the bell sounded again. Someone was about to get an eyeful. "I'm coming. I'm coming."

As he opened the door, he found Claire standing on the steps, reaching one arm across her body to clutch her purse strap on her shoulder. She'd cleaned herself up and applied a coat of makeup, the redness in her eyes the only indication of the hangover she was surely battling.

"Hey." She lowered her gaze as a blush spread across her cheeks. "Did I wake you?"

His dick instantly deflated. "It's okay. How are you feeling?"

"I've been better. Can I come in?" She moved forward, but he leaned against the jamb, blocking the entrance.

"Now's not a good time."

She stepped back, nodding. "I understand. I just…I wanted to apologize for last night."

He let out a dry laugh and crossed his arms against the chill in the morning air. "Do you remember last night?"

"Unfortunately, I do. I don't know what I was thinking, and I want you to know I would never… I mean… I know where I stand with you, so it won't happen again." She cast her gaze to the sidewalk and then blinked up at him.

Her eyes held regret, and her apology seemed sincere. He uncrossed his arms. "Thank you. I won't mention it again if you won't."

"I…" She tilted her head, narrowing her eyes as footsteps sounded behind him.

"Hi, Claire. How are you?" Sydney reached the bottom step and stood next to Blake, resting a hand on his bare back.

The contrast of her warm palm against his air-chilled skin gave him goose bumps and tightened his nipples. Why hadn't he put on a shirt?

Claire swallowed, her gaze bouncing between Sydney and him, her eyes calculating as she assessed the situation. "I didn't know you two were back together."

He wrapped an arm around Sydney. "We are."

She leaned into him, resting her hand on his chest, claiming him. "For good this time."

Claire's mouth opened and closed like a fish. "Umm… I didn't…" Her brow furrowed for a moment before she beamed a smile. "Good for you. Does this mean you figured out your vision?"

"No, but we're going to work on it together from now on," Sydney said.

"Great." Claire's smile widened, her entire demeanor shifting as if last night and this morning's awkward apology never happened. "Well, I can't wait to see the parade tomorrow. I'm sure it will be magnificent."

"I know it's last minute," Sydney said, "but you're on the guest list for my krewe's masquerade. The theme is Wonderland. If you can put together a costume in time,

I'd love for you to come. Jason, Eric, and Trish will be there too."

Claire's eyebrows disappeared into her bangs. "Really? I'm invited to a real live New Orleans masquerade?"

Sydney laughed. "What do you say?"

"Yes!" Claire bounced on her toes. "Thank you!" Her smile faded. "I don't know if Blake told you what happened before you got here last night."

"He told me." She slid her hand from his back to his side, tugging him harder against her body.

"I'm really sorry. I was so drunk, and I…"

"It's okay. We all make mistakes." She wrapped her other arm around him, linking her fingers at his hip, as if saying *he's mine now; hands off*. "Forgiveness is the best gift you can give someone."

His body warmed, and his lips tugged into a smile. The way Sydney could be kind to Claire with her words while standing her ground with her body language amazed him. Was there anything this woman couldn't do?

"Thank you." Claire nodded toward the museum entrance. "Looks like your resident crow won't be bothering you anymore. Anyway, I'm going to call my mom and beg for a costume. See you guys tomorrow."

Blake stepped out the door and onto the sidewalk, cringing at the feel of the cold concrete on his bare feet as Claire strode away. The crow lay on its side, its neck bent at an unnatural angle, the light in its eyes gone.

Sydney gripped his arm. "Did you call the exterminator already? Maybe it ate some poison."

He shook his head. "I haven't called yet. It looks like its neck is broken."

"Maybe it flew into the wall? Can you read its energy to see what happened to it?"

"I can only read energy absorbed by inanimate objects. Living things make their own, and I can't access that." His stomach sank. "Claire mentioned crows are bad omens. What does it mean when one dies on your doorstep?"

She slipped her hand into his, tightening her grip as she stared at the animal. "I have no idea."

CHAPTER EIGHTEEN

Leaning her hip against the horizontal bar latching the door, Sydney shoved it open and inched into the warehouse. Her pulse pounded in her ears as she fumbled for the light switch, her breath coming out in a rush when the fluorescent bulbs flickered on, flooding the enormous room in yellow light.

She'd been investigating the paranormal for the last six years, and while a few spirits had managed to get her blood pumping a time or two, she'd never been terrified for her life.

Until now.

Her vision of her own funeral had shaken her, but Blake had soothed her frazzled nerves with his promise to stay by her side and help her figure it all out. She took solace in the fact that she didn't have to bear the burden alone anymore, but the thought that this ghost, whom she hadn't heard a peep from since she moved her out of the museum, could be responsible for both their untimely deaths was unnerving.

She'd been seeing Blake's death until they moved the

sculpture to the warehouse, adding it to the float for the parade. With the ghost away from Blake and closer to Sydney, and now the vision changing to her own death, the pieces of the puzzle were finally starting to click.

"Wow." Sean's voice made her jump. "I'm honored to have the chance to see all this before it rolls. It's magnificent."

"Yeah." Her voice trembled, so she cleared her throat. "We've outdone ourselves this year. It's going to be our best one yet…if I live long enough to see it." She jerked her head, motioning in the direction of the float, and strode through the warehouse.

"We're going to take care of you." Sean followed close behind. "If the ghost shows any signs of violence, I'll carry the sculpture out of here myself and dump it in the river."

As she turned the corner and her float came into view, the blood drained from her head to her feet. A giant yellow flower situated next to the artifact had toppled over, the petals separated from the stem and strewn about the trailer.

Sydney's hands curled into fists as she marched toward the float and climbed the short ladder to reach the platform. This float was her baby. She'd spent a month designing it, taken countless inspection trips to the warehouse when the artists were creating it, and worked her ass off on the presentation that would light up the spectators' phones as they scanned the giant QR code. Dangerous spirit or not, nobody messed with her baby.

"Listen to me, Bernadette," she growled the ghost's name. "I'm doing you a favor by bringing this half-finished, antiquated piece of faux art on my float. You have no right to destroy my creation." She shook her finger at the sculpture as if it were the spirit herself.

"Cool it, Syd." Sean climbed the ladder and picked up a petal. "I'll help you put it back together, but if you want me to talk to the ghost, you need to stop scaring her off. I can't sense her."

Sydney clenched her teeth, swallowing the bile in the back of her throat. What if she—or one of her krewe members—had been here when the ghost went poltergeist on the float? Someone could have been hurt.

Or killed.

Her heart sank into her stomach. "Here I was, trying to do something nice for a dead lady, and she's going to kill me for it. So much for the ghost not being dangerous." She dropped onto a bench, leaning her elbows on her knees. "We have to get this thing out of here. I'll call Jason and see if he'll bring his truck."

"Wait." Sean held up a hand, closing his eyes and inhaling deeply. "Calm down. You're going to use up all your energy before you tell me what you have to say." He stared straight in front of him, but Sydney couldn't see anything except her destroyed float.

"Is it Bernadette?" Coldness crept toward her, making her arm hairs stand on end, a classic sign of a spirit trying to manifest. She tugged her phone from her pocket and turned on the audio recorder, setting the device on the bench and watching Sean expectantly. With any luck, she could catch some of the ghost's words on the device.

Sean's brow furrowed, and he nodded his head. "I believe you, but you've got to calm down. Take a minute to gather your strength. I'm not going anywhere." He blinked. "She's gone."

"What did she say?" Sydney didn't wait for an answer. She clicked play on her phone and turned the volume full blast. The recording of her own voice echoed in the warehouse, followed by the faint, hollow sound of a woman saying, "Didn't do it."

She stopped the playback and crossed her arms. "Well, if she didn't do it… Oh no." *Damon.*

Sean sank onto the bench next to her. "She was frantic when she appeared. She said, 'It wasn't me. Someone. A mask. I didn't do it.'"

Aside from knocking the box cutter to the floor when Claire accused her of planning Blake's murder, Bernadette hadn't shown any signs of violence. It didn't make sense for her to destroy the float the day before the parade she'd waited decades for. "A ghost didn't do this."

"I'm not sensing any hostility from her. Just panic."

The overhead lights flickered as the ghost drew in more energy to manifest, and Sydney glanced at the float behind hers. A nine of hearts playing card that should have been upright lay flat on its face, a huge crack running through the papier mâché on its back.

Rising to her feet, Sydney scanned the other floats near hers. Two others had broken pieces, while another sported four flat tires. "You've got to be kidding me."

She jumped to the ground and inspected the other floats from one end of the hall to the other. Seven in total had been damaged. "There's no way a ghost did all this."

But surely Damon and his krewe wouldn't stoop this low. They could have hurt someone. Nausea churned in her stomach as she crept through the warehouse toward her float and Sean. Suddenly the shadows stretching across the ground grew ominous, their shapes no longer reflecting the whimsical nature of Wonderland, but a more macabre underworld where danger lurked in the darkness.

Adrenaline coursed through her system, her fight or flight instinct kicking in, making her want to run. This was ridiculous. She wasn't afraid of ghosts or that sorry excuse for a krewe. *Get a grip, Syd.*

"Three men in masks…" Sean's voice cut through the eerie silence, and she gasped. "Sorry. Didn't mean to scare you." He hopped off the float and strode toward her.

"I'm not scared. I've merely seen a premonition of my own funeral, and now something has gone poltergeist in my warehouse. Nothing to be frightened of." A nervous giggle escaped her throat, so she clamped her mouth shut. *Stop being absurd.*

"Ghosts didn't do this. Come on." He motioned toward the back of the warehouse. "Let me show you."

She followed him past the floats, averting her gaze so the shadows couldn't take on any more ghoulish shapes.

He stopped in front of a cargo door. "Does it feel colder in here than usual?" He pointed at the floor where the massive rolling door should have met the concrete. Cold winter air flowed in through a gap about a foot and a half high.

"Would you look at that?" She knelt to examine the open door. A block of wood sat wedged in the corner, holding it up. "Now that I think about it, I did notice the temperature difference. I was more concerned with the ghost though, so I didn't pay attention."

"I think y'all have been sabotaged. Bernadette said three men in masks came in last night and did all this."

"Those assholes." She turned the knob to lift the door and kicked the wood block out of the way before lowering it completely. "We've got a rival krewe that's after our two o'clock parade slot. They've made some hollow threats, but this…" She flung her arms in the direction of the damaged floats. "If we don't get this fixed, we won't roll on time, and they'll be able to take it from us."

"I didn't realize the rivalries were so vicious."

"It's just this one. They haven't been around for long, and they won't be much longer if this is how they're going to play." Her nails cut into her palms as she ground her teeth.

"Well, the good news is Bernadette has no ill feelings toward you, and I don't think she's capable of doing anything that could cause you to die…except scare you to death maybe." He winked.

"Ha ha. Very funny."

His face turned serious. "I really wish there was something I could do to help you."

"Me too." With Bernadette ruled out as the culprit, that only left 999 different ways both Sydney and Blake could kick the bucket. The ominous dread that had been weighing her down since the premonition began ignited into anger. Screw the universe and its sorry attempt to portend. She refused to live in fear.

She straightened her spine. "I…guess I know how Courtney felt. I can't sit around waiting for it to happen."

He smiled sadly. "Lives are meant to be lived, aren't they?"

"You better get out of here. I've got to call the girls in to get this fixed. No way are we going to let another krewe take our slot."

He laughed. "Go get 'em."

After getting word to the krewe that they had work to do, she sent a text to Blake, letting him know she'd be indisposed for the rest of the day. Her phone rang a few seconds later.

"Is everything okay?" Blake's voice held an edge of panic.

"It will be." She told him about the saboteurs and that

Sean still believed the ghost wasn't their problem. "The good news is the parade can go forward, and we can take Bernadette along as planned."

"But we still don't have a clue why you keep seeing us dead."

She sighed. "True."

"Damn. I really thought it was the ghost. At least then we'd have known what we were up against."

She chewed her bottom lip. "I know."

"Oh my God." Erin's mouth dropped open as she strutted through the door. "I'm going to kill whoever did this. I talked to the police outside. The bastards took out the security camera two days ago."

Sydney lowered her voice. "The krewe is here. I have to go."

"Stay safe and call me if you need anything…or if… just call me."

"I will." Her heart warmed at the concern in his voice, and she had no doubt they would figure things out together. Right now, though, the first order of business was fixing these floats. They rolled in twenty-four hours.

CHAPTER NINETEEN

Sydney adjusted the apron on her Alice costume, pulling her phone from the pocket to scan the massive QR code on the float one last time. The device beeped, and the digital prize wheel lit up her screen in live mode, ready to award prizes. A bit of the pressure in her chest released with her sigh, and she turned to the driver, giving him a thumbs up.

A chill shimmied up her spine, making her neck hairs stand on end, and she smiled. After more than fifty years, Bernadette was finally getting her chance to ride in a parade.

"Everything good to go?" Erin called up to Sydney from below. Her brow pinched, and her right eye twitched.

Sydney leaned over the railing. "We're good. You okay?"

Erin's nostrils flared as she rested a hand on the side of the float. "That asshole Damon came up to me and said, 'Glad to see you could make it on time.'" She mocked him with a stupid-sounding voice. "I know they're responsible, but we've got zero evidence and no witnesses. I hope they don't try to screw with our ball too."

There was one witness, but the testimony of a ghost wouldn't stand up in court. "I doubt they will. They wanted our roll time. What would crashing our ball get them?"

"Jail time." She crossed her arms.

"Exactly." Sydney grabbed a set of beads from one of the many hooks positioned around the float and slipped them over her forearm. "Forget about that sorry excuse for a krewe. This is Horae's time."

"You're right." Erin nodded. "Let's roll."

Engines rumbled to life, and a high school marching band filed in front of Sydney's float, dancing to the drum cadence as the parade rolled up St. Charles Avenue. Thousands upon thousands of revelers, both locals and tourists alike, lined the streets to watch the spectacle. Krewe members tossed colorful beads and doubloons to screaming, cheering spectators, and Sydney smiled as people whipped out their phones to scan her code and see the interactive display she created for them.

Seasoned veterans had positioned lawn chairs along the route, reserving the front row for themselves, while newbies gathered under awnings that blocked the throws from making it to the crowd. Crafty parents decorated ladders in shades of purple, green, and gold, and created seats at the top for their children to tower above the crowd, not only to see better, but to have the best position for catching the coveted throws.

The colorful, elaborate floats. The cheers from the crowd. The music. The reverie… It was enough to put even the most experienced partiers on sensory overload.

Mardi Gras in New Orleans was a magical time of year, and Sydney felt almost drunk on the energy in the air.

As she tossed a handful of doubloons to the spectators, her own energy shifted, a familiar sinking sensation threatening to drag her under. Her peripheral sparkled in blue and gold mosaics briefly, and she swayed, clutching the railing. *I can't black out now.* She fought it, and the vision that tried to whisk her away to Wonderland threw her back out as quickly as it had begun.

She blinked, shaking her head, then stumbled slightly, catching her apron pocket on a hook and tearing a hole in the fabric. Her keys and phone slipped out, clattering on the float platform, but she caught them before they could topple over the edge.

She secured them on a shelf and straightened, picking up another bunch of beads to toss to the crowd. Whatever the universe was trying to tell her, it could wait. She couldn't handle another blackout. Not when she stood atop a moving vehicle with enough adrenaline running through her veins to keep her awake and alert for days.

Blake stood behind Claire, shielding her from the group of guys who'd been leering at her since the parade started. She wore a tiny tank top and leggings, but that didn't give the perverts the right to ogle her like an expensive sports car.

She squealed and jumped, catching a strand of beads with her fingertips. Spinning around, she slipped them over his head. "These look like beer mugs. They suit you better than dicks."

He chuckled. "I'm glad you think so."

"Look! There's Sydney." She flung her arms into the air, waving like a maniac.

Blake scanned the QR code on the float, and his phone lit up with Sydney's creation. He grinned and lifted his gaze as she tossed a stuffed bear to a little girl in the front row.

Her Alice costume suited her perfectly, and the beaming smile on her face sent a jolt of electricity straight through his heart. His nerves had been on edge all day, her vision about her funeral concerning him way more than his own impending death.

If he'd had his way, he'd have been up there on that float with her, protecting her from…whatever it was she needed protecting from. Looking out for Claire in this swarm of people had occupied his mind enough to keep him grounded, but seeing Sydney up there on the float, in her element, and hearing the *oohs* and *ahhs* of the spectators as they spun the wheel on their phones, filled him with so many emotions, he felt like a train wreck waiting to happen.

He loved Sydney with every fiber of his being, and he wouldn't rest until her premonitions subsided. They would change the future. They had no other choice.

He caught her gaze, and her smile widened. Holding up a finger, she ducked behind the railing and reappeared with a handful of beads. Pointing with her left hand, she reared back and hurled the necklace toward him.

He jumped to catch it, and the hard-ceramic pendant slapped into his palm, stinging his skin. He unwound the gold beads and found a white rabbit wearing a blue waistcoat and holding a pocket watch.

He slipped the necklace over his head and took off the beer mug beads, handing them to Claire. "Here. You can have this one back." His lips tugged into a smile as he gazed at the rabbit.

The mass of beads Claire wore had grown so thick he couldn't see her neck. She frowned. "You don't want it?"

"Syd tossed me this one." He held up the ceramic rabbit.

"Oh." She shrugged one shoulder and whirled around, flipping her hair into his face.

Two more floats passed after Sydney's, and it was time to relinquish their second-row spots on St. Charles Avenue and make their way over to Tchoupitoulas and Poydras where the parade ended.

"Time to go." He grabbed Claire's hand and guided her through the crowd. The guys from earlier whistled at her, and the short, stocky one grabbed her other hand as she passed.

"Hey, baby. You look good."

Claire paused to giggle, while Blake stepped between them. "Hey, man. Lay off."

"Whatever." The short dude stumbled, and his friends caught him by the arms.

Blake dragged Claire away as she protested. "They were just saying 'hi.'"

"You're better than them. Don't settle for anyone who's going to treat you like a piece of property."

"Why, Blake." She pressed a hand to her chest and mimicked a Southern accent. "I didn't know you cared."

"Of course I care." He tugged her up a side street toward the parade's end. "You're family."

The corners of her mouth twitched.

They made it to Tchoupitoulas, and he zigzagged through the throng of people to the corner of Poydras, where the krewe disembarked from their floats. As

Sydney's approached the stop, he elbowed his way to the front and waved.

She smiled, ducking behind the railing again and appearing near the ladder, her hands full of personal belongings. "Can you hold this?" She offered him her keys, wallet, and phone.

"I'll take them." Claire scooped the items from Sydney's hands, dropping them into her purse.

"Thanks." Sydney climbed down the ladder and stepped into Blake's arms. "I ripped the pocket on my apron. Caught it on a hook on the railing."

"So, what happens next?" Claire asked as they followed the crowd toward Canal Street.

"The drivers will return the floats to the warehouse, and later next week, we'll start disassembling them and getting them ready for next year." Sydney leaned into his side, tightening her arm around his waist. "Did you scan the code?"

"You know it." He kissed her cheek. "Your presentation was fantastic. Brilliant idea about including a coupon for the museum opening too."

"Most of the tourists will be gone by then, but plenty of locals watch the parades too."

"You're amazing."

She grinned. "You're not so bad yourself."

Claire rolled her eyes. "You're both so sickly sweet, it's disgusting. I have to pee."

Sydney laughed. "I could use a trip to the little girls' room too."

"There's some Porta Potties over there." He pointed with his thumb.

"Perfect." Claire dashed into one and locked the door.

"Is she okay?" Sydney rose onto her toes and planted a

kiss on him before he could answer. Her lips were soft, and a faint hint of strawberry lip balm tickled his taste buds as he opened his mouth and drank her in.

She snaked her arms around his neck and pressed her body into his, her soft curves conforming to his frame like she was made for him. Fire ignited in his core, concentrated below his waist as he held her close, losing himself in the kiss.

When she finally came up for air, she laughed, pressing her hips harder into his. "I'm happy to see you too."

"You have no idea."

"How about I meet you at your apartment before the masquerade tonight, since you live closer to the ballroom? We can spend the night at your place after." She traced a finger down his shirt, stopping at the waistband of his jeans.

"I like the way you think." He was looking forward to finally going to this ball with her, seeing her all dressed up, but all he could think about now was how good her dress would look on his bedroom floor. He cleared his throat. "Any new visions?"

She shook her head. "I started to get one during the parade, but it didn't pull me all the way under."

His brow furrowed as he searched her eyes, asking his next question silently.

"Nothing else has changed." She kissed his cheek. "Is Claire okay? She's been in there for a while."

"It's her first Mardi Gras. I'm sure she's overwhelmed. Go ahead and go. I'll wait right here."

He shoved his hands into his pockets as Sydney disappeared into a stall. A few minutes later, Claire appeared, clutching her purse, her gaze flitting about like a nervous bird searching for predators.

"Everything all right?"

"Yeah. Stomachache." She adjusted her purse strap. "Where's Sydney? I have her phone."

"Here she is." He gestured toward Sydney exiting the stall.

Sweat beaded on Claire's forehead. "I thought you left without your stuff."

Sydney cocked her head. "Blake's taking me home."

"Oh, right. I forgot. Duh." She laughed and hit herself on the forehead.

They reached the parking lot and piled into Blake's car. Sydney chatted about the parade on the short drive across the Mississippi to her house, and as he pulled into the driveway behind her car to drop her off, she leaned over and kissed him.

"I'll be at your place at six-thirty."

He glanced at the clock. "That doesn't give you much time to get ready."

"I'm low maintenance." She kissed him again, her lips lingering near his, her breath warming his skin.

He brushed his nose to hers. "I love that about you."

"Do you mind if I come in and use your restroom?" Claire opened the car door. "I'm feeling a little nauseated."

"Sure. Are you getting sick?" Sydney glanced into the back seat.

"I don't think so. I had a greasy lunch. I'm sure I'll be fine before the ball." She slid out and scurried to the front door.

Blake sighed. "I'm sorry about that."

Sydney shrugged. "I thought she seemed off. You might as well come in too."

He followed her to the house and waited in the living room as Claire dumped Sydney's things on a table and followed her down the hall to the bathroom. A flat-screen TV sat atop an oak cabinet, and surround sound speakers hung in strategic locations around the perimeter. A separate audio system occupied the shelves below the TV, and a computer workstation with multiple monitors, a trackpad, mouse, and Wacom tablet sat in the corner of the room. A white candle in a glass jar, almost used up, sat in the middle of the coffee table, and Korean-style artwork featuring elegant birds and trees adorned her walls.

He sank onto the coffee-colored sofa and picked up the candle, lifting it to his nose. A dark, earthy aroma emanated from the wax, and tension he was holding in his shoulders eased. A faucet squeaked, and a humming sound reverberated from the hallway.

Sydney strode into the room and plopped down next to him, sinking into his side.

"Is she running the exhaust fan *and* the water?"

She laughed. "I think she feels pretty bad. I hope she can make it tonight."

He took another sniff of the relaxing candle before setting it on the table.

"I've burned that down to a nub trying to figure all this out." Sydney dropped her head back on the couch. "But I don't want to think about that now. Tonight is…" Laying her head on his shoulder, she angled her face toward him. "It means a lot for our relationship. I think it's symbolic."

"I couldn't agree more." It was symbolic, a sign that from this point on, they'd be moving with a forward momentum. He wrapped an arm around her shoulders, and she rested her face against his pec.

They sat silently, the soft rise and fall of Sydney's chest bringing him comfort, helping him relax even more. He leaned his head back and closed his eyes, basking in the feel of the woman he loved wrapped in his arms.

After a while, she sucked in a sharp breath and lifted her head, glancing at the clock on the wall. "I should go check on her. She's been in there fifteen minutes."

He blinked the room into focus as Sydney rose and crossed into the hallway. He must have fallen asleep.

"Are you okay?" Sydney's voice drifted in from the hall.

"Oh, yeah. All better." Claire appeared in the entry and looked at him. "Can you take me to my dorm? I need to get ready for tonight."

"Yeah. Are you sure you're up for it?" He stood and adjusted his pants. He enjoyed cuddling with Sydney a little too much, apparently.

"No way am I missing a real Mardi Gras ball. Can I meet at your place at six-thirty, too? I'll drive there. I just don't want to show up alone."

He looked at Sydney for confirmation, and she nodded. "Sounds like a plan." He gave Syd a quick kiss on the lips. "I'll see you soon."

She smiled. "I'll be there."

CHAPTER TWENTY

Blake adjusted his ascot in the bedroom mirror and tried to flatten his mouth into a neutral expression, but he couldn't have wiped the goofy grin off his face if he wanted to. Tonight was going to be epic. A turning point in their relationship.

Going to this ball with Sydney—the event that ended their relationship last time—was symbolic like she'd said… a sign that their time had finally come. Maybe he'd needed to go to New York. Perhaps they'd both had some growing up to do before their happily ever after could happen.

And now, the culmination of their journeys had brought them back to the beginning. A fresh start. A chance at forever. *However long that may be.* He shook his head to chase away the thought. Tonight was about their love; they'd deal with the dreaded premonitions in the morning.

Sydney's sundial necklace felt cool against his chest, where it was tucked away inside his tuxedo, but the rest of him burned like a fever. Was it nerves? Excitement? He flipped the switch to turn on the ceiling fan and stepped back to check out his costume.

A short, slate blue jacket with tails covered his white button-up and dark gray vest, and an antique pocket watch he borrowed from his dad sat tucked inside the vest pocket with a gold chain attached to a buttonhole on the front. He wore matching gray pinstriped pants, and a gray mask and top hat with white ears attached would complete the outfit.

He grabbed the hat and mask from his dresser and met Claire in the living room. She perched on the edge of a chair, her hot pink stilettos peeking out from her green floor-length gown. A tuft of pink petals surrounded her waist and flowed down her hips, and the top of the dress resembled the stamen of a flower.

Her pink mask sparkled with glitter that matched her lipstick, and she smiled as he set the hat on his head. "Well, look at you, Mr. Rabbit."

"It was the best I could do on short notice. Good thing my mom is friends with a woman who designs costumes for the krewes." He pulled out his pocket watch to check the time. Six-thirty. Sydney was always early…

His heart thrummed. She should have been there already. Slipping the watch into his pocket, he checked the time against his phone. It was correct. No texts from Sydney either.

Claire rose to her feet, and as if reading his mind, she patted his shoulder and said, "She didn't have much time to get ready. She'll be here soon."

"Yeah. I'm sure she will." Claire had just arrived a few minutes before, and even Blake hadn't been ready yet. Sydney was probably on her way. Texting her now would distract her from driving.

Claire pulled her phone from her sequined handbag and typed something on the screen. "I promised Sam I'd take lots of pictures." She stood next to him and held out the phone. "Say Wonderland."

He forced a smile as she snapped a photo. His own phone buzzed with an incoming message, and he blew out a breath of relief as Sydney's name appeared when he swiped at the screen.

His relief quickly morphed into confusion as he read her message: *I'm not coming to the ball. Go ahead without me.*

"What the...?" He squinted at the screen, not believing his eyes.

Claire leaned against the counter. "Was that Sydney?"

"She says she not coming." He typed a reply: *What's going on? Is everything okay?*

Claire's brow furrowed. "Why not?"

"I'm trying to find out." He stared at the screen as the three little dots flitted near the bottom, indicating she was typing a reply. Claire's gaze was heavy, and he glanced toward her, holding up a finger before shuffling into his bedroom.

His jaw clenched, his teeth grinding together, which sent a sharp pain ricocheting through his skull. Sydney's response was taking entirely too long. He dialed her number and pressed the phone to his ear. It rang four times before going to voicemail. "Hey. Call me back." He pressed end and watched the dots bouncing on the screen while his insides tied into knots.

Her reply came through: *We're done, Blake. Don't call me.*

The room spun, and he put a hand on the dresser to steady himself. They weren't done. Was she insane?

He hit the call button again but was greeted with her voicemail. "Dammit, Syd. What's going on? Did you see something? Talk to me."

He mashed the end button and typed another message: *We're NOT done. Not even close. Tell me what you saw. We'll fix it.*

Claire appeared in the doorway. "Is everything okay?"

"No," he barked. "Everything is not okay."

"Does this mean we aren't going to the ball?" Disappointment saturated her voice.

He let out an irritated grunt. "Apparently Sydney isn't."

His phone buzzed with another message. *We can't fix this. Take Claire to the masquerade. She was looking forward to it.*

He groaned as he typed his reply, deleting and retyping as his fingers, suddenly feeling thicker, mashed the screen. *Was it a death vision? Talk to me, please.*

"Why is she doing this?" he asked through clenched teeth.

"What is she saying?"

"She's breaking up with me. Again." The three tiny dots bounced on his screen, taunting him.

"Seriously? Via text? Who does that?" Claire crossed her arms and gave him a pointed look.

He sighed. "This won't be the first time."

The final message came through: *It has nothing to do with death. We're over. I'm turning off my phone now.*

"No." He mashed the call button, but it went straight to voicemail. She'd ghosted him right before the masquerade, just like she'd done eight years ago. "Goddammit, Sydney."

The urge to hurl his phone into the wall coiled in his

muscles, tightening his grip on the device. With a sharp exhale, he shoved it in his pocket and stormed into the living room to snatch his keys from the bowl by the door.

Claire followed on his heels. "What are you doing?"

"I'm going to her house. It's not ending this way." He moved for the door, but she caught him by the arm.

"Wait a minute. Do you even know if she's at home?"

"Where else would she be?"

"I don't know. At a friend's house. Her mom's. Maybe she went to the Mardi Gras warehouse to work on taking apart the float. Maybe she's at a bar. Who knows?"

He ground his teeth.

"Look, you're upset. The last thing you need to do is get behind the wheel and drive around aimlessly looking for your ex-girlfriend."

"She's not my ex. She saw something, and if she would talk to me, we could work it out. She swore she'd always talk to me." Why was she doing this? After everything they'd been through… All the promises she'd made…

"Well, I don't know what to tell you." Claire crossed her arms. "She lied."

"No." He shook his head. He couldn't believe it. He wouldn't. Something spooked her, but there was no reason for them to break up. "She loves me."

"Does she?"

Anger burned white-hot in his chest. "Of course she does."

"Okay." Claire held up her hands. "I believe you. But if she's this upset about some premonition she had, do you think storming into her house now—if she's even at home—is the way to get her back?" She rubbed his shoulder. "Let it simmer. Give her time to process whatever it is she saw, and *then* try talking to her again."

She was right. Sydney was strong-willed. Stubborn even. If she didn't want to talk to him now, forcing her wouldn't solve anything. "Dammit, Claire. Why do you have to make so much sense?"

He flopped onto the couch and tossed his hat and keys on the coffee table. What was it about this damn masquerade? It was like fate didn't want them to attend it together…or *he* wasn't meant to attend it at all. He closed his eyes and rubbed his forehead.

Claire perched on the arm of the sofa. "So…I guess this means we aren't going to the ball either?" She smoothed her hand down the front of her dress and toyed with one of the flower petals.

"I'm not in the mood for a masquerade."

"I understand. Your time would be better spent sulking here at home. I guess I'll shove this dress in the back of my closet and hope that one day I'll get invited to another one…and that dressing like a giant flower will fit with the theme."

He sighed and eyed his cousin. Claire had been elated when Sydney told her she was on the guest list. She'd practically bubbled with excitement, calling her mom and begging for money to buy a costume. Now, she sat there, picking at a loose thread on her sequined handbag, her shoulders slumped and looking so…disappointed.

What good would sitting at home do? If he stayed here alone, he wouldn't be able to stop himself from driving to Sydney's house, and where would that get him? She needed time to process whatever she saw. He could go there tomorrow, and the next day. And the day after that. Whatever it took to get her to open up and share her visions. To remind her she didn't have to carry the burden alone.

Tonight, he needed to stay busy. He settled his mask on his face, tying it at the back of his head, and put on his top hat. "Come on, Claire. Let's go to the ball."

Her entire face lit up. "Really?"

"Why not? Sitting here isn't going to bring Sydney back."

"Okay." She took her keys from her purse. "But I'm driving."

"I'm not distraught. I can handle a car."

"I know, but it's a ball. There will be an open bar, and I'm not old enough to drink."

He laughed. "Like that's ever stopped you before."

She squared her shoulders. "I got a fake ID in New York, and it's super-high quality." She grinned, tossing her hair behind her back. "I know people."

She was smart and pretty, and she used both to her advantage. He hoped he was a responsible-enough adult to be a good influence on her, as long as she didn't follow in his relationship footsteps. "I think those *people* are the reason your parents wanted you to move out here."

"I'm glad I came."

"Me too." He grabbed his keys, but she snatched them from his hand and tossed them onto the table.

"I'm driving. You need to let loose and have fun tonight. I promise not to drink."

He started to argue, but why should he? He deserved to have some fun. Let someone else be responsible for a change.

The pink sheen on Sydney's lips glinted in the bathroom light as she smiled at her reflection. It was hard to believe that, eight years later, she was finally going to the masquerade with Blake.

While the parade was no doubt the highlight of the year for the krewe, the annual masquerade ball was the grand finale. It was the culmination of everything they'd worked toward all year long, coming together in an exciting, formal extravaganza that rivaled even the super krewes' parties.

She'd enjoyed all eight balls she'd attended so far, but every one had been laced with a tinge of sadness. A hollowness in her chest reminding her of the broken heart she'd endured before her induction into the krewe.

Tonight would be different. Blake would be by her side this time, filling the emptiness, making the night complete. "It's going to be perfect." And she planned to enjoy every second of it. If her days were numbered, she might as well make the most of the ones she had left.

She picked up her blue satin clutch and matching mask and sashayed out the front door. Her feet felt as if they barely touched the ground, her body light with giddy happiness, as she made her way to her car.

Cranking the engine, she threw it into reverse and eased on the gas. The car thumped as it rolled backward, the wheel pulling to the left against her grip. "What on earth?"

She scrambled out of the driver's seat, and her chest deflated like her front tire. "Damn it." She must have hit a nail on her way home yesterday. Blake had picked her up this morning to take her to the parade, so the hole had all day to leak out the remaining air from the tire.

She had a spare in the trunk, but she'd have to change out of her gown before she swapped the tires. It would be faster to take an Uber. Reaching across the console, she grabbed her purse and mask and pulled out her phone.

Nothing happened when she swiped at the screen. She pressed the home button, but the device remained dark. *Seriously?* She held down the power button, and it dinged, the screen lighting bright white as it turned back on.

"No wonder I haven't heard any notifications."

It powered up, and an error message lit her screen: *No SIM card installed*

"No SIM card?" She tapped on the phone, but the device insisted she put in a card. "I never took it out."

A breeze kicked up, blowing her hair across her face and raising goose bumps on her arms. She powered off the phone as she scurried to the front door and slipped into the living room. After a few minutes, she turned the device back on, but the same error message taunted her on the screen.

When her pocket ripped on the float that afternoon, the phone had taken a tumble, landing face down on the wood with a smack. The screen hadn't shattered, so she'd assumed it survived the fall. Apparently, it didn't.

"Well, what now, Syd?" Without the phone, getting a rideshare was out. She cursed under her breath and opened her laptop. The local cab company had a web-based form, so she could get a ride that way. She'd worry about the phone and the flat tire tomorrow.

She double-tapped the icon for the web browser and waited for it to pull up the search screen. An error message read: *No wi-fi connection.*

"You've got to be kidding me." She opened the control panel and tried to reconnect, but nothing worked.

She had scoffed at her mother's insistence that she have

a landline in her home for emergencies. It seemed Mother did know best about something.

She stomped to her bedroom to reset the router, but the damn thing wasn't even on. Hiking up her dress, she knelt beside the dresser, running her hand along the power cord to pull it out from behind the furniture.

The cord had been cut.

It wasn't frayed or crushed like it had been caught beneath a leg of the dresser. The cut was clean, from a sharp knife or a pair of scissors.

Her pulse thrummed, and the first hint of adrenaline trickled down her spine. The flat tire. The phone. The wi-fi. This couldn't be a coincidence.

She gasped. "My phone."

Scrambling to her feet, she rushed into the living room and scooped her phone from the computer desk. She rummaged through the drawer to find a paperclip and shoved the pointed end into the tiny hole on the side of the phone to release the SIM card slot.

It was empty.

"Son of a bitch." She dropped onto the couch and lit the meditation candle. "All right, universe. You tried to show me something earlier. Let's see it."

The flame flickered, and she focused on the orange glow. Her vision tunneled, the blue and gold kaleidoscope pattern closing in like a flash of lightning before she tumbled into Wonderland.

CHAPTER TWENTY-ONE

"Smile. It's not the end of the world." Claire patted Blake's cheek as they swayed to the music, so he twirled her under his arm to distract her from the annoying gesture.

The hotel ballroom had an enormous dance floor situated under a massive chandelier dripping with crystals. A jazz band played on a stage at one end of the room, and plush, blue carpet, dotted with tables draped in white linen, surrounded the wooden floor.

Whimsical ice sculptures shaped like characters from *Alice's Adventures in Wonderland* stood about the room, spilling out into the lobby, and an open bar and expansive buffet sat at the other end of the space. Greenery, balloons, and papier mâché flowers added to the Wonderland effect.

What was he thinking coming to a ball with this theme? Everywhere he looked, the decor screamed *Sydney*.

Not the end of the world, my ass. "Might as well be."

Claire rolled her eyes. "Don't be so melodramatic. You'll either get her back, or you won't. Life will go on either way."

"No, it won't. I love her. I can't...I don't want to live without her." And that was the god's honest truth. He couldn't imagine any kind of a future without Sydney in it.

She pressed her lips into a disapproving line. "This is what happens when you get too attached to people. You know what? If she won't take you back, then screw her. You'll always have me. We're...*family.*"

He laughed, but he couldn't force any humor into it. "I appreciate your friendship, and I'm glad you're here in New Orleans. But you've got to realize it's not the same. Being in love with someone is an entirely different ballgame."

A noncommittal sound emanated from her throat as she stepped away from him. "You need a drink. You like whiskey, right?" She dragged him to the edge of the dance floor. "Wait here, and I'll get you one."

"How?"

"Fake ID, remember?" She turned on her heel and marched toward the bar.

Blake sighed and checked the time on his pocket watch. Nearly eight p.m. What on earth could Sydney have seen in her vision to make her so upset? He'd thought their deaths were the worst things she could have predicted. Apparently, he was wrong.

He fished his phone from his pocket and dialed her number, but it went straight to voicemail again. "What am I doing?" He needed to find her. She was most likely at home, but if she wasn't, he'd look for her. He'd spend the entire night driving to every location he could think she might be to find her.

Claire would be fine without him. She never had trouble making friends, and Eric and Jason were around here somewhere. They could keep an eye on her.

He scanned the crowd, looking for one of the guys. Claire was still at the bar. He'd find one of his friends, let them know he was leaving, and he could get an Uber back to his place for his car.

He'd made up his mind just as his gaze landed on the most beautiful sight he'd ever seen. Sydney stood at the entrance wearing a long blue and white gown, slit up the side to right above her knee. Black patent leather high heels accented her black choker and bracelet, giving her Alice costume a slightly gothic flair.

She brushed her hair out of her face, and as she caught his gaze, his heart stilled in his chest. She didn't smile, but she moved toward him in hurried strides until a blonde woman stopped her with a hand on her arm. They argued briefly, the woman gesturing to Sydney's face before Sydney huffed and tied her mask around her head.

Her gaze darted about the room as she moved toward him, her long strides quickening into a jog. Stopping in front of him, she clutched his biceps. "Where's Claire?"

He blinked, his mind scrambling for a response to the question that seemed to come from nowhere. "She's at the bar. What happened? When you texted me, I thought—"

"I didn't text you. We need to leave. Now."

"Hold on." He clutched her hand. "What do you mean, you didn't text me? You told me you didn't want to be with me anymore. You said not to call you, and then you turned off your phone."

She shook her head, still searching the room. "That wasn't me, Blake. It was Claire."

He furrowed his brow. "Claire was standing right beside me when I got the texts."

"Someone did it for her, then. She took my SIM card. Listen to me." She tugged him deeper into the crowd, her voice taking on a hushed urgency. "I had another vision. I saw…" Her eyes widened.

"Sydney? What are you doing here?" Surprise lilted Claire's voice.

Sydney clutched his arm, digging her nails into the fabric of his jacket. "There's been a misunderstanding. Blake and I need to talk privately."

Claire pursed her lips, her gaze cutting from Sydney to Blake. "No problem. Here, Blake." She handed him a glass with *Drink Me* written on the side in a whimsical script. "Drink up. I'll go get you something, Sydney. I hear they have a fantastic rosé, not that I would know, since I'm not drinking tonight."

Blake lifted the glass to his lips.

"No!" Sydney snatched it from his grasp, sloshing the contents onto Claire. The liquid soaked her dress, splashing across her hand as she tried to shield herself.

"She's planning to kill you," Sydney whispered through clenched teeth. "Look at her nails; the drink must be drugged."

Claire laughed, unbelieving. "Is that what you think of me, Sydney? Clearly your premonitions are making you crazy." She wiggled her fingers. "No drugs."

Sydney frowned. "I saw you die, Blake. She has a gun in her purse."

None of this made sense. Claire was family. A nineteen-year-old girl. She wasn't capable of murder. But the feral look in Sydney's eyes told him this was no mistake. She had seen *something* in her vision.

"I don't have a gun. Look." Claire opened her purse and pulled out her phone.

"Oh, God. It's someone else then." Sydney's gaze darted about the room while the people around them stopped to stare.

"Hold on." He raised his hands. "Claire, did you somehow fake those texts from Sydney?"

"Don't be ridiculous." She glanced at her phone. "She flaked on you like she's done before. Like she *always* will. Let's move this conversation to the lobby. People are staring."

"Syd, tell me what you saw." He wrapped an arm around her and guided her out of the ballroom.

"I saw you get shot." Her voice held an edge of panic as her gaze darted about their surroundings.

"Did you see Claire do it?"

"No, I couldn't. It was in the darkness like the rabbit was, only now it was you…dressed like a rabbit." Her body trembled.

"She's obviously gone nuts, Blake." Claire crossed her arms, scanning the area as if looking for someone, but with the party inside in full swing, the lobby sat empty. "Why else would she text you to take me to the ball and then show up accusing me of murder?"

"Wait." Blake turned to Claire, a sinking sensation forming in his abdomen. "I never told you what her texts said."

"I… I just assumed…" Claire's mouth dropped open, her gaze flicking around the room. "Okay, look." She laughed nervously. "I admit it. I got Sam to send the texts. It's no big deal."

"Why?"

Sydney clutched his arm, trying to pull him away.

Claire lifted her hands and dropped them at her sides. "I wanted to break you up, but I'm not a murderer. I…"

Her bottom lip trembled. "Carmen should be here any minute. I knew Sydney would find a way to get here, and I thought if you were mad at her, and then she and your ex-boss got into it, fighting over you, then you'd see."

"What would I see?" He shook his head. "What are you talking about?"

Her voice took on an edge of hysteria. "True devotion has been standing right in front of you all this time, but you've looked right through me. All you can see is *her*. I love you, Blake."

"Claire…" She couldn't be serious. She'd hatched this elaborate scheme to try and steal him from Sydney? "You said Sydney was your friend."

"She is, but I'm in love with *you*."

"We need to leave, Blake." Sydney tugged on his sleeve.

"Blake Beaumont," a male voice growled from behind him. "My wife isn't enough for you?"

Claire's eyes widened. "That's the guy who tried to run you over."

Blake tensed, swallowing the bile from his throat as he faced the man. "William." He straightened to his full height. "To what do I owe the pleasure?"

William stood three inches taller than Blake and wore dark jeans, sneakers, and a wrinkled, untucked button-up under a navy blazer. One arm hung by his side, his thick fingers curled into a fist, while the other rested in his jacket pocket. "Carmen left me." His bloodshot eyes gleamed in the lobby lights.

Blake held his hands out at his sides, positioning himself between William and the women. "I'm sorry to hear that, man."

William scowled, adjusting his hand in his pocket,

what could only be the barrel of a gun protruding through the fabric. "What is it about you?"

"I don't know what you mean." Blake scanned his surroundings, searching for a weapon or a place for the women to hide, but all he found was an ice sculpture carved in the shape of the Cheshire Cat.

"I've been watching you. Women flock to you like flies to garbage, you wife-stealing piece of shit." He drew the gun from his pocket, pointing it at Blake's chest. "Which one are you in love with?" He pointed it at Sydney then Claire.

Blake tried not to react, but William narrowed his eyes and aimed at Sydney's heart. "I'll take her from you like you took Carmen from me."

"It's me." Claire stepped in front of her. "He's in love with me. Kill me, not her."

Blake raised his hands, moving in front of them both, inching toward the crazed man while keeping his voice calm. "I didn't steal your wife. We've talked about this."

"No?" He pulled back the hammer on the revolver, training the barrel on Blake's head. "You haven't been emailing her all week? You didn't ask her to meet you here tonight?"

His jaw tightened as he edged toward the ice sculpture, away from the others. "No, I didn't." But he knew exactly who did.

"Liar." William's voice grew louder. "I wrote those emails, not Carmen. You've been talking to *me*."

"What?" Claire gasped.

William jerked his head toward her, and Blake used the distraction to his advantage, ramming his shoulder into the ice sculpture and knocking it into William. As it crashed to the ground, the cat's body shattered, and the head rolled across the wooden floor.

William stumbled, and time slowed to a crawl as Blake tackled him, dragging his stocky frame to the ground. They wrestled, William landing a punch on Blake's right eye, making the room spin. Blake swung back, hitting the man in the jaw, knocking the gun from his grip.

Sydney lunged for the weapon, but Claire snatched it from her grasp as William wrapped an arm around Blake's neck, putting him in a chokehold and dragging him to his feet.

Trails of mascara streaked Claire's face as she lifted the gun to her head. "This is all my fault. I'm so sorry, Blake."

He tried to call out to her, to stop her, but William tightened his arm, blocking Blake's airflow. His vision tunneled, and stars danced in his gaze.

"Claire, no!" Sydney grabbed her arm, trying to wrangle the gun from her grip.

William punched Blake in the gut, knocking the breath from his lungs. His vision eclipsed, and the explosive *pop* of gunfire sounded simultaneously as his shoulder collided with another ice sculpture.

The statue toppled with both men, sending ice crashing to the ground, shattering with the impact, and panic flushed through Blake's veins. *Sydney.*

"Drop the weapon." A deep voice boomed over the chaos.

Blake looked up to find three police officers, guns drawn, closing in on them. Claire gingerly placed the revolver on the floor and raised her hands, fresh tears streaming down her face. "I didn't mean to. It was an accident."

An officer grabbed her by the arm, while another hauled Blake up, cuffing him.

The third officer cuffed William and dragged him to his feet, and Blake's gaze finally found Sydney. "No."

The crowd that had filed out from the ballroom dispersed as the paramedics arrived with a stretcher, and Blake's heart wrenched from his chest. Sydney lay on her back, a pool of thick, red blood soaking the carpet beneath her.

CHAPTER TWENTY-TWO

Blake sat with his elbows on his knees in the squeaky vinyl chair, watching the little blue line on the monitor blip up and down with each beat of Sydney's heart. Her pulse was steady, which was surprising considering the bullet missed her heart by a mere three inches.

His own heart was a mangled, shredded mess.

He dragged a hand down his face and leaned back in the chair, sucking in a shaky breath. The sharp scent of antiseptic mixed with the sickly-sweet hospital smell, and his stomach churned. That should have been him lying wounded in the bed, not Sydney.

How could he have missed the signs? The strange happenings and near-misses had begun shortly after Carmen's message about leaving her husband—or rather, William's message pretending to be Carmen—but Blake never made the connection. And Claire… Thinking back on it now, it seemed so obvious: her behavior, her clinginess, Eric's comments about how messed up her emotions were. She was obsessed, and Blake was a blind idiot.

He blew out a hard breath. That was the understatement of the century. He squeezed his eyes shut, pressing his thumb and forefinger against his lids as he replayed the night in his mind.

After the paramedics stabilized Sydney and loaded her onto the stretcher, enough witnesses testified on Blake's behalf that they let him go free. He'd made it to the hospital while Sydney was in surgery and gave his statement to multiple officers and a detective while he waited for her to come out.

She'd woken briefly, several hours ago. Long enough for her to give him a small smile and squeeze his hand before the painkillers pulled her back under. As the apology had spilled from his lips, she'd shaken her head and muttered, "Not your fault," before drifting back to sleep.

Blake hadn't slept at all. He made phone calls and watched the monitors for any signs of distress, though the doctors assured him she'd pull through with no problems; shoulder injuries weren't normally life-threatening. Still, the nauseating concoction of worry and guilt churned in his gut, refusing to allow him even a moment's respite.

This was his fault. Every bit of it.

Contacting Sydney's mom had been difficult, but he'd managed to keep his voice from quivering as he promised her that her daughter would be fine. Calling his cousin had been gut-wrenching.

When he explained what happened, a string of curses flowed through the receiver. "I knew that kid was messed up. I told Diane she needed more than time away. She needed psychological help."

"Well, you were right, man. I'm sorry I couldn't help her."

"No. I'm sorry we put this burden on you. Her mom hoped…we both hoped it was just a bout of depression that she'd pull through, but I've always thought something was off about Claire." He laughed, but there wasn't any humor in it. "How do you tell a mother you think her daughter is a psychopath?"

"You don't."

"Exactly."

Both Claire's parents and Sydney's mom intended to hop on the first flight to New Orleans they could get, and Blake sat in the quiet room, drowning in guilt as he watched the only woman he'd ever loved lying injured in bed.

Sydney stirred, inhaling a deep breath and blinking her eyes open. She squinted against the overhead light and turned her head toward him. "Hey."

He shot to his feet and was by her side in two long strides. Sinking onto the edge of the bed, he took her hand in his and brushed a stray strand of hair from her forehead. His throat thickened, and pressure built in the back of his eyes. "I'm so sorry."

"I think I already told you it wasn't your fault. Or did I dream that?" She lifted her head from the pillow and winced.

Tears collected on his lower lids. "You said it."

"But you didn't believe me." She covered his hand with her free one.

"Because it *is* my fault. I moved back to New Orleans. I brought the danger with me. I brought Claire. I…" A warm tear slid down his cheek, and he wiped it away with the back of his hand. "Can you ever forgive me?"

"You didn't do anything wrong. You never did." She cleared her throat.

"Here. You must be parched." He grabbed the water from the bedside table and held the straw to her lips. She took a sip, and he set it down. "How are you feeling? Do you need me to call the nurse? Do you need more pain meds?"

"I'm okay."

He nodded. "Sean and Emily are on their way. The others left a little while ago, and your mom is taking the first flight home she can get."

A small smile curved her lips. "She's still in Monaco?"

"Yeah, but I think there's a flight tonight. I…" He choked on a sob. She was okay. She was awake and talking to him. They'd thwarted her premonitions, and they were together.

His chest tightened as gratitude and relief joined the heady mix of emotions swirling through his core. "I thought I'd lost you." A lump wedged in his throat as more tears slid down his cheeks.

"You didn't." She ran a hand up and down his arm. "I'm here. We're both here."

"When I saw you lying on the floor, I…" He shook his head to chase the horrid image from his mind. "I swear my heart stopped beating. The entire world fell away; my whole life came crashing down around me, and I didn't… I don't even remember what happened other than they wouldn't let me go to you. I didn't know if you were alive until they put you on the stretcher, and all I could do was pray to every god I could think of for them not to cover your head. I knew if they left your head uncovered it meant you were alive."

She hit the button on the side of the bed, inclining it toward him, and she cringed as her body adjusted to the new position.

"Should you be sitting up? Should I call the nurse?" He wiped his eyes and helped her get situated.

"It's just a shoulder wound, right?"

"That's what they tell me." He scooted closer and pressed a kiss to her temple. "It could have been so much worse." He closed his eyes, resting his forehead against hers.

"It would have been if you hadn't tackled him."

"If I hadn't tackled him, Claire wouldn't have shot you."

"And you'd be dead." She placed a hand on his leg. "What happened after you realized I was alive?"

He inhaled deeply, letting her scent seep into his senses before pulling away. "I guess I *woke up* after that. They arrested William and Claire and drove me to the hospital to be with you. A detective said she'd stop by later after they questioned them."

He looked into her dark brown eyes and saw his entire world inside them. "I can't ever lose you again, Sydney. You are everything to me, and my heart…it's not in your hands. It's beating inside you. If you go, you'll be taking it with you."

"I'm not going anywhere. I love you, Blake."

"I love you too." He leaned in and took her mouth in a gentle kiss.

"Are we interrupting?" Sean's voice drifted in through the doorway, and Blake straightened.

"Hey, Sean. Emily." Sydney smiled weakly as they entered the room. "Where's Sable?"

"She's with my mom." Sean set a bouquet of yellow roses near the window.

"How are you feeling?" Emily touched Sydney's good shoulder and smiled before shifting her gaze to the monitors. "Your pulse is strong. Good oxygen levels too."

"I'm sure I'll be sore once the pain meds wear off," Sydney said.

Blake rose from the bed and lowered his voice. "Can you look at her file? The doctors said she'll be fine, but can you be sure?" Emily was a nurse practitioner. Surely, she could let him know if anything could go wrong.

"You know I can hear you, right?" Sydney laughed and then winced.

Emily gave him a sympathetic smile. "I don't work here, so, no, I can't access her file. But everything looks good."

His shoulders slumped. "Would they lie though? I'm not her family, so maybe they didn't tell me everything."

"I'll tell you what… One of the nurses on duty is a friend of mine. I'll go talk to her if it will make you feel better." Emily winked at Sydney.

"Please do," Sydney said. "He's not going to relax until you tell him I'm okay."

"Be right back." Emily slipped out the door.

Sean sank into the squeaky chair. "So, your visions? The funerals? Is that all cleared up now?"

"I think so." Sydney reached for Blake, taking his hand and tugging him onto the bed next to her. "I had another vision in the ambulance. Blake and I were babysitting a two-year-old Sable, so I think it's safe to say we won't be dying anytime soon."

A flush of relief loosened the tension in his chest, warming his heart. "You could have told me that twenty minutes ago."

"I got shot, and I'm doped up on pain meds. My brain isn't quite performing at peak level."

His heart tore in two all over again. "I'm so sorry."

She patted his cheek. "I know."

"Before that, you saw William shoot him?" Sean leaned forward, resting his elbows on his knees.

Her brows knit. "No. I only saw that he'd been shot."

"Nothing to worry about." Emily smiled as she stepped through the door, and Sydney blew out a breath, thankful for the distraction. "They're planning to release her as soon as the doctor signs off on it."

"See?" She squeezed Blake's hand. "I told you I'll be fine." She'd take a shoulder wound over what could have happened to him any day.

Blake swallowed hard. "Thanks, Emily." He turned his gaze to Sydney. "What did you see?"

Bile burned its way up her throat as her stomach churned at the image. The horrid vision would be seared into her mind for the rest of her life. "A bullet to the head. Your mask lay off to the side, blown off by the impact, and your face…" She closed her eyes for a long blink, searching for the words to describe the bloody scene.

Her insides quivered, her throat thickening, making it hard to drag in a breath. As she opened her mouth, her jaw trembled, so she snapped it shut.

Blake cupped her cheek in his warm palm. "I can imagine the rest. You don't have to say it."

She covered his hand with hers, holding it to her face as she sagged with relief. "Thank you."

Emily sank onto the arm of the chair, resting a hand on Sean's shoulder. "What a horrifying thing to see happen. I can't imagine."

"I really thought it was Claire. After everything she did to keep me from the ball, I assumed…" She smoothed the blanket down her stomach. "I suppose my accusation sent her over the edge."

"No, she'd already crossed it. She was trying to break us up, and she went to psychotic lengths to do it." Blake shook his head. "I never pegged her as being so conniving, but to shoot you? And William… I should have seen this coming. I put everyone in danger." His eyes darkened as he slipped back into his pit of guilt.

"No, Blake." She wouldn't let him shoulder the blame for this. "People get divorced every day, and they don't resort to murder. There's no way you could have known."

A knock sounded on the door before a cheerful nurse in pink scrubs shuffled into the room. "Hello, Ms. Sydney." She glanced at Emily. "I guess you heard the good news?"

"I'm going home."

"As soon as we get the doctor's signature."

They remained silent as the nurse checked her vitals and typed something into the computer. "We sent a script for pain meds to your pharmacy. You'll want to pick it up on your way home." She logged out of the computer and clasped her hands together. "I'll be by with your release instructions soon. It was good seeing you, Emily." She smiled and left the room.

Sydney leaned her head against the pillow, fatigue from her injury mixing with the muddiness in her mind from the pain medication, making it hard to keep her eyes open. She let them flutter shut for a moment, and when she opened them, Blake, Sean, and Emily settled heavy gazes on her, their silent question hanging in the air.

"I'll be fine." She could never unsee the image of Blake

lying dead, but she'd stopped it from happening. She'd heal.

Another knock sounded on the door. "Mr. Beaumont?" A petite blonde woman stepped through the threshold. She wore black slacks with a light blue long-sleeve button-up, a pistol holstered at her hip.

Blake rose and strode toward her, shaking her hand. "Detective Mason, this is Sydney." He gestured toward her, and the detective nodded.

"Please, call me Macey. I'm glad you're okay." She glanced at Sean and Emily. "Hello."

"We better get home to Sable." Emily stood and tugged Sean to his feet.

"Call us if you need anything." Sean followed her to the door, pausing before crossing the threshold. "I mean it. Both of you."

"Thanks, Sean." Sydney lifted a hand to wave as her friends left the room.

Detective Mason's face was serious. "You may want to sit down, Mr. Beaumont."

"Okay." Blake sank onto the bed next to Sydney and motioned toward the chair for the detective to sit.

"Mr. Stone has confessed to attempted murder."

Sydney's chest tightened, her breaths growing shallow. "How long had he been planning it?"

The detective pulled a small notepad from her pocket and scanned a page. "His wife left him three weeks ago, and he came to New Orleans looking for her. When he couldn't find her, he took out his frustration on you, Mr. Beaumont. He stated his original intent was merely to scare you, to 'teach you a lesson.'" She made air quotes with her fingers. "It escalated from there."

"Jesus Christ." Blake slumped, and Sydney rubbed his back. "What else did he do?"

"He admitted to killing a bird and leaving it on your doorstep, in addition to nearly hitting you with his car."

Sydney let out a slow breath. *Poor bird.*

"You're safe. He will remain in custody, as will Ms. Fontane." The detective paused. "How are you related to her?"

"She's my cousin's step-daughter."

Detective Mason nodded. "In addition to assault with a deadly weapon, her confession has led to charges of theft, vandalism, and breaking and entering. She's been stalking both of you."

"My God." Blake shifted on the bed toward Sydney. "I can't believe we didn't see this coming."

She pressed her lips together, trying to ignore the sting of his words. It was obvious from his expression that he meant he couldn't believe *they*, as Claire's friends, didn't see it coming, but Sydney was a clairvoyant, for goodness' sake. She *should* have seen it.

Whatever the universe was thinking when it chose her to have this gift, she *had* been chosen. Her *why me?* attitude ended today. It was time she took control of her ability and learned how to harness her visions. "I think I need to make a standing appointment with Natasha," she mumbled to herself.

The detective cocked her head, narrowing her eyes. "Are you referring to Natasha Delandre?"

Sydney pressed her lips together. She hadn't meant to say that out loud. "She's umm…been helping me learn to meditate." She forced a smile, praying the detective wouldn't press her further. The last thing she needed was the police officer in charge of the case questioning her sanity.

Detective Mason nodded. "I know her well." She turned to Blake. "We're going to need access to your apartment and museum." The detective swiped at her phone. "Are you still on St. Ann? That's the maroon building with the paper in the windows, right?"

Blake nodded. "Do you think she left evidence in the office? She didn't have a key."

"She didn't need one." Detective Mason stood. "When can we expect you home, Mr. Beaumont? The sooner the better."

Blake squeezed Sydney's hand tighter. "Not until Sydney is released."

"How long will that be?"

The nurse in pink scrubs shuffled in carrying Sydney's dress and a stack of paperwork. "You're free to go, Ms. Sydney. I just need your signature on a few of these documents, and you'll be all set."

"Give us an hour?" Blake said to the detective.

"Sounds good." Detective Mason gave a curt nod. "Ms. Park, we'll be in touch."

Blake scanned the paperwork before Sydney signed it, not moving from his spot on the bed next to her. "You can stay with me tonight. For as many nights as you need to."

The nurse took the papers, leaving the release instructions on the table as she exited the room.

Blake scooted closer to Sydney on the bed, wrapping his arm around her waist and leaning his head on her pillow. "The first thing I'm going to do after this investigation is done is get the best security system I can find. With cameras. This situation never should have escalated this far."

"I'm going to visit the Voodoo priestess and really work to develop my ability. Curse or gift, whichever it is, I've got to learn how to use it properly."

"Neither of our abilities were very useful in this situation."

"Not until it was almost too late." Her chest tightened, and now it was her turn for the tears. Since she woke up this morning, she'd been focusing on consoling Blake, making sure he didn't shoulder all the blame. But she'd almost lost him too.

A sob bubbled into her throat, spilling a tear down her cheek. "I feel so stupid. I've never been more angry with myself."

He wiped the tear away with his thumb and held her face in his hands. "I think all of this is going to take time to process. The important thing is we're both alive and together now."

She nodded, swallowing the thickness from her throat. "And it's for good this time. No matter what I see about the future, I'm yours."

"That's all I've ever wanted. Let's get you home."

Blake helped Sydney change into a pair of his sweatpants and a t-shirt before getting her situated on the couch. "I'll run to your place in the morning to get you some clothes."

She lifted the shirt to her nose and inhaled deeply. "I kinda like wearing yours."

"They look good on you." So good he was tempted to peel them off her and toss them on the floor. *Cool it, horn dog.* She was injured. There'd be plenty of time for those thoughts when she healed.

With Sydney resting comfortably, he took a quick shower and changed into normal clothes before the detective knocked on his front door. He hurried down the stairs and invited her in.

"I'd like to start at the back entrance," Mason said. "That's where she claims she got inside."

"Right." He stepped onto the small porch and closed the door, locking it behind him. "It's around this way." He led her through a gate and into the back courtyard, past the fountain he'd be fixing for Sydney as soon as things settled down. "The door back here has an alarm, but it never went off."

"That's because she never opened it." Detective Mason knelt in front of the door, running her finger along the edge of the bottom right panel. As she pressed two fingers into the corner, the wooden slat popped loose. The entire thing came off, creating an opening in the door roughly two feet by eighteen inches, just big enough for a person to squeeze through.

Exactly the way Claire had told him The Axeman broke into his victims' homes. A shudder ran up his spine. "I'll be damned."

The detective tried the knob. "Do you have the key?"

"Yeah." He pulled the ring from his pocket and opened the door.

She led the way up the stairs, running her hand along the wall. "She said there was a hidden doorway that had been painted over?"

"It's through there." He pointed down the tight passage leading back toward a shuttered window.

Mason slipped through, and he followed, stopping beside her as she pressed her palms flat against the panel and closed her eyes. Her body swayed slightly, her deep inhalations and the way her eyes darted about beneath her closed lids seeming eerily similar to the way people had described him when he used his ability.

She opened her eyes and shook her head. "She's been using this entrance for months to watch you sleep."

He laid his hand on the squat door, allowing its energy to seep into his skin. Sure enough, an image of his cousin creeping through in the darkness flitted through his mind's eye. "That's…unsettling."

"May I?" She opened the panel and gestured inside.

"Be my guest. It leads through a crawl space to my bedroom closet." He followed her through the space as she again ran her hands along the walls.

When they exited into his closet, she paused in the threshold to his bedroom, resting her hands on the door jamb. "She was infatuated in the beginning. You were like a savior to her." She stepped into the room and touched his dresser. "Then you became an obsession. Ms. Park too."

"Is that what she told you, or are you reading her energy in the walls?"

Her eyes widened briefly. "What do you mean?"

He stepped toward her, lowering his voice. "I have that ability too. Psychometry? Is that what you're doing?"

She studied him, narrowing her eyes. "Something like that, yes. I spoke to Natasha about you both, which is the only reason I'm confiding in you."

He laughed. "Wow. I've never met anyone else who could do that."

"It comes in handy in my line of work." She walked into the hallway toward the living room. "Though it's sometimes hard to explain how I know things."

"I can imagine." He followed her, and Sydney's eyes fluttered open as he entered the room.

She winced as she pushed to a sitting position. "Did I fall asleep or did you sneak in through the secret passageway?"

He rushed to the sofa and knelt beside her. "We came in through the back. How are you doing? Can I get you anything?"

"A pain pill and some water would be nice."

"You got it." He pressed a kiss to her forehead, letting out a breath of relief at the coolness of her skin.

Detective Mason stopped in the kitchen and tilted her head. "Do you make a habit of leaving knives on the floor?" She stooped to pick up the same knife he'd found on his counter several times. The one he was certain he'd shoved into the drawer.

"I assume that's Claire's doing. It was falling out of the block onto the counter, so I stuffed it in a drawer. She must have been messing with me." He filled a glass with water and took a pain pill to Sydney in the living room.

Detective Mason clutched the knife, closing her eyes and swaying.

Sydney swallowed the pill and drained the glass. "Is she…?"

"She can read energy."

"Wow." She settled back on the pillow.

"I know."

"I wonder how that kind of evidence works in court."

"I'm not sure it does."

Detective Mason's lids flew open as she gasped. "Have you been experiencing any kind of…haunting?"

Blake locked eyes with Sydney. "We have…"

"You need to see this." She held the knife handle toward him.

Letting out a slow breath, he shuffled across the small living room into the kitchen. He needed to see it, but did he want to? Taking the cold steel into his palm, he wrapped his fingers around the handle and closed his eyes.

His skin tingled where it touched the metal, and blurry images wavered in his mind before coming into focus. He saw himself cooking, and as he pushed further back, the manufacturing process came into view. Nothing unusual.

He opened his eyes. "What am I looking for? All I see is the normal life of a kitchen knife."

The detective arched a brow. "You don't feel the spirit energy?"

"I can only feel energy the living have left behind." He set the knife on the counter. "Ghosts aren't my forte."

Her brow furrowed as she tugged on her bottom lip. "If you can read energy in objects, you should be able to read *any* energy attached to it. Try again, but look for a higher vibration. You should feel it buzzing around your senses."

"I've never been able to—"

"Natasha wasn't kidding about you two." The detective put her hands on her hips. "A ghost left a message for you in that knife, Mr. Beaumont. Listen to it."

His nostrils flared as he blew out a frustrated breath and gripped the handle. Closing his eyes again, he focused on the energy in the object. Immediately, images of his own life since he purchased the knife flashed in his mind. Not helpful.

He let the scenes play out like a movie and expanded his perception. A faint, buzzing energy danced around the edges of his senses, but when he tried to latch on to it, it drifted further away. He clenched his jaw, grinding his teeth as he tried again to grab hold of the energy.

"Relax your mind," the detective said. "Let it come to you."

Inhaling a deep breath, he gave up the struggle and relaxed, letting the energy simmer and gently stroking it with his mind. It yielded, opening up to a gruesome sight. A woman with a tangled mass of short blonde hair reached a hand toward him. Blood oozed from an angry gash across her throat as she opened her mouth and forced out the word, "Air." She looked exactly like the spirit Sean had described trying to come through in the museum weeks ago.

The vision shifted, showing him scenes of Claire watching him from the shadows of his closet, following him on his date with Sydney, using his computer when he wasn't in the office. He shuffled through the images and saw the ghost knocking the book from the shelf, shattering the necklace he'd given Claire, and finally a scene of the woman when she was alive, carrying a moving box to the trunk of a car, tears streaming down Claire's cheeks as she begged her not to leave.

He sucked in a sharp breath and dropped the knife on the counter. "Oh my God."

Sydney shuffled into the kitchen and lowered into a chair. "Who is it?"

"It's the other ghost Sean tried to communicate with. The one who couldn't say anything but 'air.'" He locked eyes with Sydney. "She was saying, 'Claire.'"

Detective Mason nodded. "I don't know a lot about ghosts, but it probably took a lot of energy to infuse this much of a message into an object in a short amount of time."

"It's Claire's friend." He sank into the seat next to Sydney, resting a hand on her knee. "She's been trying to warn us the whole time."

"And we've been focusing on Bernadette." Sydney covered his hand with hers and looked at the detective. "Now that her message has been received, will she move on?"

Mason cut her gaze between them, as if sizing them up. "I don't sense any spirits here, but I'm not a medium. If I had to guess, I'd say she's either moved on already, or she'll be sticking by Claire for a while. I can put you in contact with a medium if you want."

"We know one. Thanks." He'd have to get Sean over to check things out again before the museum opened.

The detective strode through the living room toward the door. "Thank you for your time, Mr. Beaumont. Ms. Park. We'll be in touch."

Blake closed the door behind her and turned to Sydney. "She was mysterious."

She nodded. "I get the feeling she knows more than she's letting on."

"When you make that standing appointment with the priestess, will you see if she can help me too?"

"Sounds like we've both got a lot to learn about our abilities."

He sidled next to her, taking her in his arms. "And we have all the time in the world to do it, right?"

Sydney smiled. "I believe we do."

EPILOGUE

ONE YEAR LATER

"That was an event worth waiting for," Blake said.

"It was fun, wasn't it?" Sydney picked up her mask and slipped her hand into Blake's as she stepped out of the mule-drawn buggy. "Thanks, Jack."

The driver smiled. "Always a pleasure, Ms. Sydney."

"We appreciate it, man." Blake shook Jack's hand and guided Sydney up the sidewalk toward his home.

A warm March breeze tickled her bare shoulders as she admired the full moon glowing dimly in the cloudless sky. Finally attending her krewe's Mardi Gras ball with Blake had been magical, and she swayed softly to the music still playing in her mind as they made their way up the path.

She adjusted her tiara and smiled at the crown sitting crooked atop Blake's head. She'd dressed like a queen for the Regal Royalty-themed masquerade, but Blake had treated her like one every day for the past year.

They'd postponed the museum opening until things settled down, but once Sydney had healed and the trial concluded, they moved forward, and the most popular tour company in the French Quarter became even more popular.

After riding in the parade last year, she'd thought the ghost would have moved on quickly, but Bernadette enjoyed the parade so much she decided to stick around. She haunted the museum, teasing guests who visited her Mardi Gras artwork with chills and cool breezes. Sean checked in with her occasionally, reminding her of her promise to stay quiet after closing time, and the spirit seemed content to remain in the museum.

Claire spent the past year in a psychiatric facility, hopefully getting the help she needed. It had taken a while to process everything that happened, but things were slowly getting back to normal, and Sydney treasured every minute she spent with Blake.

He walked past his front door, pausing by the gate that led to the back courtyard. They wouldn't be heading up to his apartment yet, and she'd seen the reason why in a vision. She'd have preferred the surprise not be spoiled, but that was what she got for poking around in her own future.

"I want to show you something." He rested his hands on her hips and placed a soft kiss on her cheek.

She bit her bottom lip, fighting her smile, and pulled him into a hug. "Okay."

"You know, don't you?" he whispered into her ear.

"I haven't a clue what you're talking about."

He leaned away, narrowing his eyes at her, and she batted her lashes, feigning innocence as anticipation wound tight like a spring in her core.

She'd kept up her weekly appointments with the Voodoo priestess, and while learning to control her gift often felt like riding a bicycle with a flat tire uphill in the mud, the progress she'd made astonished her.

The vision she'd squelched during last year's Mardi Gras parade, while dire, had been her first foray into taking control and not blacking out randomly. Now, she was learning how to feel the visions, paying attention to the vibrational energy to determine if what the universe wanted to show her was urgent or if it could wait for a more convenient time. The urgent ones—like the Mardi Gras vision—had a sharp, stinging sensation when they pulled her under, while less pressing matters felt soft and vibrated slowly.

Blake took her hand, lacing his fingers through hers. "If you're telling the truth, I *might* have a surprise for you."

She grinned. "I can't wait to see it."

He gave her another skeptical look before leading her through the gate and down the alley toward the back of the building. He paused before rounding the corner, facing her and brushing her hair from her forehead. "Don't fake being surprised if you know. I want your real reaction, *cher*. It's important."

She rose onto her toes and kissed his lips. "I promise."

Part of her psychic training included bringing on premonitions purposely. It felt wrong to pry into other's lives without their permission, so she'd been practicing on her own future…which was why she knew exactly what she would see when she stepped around the building.

She couldn't wait.

"No peeking." Moving behind her, Blake put his hands over her eyes and guided her into the courtyard.

The uneven cobblestone threw off her balance, so she reached behind to hold Blake's hips as they shuffled forward. The sound of water bubbling from a fountain and cascading down into a pool drifted toward her, drawing the corners of her mouth into a smile.

Blake stopped, and, keeping her eyes covered, he pressed his lips to the back of her neck, sending a shiver down her spine. That, she hadn't seen coming.

"Are you ready, *cher*?" he whispered against her ear.

She nodded, and he uncovered her eyes.

Though she'd seen it in her premonition, her breath caught at the beauty of the fountain. A series of lights installed in the reservoir illuminated the structure, making the water glow as it tumbled from pedestal to pedestal before splashing into the pool at the bottom. A stone rabbit wearing a waistcoat sat atop the center column, its pocket watch tucked neatly into its vest.

Blake slid his arms around her from behind. "What do you think?"

"It's beautiful. I love it."

"Good. I had the rabbit commissioned just for you. It'll be nice to sit out here in the springtime." He kissed her cheek and stepped back as she took in the rest of the courtyard.

He'd had the whole space renovated, with new greenery planted along the walls and strings of lights draped across the center. A stone bench sat against the back wall, and an elaborate wrought-iron table with two chairs stood in the corner beneath the shade of a massive magnolia tree.

Her pulse quickened, her hands trembling as she prepared to turn around. She knew exactly what to expect and what her answer would be, but that didn't take away from the thrilling excitement rushing through her veins.

She turned and bit her bottom lip as she found Blake

on one knee, a black velvet box in his hand. Her legs wobbled, and she sank onto the edge of the fountain.

"I may not be able to see the future like you, but I do know one thing for certain. I can't even *imagine* a future without you in my life. This courtyard is yours, and so is my heart."

Her throat thickened, and tears collected on her lower lids.

Blake opened the box and pulled out a diamond ring. "I love you, Sydney. I will love you for the rest of my life, and then some. Will you be my wife?"

"Yes," she whispered, and a tear rolled down her cheek.

He smiled. "What was that? I'm not sure I heard you."

She laughed. "Yes. Yes!"

He slid the ring on her finger and stood, pulling her into a tight embrace. "You've just made me the happiest man alive."

"I love you, Blake."

"I love you too." He linked his fingers behind her lower back and leaned away to look in her eyes. "Be honest. Did you know it was coming?"

She nodded. "Doesn't make it any less special, though. I see how things are going to turn out a lot, and there's something you should know."

"I'm listening."

She smiled. "For you and me, there's no end in sight."

ALSO BY CARRIE PULKINEN

Crescent City Wolf Pack Series

Werewolves Only

Beneath a Blue Moon

Bound by Blood

A Deal with Death

A Song to Remember

Crescent City Ghost Tours Series

Love & Ghosts

Love & Omens

Spirit Chasers Series

To Catch a Spirit

To Stop a Shadow

To Free a Phantom

Stand Alone Books

The Rest of Forever

Soul Catchers

Reawakened

Bewitching the Vampire

ABOUT THE AUTHOR

Carrie Pulkinen is a paranormal romance author who has always been fascinated with things that go bump in the night. Of course, when you grow up next door to a cemetery, the dead (and the undead) are hard to ignore. Pair that with her passion for writing and her love of a good happily-ever-after, and becoming a paranormal romance author seems like the only logical career choice.

Before she decided to turn her love of the written word into a career, Carrie spent the first part of her professional life as a high school journalism and yearbook teacher. She loves good chocolate and bad puns, and in her free time, she likes to read, drink wine, and travel with her family.

Connect with Carrie online:
www.CarriePulkinen.com

Made in the USA
Monee, IL
26 May 2020